the ANGEL'S SONG

KAREN SPARNON

Published by Sanctuary Publishing

Cover and internal design by Coven Press

www.covenpress.com.au

First printing: May 2026

Paperback ISBN 978-0-6483108-3-9

eBook ISBN 978-0-6483108-2-2

www.karensparnon.com

A catalogue record for this work is available from the National Library of Australia

Distributed by Lightning Source Global

Also by Karen Sparnon

Madonna of the Eucalypts (2006)

A Note from the Author

I truly believe art has the power to change lives. And what better art to look towards than that of the Italian Renaissance – that glorious artistic flowering that in all probability will never be surpassed.

The following paintings feature in *The Angel's Song*. For those inclined, it would be useful – although not necessary – to view images of the paintings listed below. I have also posted images on my website: www.karensparnon.com

The Coronation of the Virgin by Lorenzo Monaco
Uffizi Galleries, Florence, Italy

Primavera by Sandro Botticelli
Uffizi Galleries, Florence, Italy

Expulsion from the Garden of Eden by Masaccio
Cappella Brancacci, Florence, Italy

Allegory of Prudence by Giovanni Bellini
Gallerie dell'Accademia, Venice, Italy

San Zaccaria Altarpiece by Giovanni Bellini
Chiesa di San Zaccaria, Venice, Italy

The Visitation by Jacopo Pontormo
Pieve di San Michele Arcangelo, Carmignano, Italy

'A mother is she who can take the place of all others
but whose place no one else can take.'
Unknown

'Motherhood: All love begins and ends there.'
Robert Browning

'A mother is always the beginning. She is how
things begin.'
Amy Tan

Peterborough

Australia

2005

From my vantage point on the hill behind our ramshackle house, I can see my father's grey head through the open louvred windows of his studio. He takes on fewer commissions these days, but his work is richer, seamed by experience in the same way gold threads quartz. The distant sea is grey and small waves relentlessly pound the rocky coastline. For most of my life, I called my father by his first name, Lawrence. It seemed a natural thing to do. In the absence of a mother, it was just the two of us: Lawrence and Iris. But the events of recent years have weighed heavily on both of us, bringing into sharp focus our roles as father and daughter.

Today, Marcus has taken our daughter Amadora along the poplar walk to the bay that during my childhood my father and I claimed as our own. They wanted me to go with them. Twelve-year-old Amadora pouted and frowned and then lapsed into silence, in the same way her grandfather used to when things were not to his liking. But I took no notice. I wanted to be alone to write my story.

Thirteen years ago, I sat on a grassy patch on this same stony hillside, watching my father as he returned to his studio after many months absence. I didn't begrudge him the safe harbour of his work. I was truly glad that once again the house would be filled with the earthy, resinous scent of wood shavings.

It was the December of 1991 and I'd not long returned from Italy. Marcus had arrived a few days earlier to meet the man who would become his father-in-law.

I remember gazing towards the ocean and placing a hand on my belly. I'd had no tests but knew with certainty that my child was a girl. I knew by the feel of her and by the soft, spreading roundness of my hips. As I sat with my unborn child, I realised that the anger I felt towards my father had faded, and I now understood enough about what had happened to care about his feelings. Anger and love had fought each other ever since my return to Australia, and I often felt a pawn in their game.

Early that morning, my father and I had talked and dragged more ghosts into the light. He told me that after I discovered his secret, he went to Curdies River Cemetery and righted his wrongs. He said he took the wooden plaque from my mother's grave, drove back to our bay, and threw it into the sea. He watched it bob about until it was no longer in view.

Then, I'd decided not to go to the grave to check if he was telling the truth. In Italy, I'd uncovered all I needed to know, and no matter what was said or done, we both knew the price to pay for the uncovering of this secret was sadness that only time could heal.

I learned from my father's deception and my mother's journal that sometimes it is necessary to travel back in time to discover the truth. Wallowing amongst family sins is painful but yields surprising fruit. Such behaviour ran contrary to every carefully cultivated, literal bone in my body, and without Marcus I'm not certain I could have done it. He taught me not to pick over the carcasses of broken dreams and promises but to reassemble them into patterns and see their possibilities.

Allegra's journal taught me that some women's stories are subtle and multi-hued, the colours merging and separating. My mother's story was also labyrinthine. It twisted and turned, and like all good mazes, I learned that an end can be a beginning and a beginning an end. I was only a child when I found her journal, and as I couldn't read Italian, it wasn't the writing in it that set me on my path but the four postcards pasted inside. Perhaps this was serendipitous. With writing, one sentence leads to the next and I could have been easily duped into believing there was no need to explore the spaces in between. Instead, I found myself searching for my mother in the shifting colours of her postcard paintings.

They say there will never be a close to a story as long as there is somebody left who wants to tell it.

Next month, Amadora will turn thirteen, and on this milestone birthday, I will give her what I now write. I want our story to be known by the generations that come after us. I write not to expose our family's lies but to find our truth. I write to leave Amadora a path as broad and strong as a Roman road.

Peterborough

Australia

1976

1

My home town of Peterborough stands on a cliff above the mouth of Curdies Inlet in southwest Victoria. Australia's Great Ocean Road bypasses our town centre. Peterborough is a sleepy hamlet, and even though the first parcels of land were surveyed in 1866, no building took place for almost ten years. Its few houses blend into the high dunes, which then catapult down to the ocean.

A golf course crisscrosses between these dunes and the town. It takes no notice of Schomberg Road, which slices the seventh and eighth holes. This anomaly has made our course infamous and draws a regular parade of golfing enthusiasts. Small stores compete for business in Macs Street, but for most of the year the town sleeps, relying on summer holidaymakers and passing travellers. There is no school and from the age of five I travelled by bus to the inland town of Timboon, leaving Lawrence to the precarious living he made from his sculptures and the casual work he received from nearby farming properties.

Lawrence and I lived a kilometre from the town; far enough away to discourage casual visitors but close enough to meet our everyday needs. Our lives were predictable and I knew that this was how Lawrence liked it. But in the summer of 1976 – when I was eleven years old – everything changed.

Lawrence took me to visit my mother's grave.

Lawrence had told me of my mother's death just before I began my school life. Until then, I'd spent most of that first five years of my life alone with him, roaming the nearby dunes, and sitting with him in the studio as he worked on his sculptures. Our isolation meant that the subject of mothers simply never arose. As he worked, Lawrence told me stories about paintings and artists, and in my mind images of his much-loved Florence and Italy grew year by year until they were as clear to me as was my home town of Peterborough.

The fact that I didn't have a mother was never a cause for concern. I'd always been aware of her absence, but its true reality was brought home when I saw the small cluster of mothers chatting and laughing while they waited with their children at the Peterborough school bus stop. I watched as they exchanged hugs and kisses, and the children's new school jumpers and socks were fussily straightened. My second-hand jumper had a stain on the cuff of the left sleeve, and its navy-blue colour had faded with washing. My dress was new but too long. When I mentioned this, Lawrence looked worried before saying with relief that the length would make it last a good few years.

Lawrence never joined in with the mothers. He usually stood to one side, leaning on a fence with his hands in his pockets. One day, as we walked slowly home, I plucked up my courage and asked him about my mother. He hesitated and then the words tumbled from his mouth. *She died, honey. There's no need for you to worry. She had no pain, really. It was very quick.* And, finally – *When you're a big girl, I'll take you to the cemetery.* That was the end of it. This had been enough information for a five-year-old child, the concept of death too abstract and overwhelming to allow further discussion.

I slept badly the night before our visit to the grave. I woke in pitch dark, sensing it was past midnight because of the waves. During the day the white caps broke relentlessly against our Peterborough shoreline. At night they retreated with the moon to a place near the horizon, soothing me with their rhythmic but distant rush. I could hear soft music and knew Lawrence was still awake. I laid for a long time in the blackness, and just as I was about to drift back to sleep, I heard the low hoot of a barn owl and scrambled out of bed to peer through the window. My bedroom was at the front of the house. The bird sat on the high wire that ran along the narrow gravel lane that linked us to the Great Ocean Road, its eyes wide in a white heart-shaped face. My heart thumped. It was staring straight at me. The owl inclined its head and lifted one wing as if it were opening a fan. It was still for a moment and then shook itself, transfixing me with its stare. Lawrence said that owls were wise, but I thought this one looked sad, like the Pierrot doll Aunt Monica – my mother's twin sister – brought me home after her last overseas trip. I went back to bed then and dreamed confusedly of waves and owls until daybreak.

I woke at first light and lay in bed thinking of the day ahead. I pulled my blankets up and around my neck, chewed thoughtfully on the tattered binding, and let my thoughts drift to the sea.

First light in Peterborough was the best time of the day. In winter, clouds scudded across the horizon backlit by a weak sun. Below them, the sea might be grey and sleepy or a deep blue with high waves that heralded danger to the local fishermen. But now, in summer, sunlight streamed through blue sky down to the water and silvery rays darted in blinding flashes. I loved to get up early and run to the still silent beach before the summer holidaymakers arrived with their coloured towels and striped umbrellas. And it seemed especially important that I go this morning.

I thought there was enough time to walk to the beach and back before Lawrence woke. I knew he would sleep on for at least another hour because he had been up so late.

I dressed hurriedly and tiptoed through the living room on my way to the back door. The room hummed with trapped heat from the previous day. I stopped and stared at my parents' photograph on the mantelpiece. The curtains were drawn against the early sun, but a beam of light had threaded its way between the velvet folds and been caught by the glass protecting the photo. My mother stared out at me from the silver frame. I looked from my mother to the print on the wall above. It was Botticelli's *Primavera*; a pretty painting guaranteed to attract a child's attention.

In the centre of the print was beautiful, full-bellied Venus – Aunt Monica had told me her name – with her filmy white gown and red drapery, her fine latticed sandals, which I thought must have been useless for walking, and her tilted head with its lopsided right eye. I was sure that even if she straightened her head, this eye would still be lower than her left. The effect was a sleepy otherworldliness, and I often wondered what she was thinking about. To her right, three blond-haired women in see-through gowns twirled in a graceful circle. I knew little of sex but thought it strange that the man on their right was more interested in whatever was above his head than in the near-naked women next to him. On Venus's left were three more figures. A blue man with puffed-out cheeks held another woman in a see-through gown, who in turn reached for another woman wearing a dress covered in flowers. These flowers were so thick around the neck of her close-fitting bodice that they looked like a miniature garden. Her right hand plunged into an abundance of pink rose petals cradled in the folds of her dress. My aunt had also told me that her name was Flora.

As usual, my gaze stayed not on the central figure of Venus but on Flora and her flower-strewn dress. With her delicate, pointed chin, cupid lips, and dream-laden eyes, she was my mother's mirror image. For a moment I thought Flora might step from her print and take me in her arms, just as I had often wished for Allegra to spring from her photograph, lift me by the underarms and spin me around, my arms stretched but comfortably supporting my infant weight and my feet flying just above the floor.

I swayed and reached for the back of the lounge chair. The proposed visit to the cemetery had brought my mother strangely to life, and I swung between uneasiness and a small child's placid acceptance. Blood pulsed at my temples, but then I was jolted back to reality. My mother was dead. I had Lawrence; so why did I need a mother? The world settled on its axis and I again looked at the photograph.

I put my head on one side and considered Lawrence, who stood stiffly beside Allegra in the photograph. He was staring forward. My parents' shoulders touched, but Lawrence's hands were pushed low in his pockets. Lawrence, I decided, belonged in the frame. But then I was struck that my mother looked far too alive to be in such a small place.

I held my breath as I opened the kitchen screen door at the side of the house and the latch clicked shut loudly behind me. I skirted around the back of the house, past Lawrence's studio, and onto the poplar-lined track that led from the gravel lane to the beach. Starting near the corner of the lane, there were eight poplars planted symmetrically on either side of the track. The track rose steadily the length of these poplars and then dipped down to the ocean, with little vegetation other than a few drooping sheoaks and low prickly coastal scrub.

When I was halfway along, I stopped and let my eyes scan one conical form to its apex high above. These trees were the shifting points in my otherwise unchanging horizon. I watched through late summer and autumn as their leaves blazed and yellowed until only the stubborn trembled on almost naked branches. The coastal winds were bitter and the winter gusts unforgiving. I was always surprised when each spring unfurled new growth. Now, in summer, paper-thin leaves flickered against a bright blue sky.

When I reached the dunes, I took the track between the low tea tree to the secluded bay Lawrence and I considered our own. That early in the morning, the bay was freshly washed; only the star-like imprints of seagulls patterned the sand. The waves lapped rather than surged, and the high cliffs threw misshapen shadows over the water.

I felt my shifting unease settle. Ever since Lawrence decided to take me to the grave, our days had been underpinned, strangled almost, by this nameless fear. Here, I could think about what the day might hold without the risk of looking up and finding Lawrence's sombre gaze on me. Lawrence rarely smiled. I reasoned that this was because he was an artist and worry about the shape of his sculptures occupied the spaces where other people held laughter. When asked what Lawrence did for a living, there was a certain pride in being able to say gravely that he was an artist. It set us apart, made us special. It compensated in a small way for the silence that sat at the core of our lives, in the place where other people had mothers. I began the steady climb to the high sea cliffs above.

The upper reaches of the cliffs were stepped with deep rises and wide ledges. The rises were pitted with crannies large enough for a child to crawl into, and when I was unsure of what was going on, I often used them as refuge.

That morning, I crawled to the edge of the first ledge. A wide platform of rock separated me from the next step with its flat ledge that fell away abruptly to the sea below. I did not stop to think about my footing on this dangerous precipice but swung my body over and into a child-sized nook and nestled against the sand. I raised my face to the warm summer sun and let it calm my thudding heart.

A still sea belied the area's reputation as the shipwreck coast. I squinted and imagined the indigo outline of the *Schomberg* as clear in the glassy water, small fish swimming through her barnacle-encrusted hull. But I knew that the ship with her rosewood drawing room lay scattered along the coastline. There were no longer soft voices and swishing gowns on the decks; the ship was broken, much as my family had been ever since my mother went away.

I closed my eyes and smelled on the breeze my mother's scent of violets. In my first year of school, I had a teacher who encouraged us to ask questions of the adults in our lives. But, even then, I instinctively knew that this did not include Lawrence. When I turned six, midway through the year, I asked Aunt Monica why Lawrence kept an ornate, empty bottle on his bedside table. The word 'Violet' was etched into the greenish glass in gold script. My aunt was silent for a time and then told me that it had held my mother's favourite perfume. After that I visited it like a shrine and one day pulled out the stopper and held the bottle to my nose. It was like nothing I had smelled before – a scent like lush purple velvet – a scent in which you could drown. I had replaced the stopper and the bottle carefully.

But the scent stayed and now – five years later – again brushed by me and I scrabbled through infant memories for my mother's touch. But there was little for me to hold onto, only her blond hair like silk against my cheek before she pulled away.

Then the anger bubbled up and I slapped my palm hard on the sand and winced.

I laid on my stomach with my hips pressed to the ground and my chin cupped in my palms until I heard the crunch of shoes on sand, followed by a tired-sounding disembodied voice.

'How many times have I told you?'

I peered out guiltily from my hidey-hole. Lawrence was standing above me, feet astride and hands on his hips.

He wore blue jeans and a pale-blue fine cotton shirt and looked like the men on the covers of the records he played late at night when he thought I was asleep. He was thin and the outlines of his collarbone and hipbones were visible through his clothes. Dark hair reached his shoulders and a few days growth stubbled his chin. To me he was just Lawrence Maddison – my father – but even I was aware that the women we met looked at him in a way I didn't like or understand. I also knew that he never looked back. He was frozen by the woman who had changed his life and then left us. The week before, I had made a cake for his thirty-fifth birthday. It sank in the middle and I filled the centre with cream whipped almost to butter and watched as he ate. When he smiled, my heart swelled with pride. I loved Lawrence, and knowing that once again I had disobeyed him, I flushed and stared at his feet.

'You know this is dangerous,' he said. 'I've told you these holes are too close to the edge. You must promise me you'll stay away.'

For a moment we both looked down at the sea and then Lawrence ran his hands through his hair and I wanted to run to him. Instead, determined to prove that I was sensible, I climbed slowly from my hole, walked over to him, and slipped my hand into his. He squeezed it.

'You promise me?' he said.

'Okay,' I lied.

'How about pancakes for breakfast?' Lawrence said as we clambered down the cliff face.

I grinned. 'With honey and cream?'

'Okay. You can have cream today, but don't expect it all the time.'

After breakfast we made a list of groceries and set off to walk to Macs Street. Our Holden was garaged at Jim's Place at the far end of the street, just where it curved in the direction of the Great Ocean Road. Jim was good at repairing cars, especially old ones. I thought this made sense, as Jim was pretty old himself. As we passed the general store, I tugged at Lawrence's sleeve and said, 'I want to take my mother something.'

Lawrence fished in his pocket for some change and then held out a closed fist. I tried to loosen his clawed fingers, but just as I had one or two straight, he sprang them shut. Finally, I managed to hold three flat, and he let me open his hand and gather the contents. When I lifted the coins from his palm, I noticed the half-moons left by his nails in the flesh.

'Do you want to come in with me?' I said.

'You go. You're a big girl now,' he replied.

I drifted down the aisles in search of the right gift. There were rows of tinned fruits and vegetables, household products and fishing tackle, writing pads and envelopes coated in dust, and then the brilliant display of foil-wrapped sweets. But there was nothing for my mother and I frowned and let my eyes wander. Through the smeared glass of a display case, I saw a frosted vase filled with stiff pink daisies, their stalks arranged symmetrically in floral foam.

'How much are the flowers?' I asked Mr Calder.

He peered at me from over his glasses. 'How much have you got?'

I held out my hand, shaking the few coins so he could see them clearly.

'Just enough, I reckon,' he said.

We walked on towards Jim's garage in silence. Goosebumps erupted on my arms and my skin began to feel cold. My gait changed from a hop-skip to an awkward scramble to keep up with Lawrence's long legs. I knew that anything to do with my mother brought on these silences. Like huge clouds, they descended on the brightest horizon and blocked out the sun. If they went on for too long and I couldn't distract him, Lawrence disappeared inside the silence, and I was left to wait anxiously on the outside. But this time there was nothing I could do for him. That afternoon we were heading straight for my mother's grave, and I could only let the silence deepen.

I could not understand why mothers burrowed deep into the softest part of your being and made you believe that the world was safe and then tore it apart. It made me angry that Allegra's death had left me with a shipwrecked father, torn apart just like the *Schomberg*. She still shaped our lives, even though she was no longer in them. Everybody told me that my mother had loved me, but I was amazed at their stupidity. It was quite simple. If she loved me, I thought crossly, why did she die?

I was glad when we reached the end of the street and entered the garage. It was dim and smelled of oil and paint, and the floor was littered with rusted bits of cars and farm machinery.

'The old girl lives to run another day,' Jim said. And he rubbed his hands together in a show of triumph.

'Thank God,' Lawrence said. I heard the relief in his voice and breathed easier. A new car would have strained our money to breaking point.

We drove back up the street and parked outside the grocery shop. Once a month we drove to a supermarket in nearby Warrnambool for the bulk of our supplies, and in between excursions topped up anything we might have forgotten or run out of from the shop. The stock was sparse, over time whittled to bare necessities, but we could usually get what we wanted. Lawrence glanced at our list, moved quickly along the shelves and we were out within ten minutes.

At home we unpacked and, as usual, I set six slices of bread on the bench and went to the fridge for butter and some filling for our sandwiches. I opened the door and stared inside.

'What do you want on yours, Dad?'

When there was no answer, I swung around impatiently and called, 'Dad!'

Lawrence turned towards me as if pulled from a dream. His lips moved but there was no sound. It was the first time I experienced one of those moments which are full of feeling but without words, which pluck you from the everyday world of time and logic and leave you suspended – briefly – in some parallel space. My goosebumps returned along with a strange sinking sensation in the pit of my stomach.

'Cheese and tomato,' Lawrence finally said.

I pulled out one of Lawrence's favourite egg-shaped tomatoes and a packet of cheese slices, and the moment passed.

Early that afternoon, we drove inland from the beach along a straight road lined with stands of drooping sheoaks, their blue-green foliage tinged with summer yellow. The sky was a dazzling blue and the distant sea shimmered darkly. Clusters of cows grazed the shorn paddocks, heads down amongst the dry grass. I looked sideways at Lawrence. He hadn't spoken since we turned off the highway.

'When will we get there?' I said.

Lawrence glanced at me. He wore a forced smile that stretched his lips into a thin line and he gripped the steering wheel tightly.

'It's not a very long drive,' he said. 'But long enough for you to have a sleep on the way, if you like.' After a pause he added, 'You do understand that it's time you visited your mother's grave, don't you? *I* think it's time you did.' There was a longer pause and then he said, 'And your Aunt Monica thinks it's time too.'

Lulled by the warmth, I closed my eyes and slept until the car slowed to a halt and I heard the grind of the handbrake. Lawrence still didn't speak, and something about his fierce concentration stopped me from chattering. Instead, at his signal, I got out, leaned against the side of the car, and waited for directions.

It was a lonely road with only one house visible near a distant bend. We waited while a car and its bulbous white caravan chugged past, followed by a truck packed with braying lambs. On the opposite side of the road was a dirt track, flanked by gum trees. I shaded my eyes from the sun and tried to see what lay ahead, but the track veered to the left and, this far back, I could only see the cropped bump signposted as Ashley's Hill in the distance. We crossed the road and followed the sweep of the track around the base of the hill until we reached a wooden gate set between two tall cypress pines. I noticed that its paint was peeling off in curls. One hinge was broken, and I watched anxiously as Lawrence wedged his shoulder against the gate, lifted it slightly and pushed inwards. A walkway crackling with pine needles led past a rickety wooden outhouse. The smell of crushed pine resin burned through my nerve ends like fire.

The graves in the cemetery's stony ground followed no regular pattern as they had been dug into any part of the earth that proved pliable. They were mostly rustic graves with no clearly defined outlines and small tilted headstones with brief epitaphs. Abruptly – and for no reason – I stopped walking, checking Lawrence, who was forced to look behind to see what I was doing. His face was grey. He hadn't shaven. He seemed smaller.

Still without speaking, Lawrence took my hand and led me to a grave where another cypress cast a thin length of shadow along an oblong marble slab. A piece of greying wood was fixed to the upright granite headstone and carved into it were the words:

To Our Beloved Allegra Maddison
Wife of Lawrence
Mother of Iris
1943-1967

Under this inscription was a stylised weeping willow. I knew this was a symbol of sorrow. It was part of the trivia I had picked up through living with a sculptor, and I ran my finger along the willow's grooves. But the flat gravestones made me sad. And the way they spread haphazardly over the parched Australian hill, beaten on by a high sun, made it seem as though no one cared about them.

I sat my vase in the centre of the marble slab. The sun refracted off the quartz crystals in the surface and my eyes watered. When I had been little more than a baby, Aunt Monica told me to imagine that Allegra had gone to a magic world. With my head on her knees and the lamplight soft behind us, all this seemed possible. But here, no matter how hard I tried, I couldn't imagine any way for my mother to push past the slab that buried her and rise up and into this other world. The easy slide from life to death to other life collapsed under the weight of my mother's slab and I panicked. Fear rippled through me, but I couldn't move or open my mouth to tell Lawrence of my distress.

When I felt calmer, I walked over to Lawrence, who had knelt down and was plucking a few weeds from the base of the grave.

I tapped his shoulder. 'Should I say a prayer, Daddy?' My teacher was fond of prayers. Miss Larkin was a no-nonsense woman who veered between telling us to try harder or, if things were beyond fixing, to say a prayer. The stony cemetery struck me as the perfect place for prayers.

Lawrence looked up at me, shrugged, sighed and said, 'If you like.'

'God bless my mother,' I muttered and looked at Lawrence for approval. I waited for him to add to my prayer, but he only stood up and held out his hand for us to leave.

As we walked down the track, I looked back and felt sad that we had to leave my mother in this lonely place. It was now late in the day and the afternoon sun had disappeared, casting the cemetery into shadow. The only sounds were the lowing of cows from a nearby farm and the crunch of our footsteps on the gravel path as we walked back to the car.

2

On the return journey from the cemetery, we took a different route back to our house along the twisting coastal road. The tide was high and waves foamed between the jagged rocks. When we neared the gravel track and our house came into view, Lawrence grunted under his breath and his body stiffened. I followed his gaze, saw Aunt Monica's car, and smiled. It was tilting sideways, one wheel parked on the high verge and the other three on the road in front of our house.

'Airy-fairy land,' Lawrence said and shook his head. 'Look at that car!' His voice had the crisp edge to it that crept in every time my aunt came to visit.

When we reached the back door, he hesitated before turning the handle, but Aunt Monica had seen us first, and before I knew it, she was out the door and her arms were around me. '*Mia cara figliola*,' she said, as she pulled my head to her chest and squeezed me.

Then she held me at arm's length, and we looked at each other. I liked that she was different from the other women I knew. Today, she wore her dark hair piled high. Her lipstick was carmine, and her perfect, almond-shaped eyes were highlighted with smoky eyeshadow, which made them seem even larger. Her dress was a profusion of flowers in shades of red and pink, and she wore high-heeled red shoes. But despite her love of fashion and clothes, my aunt was clever. I had seen the framed awards and prizes for obscure studies of medieval and renaissance saints on her study wall. I was proud that people admired her. She lived and worked at a university in Melbourne but had visited us for one weekend each month ever since I could remember. Now, she saw me appraise her dress and shoes, laughed, and pirouetted.

'You like?' she said.

I nodded.

'I've a present for you.' She turned to Lawrence. 'Can I give it to her, Lawrence?' Something in his expression stopped her in her tracks and I watched, bewildered, as her gaiety drained away and her face grew pale. 'Oh, Lawrence,' she said in a low voice. 'You didn't? You said you wouldn't.'

'It's none of your business.' Lawrence's answer was firm and sharp. He turned on his heel and walked down the hallway to the kitchen, leaving us standing in the open front doorway.

'Oh, Lawrence,' my aunt repeated – this time under her breath – as she put her arm around me and guided me down the hallway. I could hear Lawrence busying himself in the kitchen. There was a rush of water into the kettle, followed by the clink of mugs as they landed on the laminate tabletop. Aunt Monica turned to me with a forced smile. She reached into her carry bag, pulled out a small, red cardboard box, and handed it to me. The box was fragile, made from the same material as an egg carton.

'Can I open it?' I said.

'Of course!' My aunt's voice was a pitch higher than usual, and I looked up at her and frowned, holding the box so tightly that its soft edges crushed under my fingers.

'Go on,' she encouraged. 'You told me you wanted one of these. Remember, we talked about them after I gave you the Pierrot doll?'

I thought for a moment and a smile broke out on my face as I said, 'A Pinocchio!'

Aunt Monica nodded and I opened the box and pulled out the little wooden figure with its thin cylinder for a nose and yelped with excitement. When she first gave me the Pierrot doll, Aunt Monica told me about its human function as a pantomime artist in France, and this had led on to a discussion of other dolls in other countries and Italy's little Pinocchio, the boy whose nose grew when he lied. This idea had both intrigued and frightened me. I knew all about white lies, and the thought that my nose, too, might grow was alarming – even though the sensible part of me knew this was impossible. I'd asked my aunt to bring me a Pinocchio, half-expecting her to forget all about it.

'Look, Dad!' I placed the figure carefully on the table and looked up, but Lawrence didn't comment and, disappointed, I returned my attention to the wooden figure with its loose limbs and that extraordinary nose.

That evening, Lawrence and Aunt Monica prepared dinner in near silence. I sat at the kitchen table watching as Lawrence made our favourite chilli and garlic pasta sauce and then set our pasta pot full of water on the stove to boil. My aunt moved about quietly, setting the table, grating the parmesan cheese into a small bowl, and then placing six, cream-filled cannoli on a floral, ceramic plate. The uneasy silence continued even as we ate. My aunt asked Lawrence questions about his work, but his replies were terse. Eventually, she gave up, asked me about school, and told me about the play she'd recently seen at the theatre. Then we all cleared the table and washed the dishes, again with hardly a word spoken. I was confused. Usually, we laughed and joked, and Lawrence lightened in a way that made me happy. My aunt's few words on arrival hinted that Lawrence had done something that she wasn't pleased about. But they'd said no more on the subject, and I sensed this was not a time for me to ask questions.

I was sent to bed early, and by the time Aunt Monica came to tell me another of her stories, I was tired and irritable. For the last two years she had stopped reading to me from children's books and, deeming I was old enough, had chronicled the life of a different saint each time she visited Peterborough. Her stories filled my dreams with saints and sinners, and I knew about sacred and secular love and the sacrifices made in their names. I loved these tales of visions and flames and fabulous beasts.

Because my aunt believed in telling children history's truths, even the dubious – and perhaps imaginary – truths of an age given to martyrdom, I had accrued over time a colourful and disordered sense of history where chronology took second place to passion. Throughout time, she told me, people have lived by many different creeds and can live with anything so long as it has meaning for them. It was Aunt Monica who told me that all of our truths are different and have been that way for centuries. That it is living a lie that takes away meaning.

My aunt settled beside me on the bed, pulled my brightly coloured crochet blanket over both of us, and

I rested my head on her shoulder. She reached across, grabbed my hairbrush from the side table, and began to tame my unruly hair. We were both silent. The room was dim except for my blue and aqua lava lamp, its soft, waxy blobs gently undulating. I loved this lamp. I loved the way it caught the eye and quietened the mind. The minutes ticked by and I began to feel drowsy. Finally, Aunt Monica put down the brush and said, 'So, Lawrence took you to the cemetery today to visit your mother's grave?'

There was a long pause. I felt a comment was expected of me but, in truth, I couldn't think of anything to say. The drowsiness of a few minutes prior vanished, replaced by an unpleasant squirming sensation in the pit of my stomach. Eventually, I said, 'It was lonely.'

Aunt Monica sighed and said, 'Yes, I'm sure ...'

'I took flowers. But they were plastic.'

My aunt laughed. 'Allegra loved flowers. They always made her happy.' She tilted my face upwards and looked searchingly into my eyes. 'Are you okay?'

I nodded and returned my gaze to the shifting forms of the lava lamp.

Monica hugged me gently. 'Who would you like to hear about tonight?'

I thought for moment. 'Saint Francis of Assisi, I think.'

'Hmm ... That's a good choice for today.'

But that night, even Saint Francis, with his love of all birds and animals, couldn't distract me from the heaviness that blanketed the house. Lawrence and my aunt were keeping something from me. Something was seriously wrong.

After telling of how Saint Francis had established his order of brothers, my aunt turned so she could see me full in the face. 'Iris, you know how I'm working on the life of Saint Ursula?'

'The one with the eleven thousand virgins for friends?' I said.

Aunt Monica smiled and nodded. 'Well, a new, or should I say old, manuscript has been found that adds details to what we already know about her.' She put her arm around me. I knew I wasn't going to like what came next. Even so, her eyes didn't slide sideways, as people's do when they feel guilty about what they are about to say. Instead, she held my gaze. 'Iris, I have to go away for a while. The university is very excited about this manuscript and want me to go to Italy to do some research on it. I have to add this story to all my other stories about Ursula and there might just be enough to complete the book I told you about.' She fondled my hair and smiled. 'I guess I'm making one very big story about Ursula for the whole world to read. I'll be living just near your nonna and nonno, and we'll write lots of letters, eh?'

I nodded obediently but my body felt limp. At school one day my teacher had drawn a family tree on the blackboard and dotted it with parents and grandparents, aunts and cousins in coloured chalk. They sat on the bare branches like bright birds. Now it occurred to me that my family was like this bare tree before the birds alighted. After my mother died, my grandparents returned to their home just south of Florence. Too grief-stricken, I suppose, to withstand the loss of homeland as well as the loss of daughter. Now my aunt was to leave me too.

As for Lawrence's family – there was none. He had been orphaned as a child after his parents died in a car crash and been brought up by his father's only sister. She died when he was seventeen and he never spoke of the years before he met Allegra. I knew there was a lot Lawrence didn't talk about.

I looked steadily at my aunt, whose forehead was creased with anxiety. I wanted to tell her that it was all right, that I was a big girl now and knew that mothers and families made a habit of going missing. But I kept silent and held her gaze until she crushed me to her chest and I could hear the erratic beat of her heart.

'Lots of letters, eh?' she said.

I nodded again, my body stiff like a peg doll.

Later I crept down the hall to the kitchen door and pressed my ear to the crack. I could hear low, angry voices.

'What on earth did you do that for?' Aunt Monica's voice was tight. 'I know you said you were going to, but I thought it was just a bad mood. A fit of pique. I thought you were joking ...'

'Why do you care?' Lawrence interrupted. 'Your mother and father saw no reason to stay around. Did they? They blamed me for what happened.' Lawrence's anger bloomed. 'Sometimes things need to have an end put to them. A line that we can work up from.'

'But to take her to the cemetery!' My aunt sounded incredulous. 'I trusted you – we all trusted you – to handle things gently. And Iris has no choice but to trust you.'

There was a long silence and then Lawrence continued, 'It's all right for you. You'll keep going away and coming back and I'll be here just waiting for the right time. Instead of waiting, I made a decision and now' – in my mind's eye I could see Lawrence flinging out his arms to make a point – 'we can close that door.'

'You'd just better hope Iris will forgive you if anyone ever opens that door,' Aunt Monica said.

My aunt left the next morning. I was confused. Usually, she got up early on the Monday morning as her work was flexible, and she said she liked to spend as much time with me as possible. I waved frantically until her car disappeared from view.

Lawrence and I returned to the house, and we went straight to the kitchen to wash the breakfast dishes. I took my time dragging the tea towel from the rack on the far side of the room. I wanted to ask Lawrence about my mother but had no idea how to begin. When he was bent over the frying pan, I tugged at his sleeve and asked what seemed to me a safe question. 'Lawrence, was my mother beautiful?'

Lawrence dropped the pan into the suds, turned, and put his hands on my shoulders. I felt dampness through my T-shirt, and then his long fingers spread and settled.

'As beautiful as, as' – he stumbled for words and his eyes drifted away from me to the ocean visible through the glass side door – 'as beautiful as the sea.'

Other questions leapt into my mind. Did my mother love me? What was it like when there were three of us? Do you long for her like I do? But Lawrence's response to my first question silenced me. It was too poetic, too abstract, and the door between us that had briefly opened snapped shut.

Sunday dragged after Aunt Monica left. I looked forward to our long walks and to having someone to listen to my chatter after the isolation of my usual daily routine, so I was glad when night fell and I retreated to my room. I was turning the pages of an old picture book when I heard the back door slam and Lawrence's footsteps cross to where we kept our rubbish bin. When he didn't return after the usual amount of time, I got out of bed and peeked through my bedroom curtains. Lawrence was standing in a pool of light with a book angled high so he could read its contents. He turned the pages slowly and something made me feel that the book was important. I watched in astonishment as he suddenly slammed the cover shut and pelted it into the bin, pushed tight the tin lid, and strode back to the house.

In the early hours of the morning, I crept outside, tipped the bin on its side, and sifted through the rubbish until I found the book. I took it inside, sat on my bed, and ran my hand over its crimson leather cover. There were three vertical cracks with vein-like tributaries also branching downwards. I closed my eyes, opened the book, and pressed my nose to the cream, mottled handmade pages. They were cool and smelled musty and old and, somehow, magical. I sat this way for some time, and when I opened my eyes, the first thing I saw were the words: 'Allegra Maddison's Musings'. My spine tingled. I began turning the pages, slowly at first because they crackled under my touch, and this made me nervous. I was worried that the old book would break. But then I leafed faster as I realised that the book was a journal – my mother's journal.

The first few pages were filled with close script, which I recognised as Italian. Letters from my grandparents were rare but enough to make me familiar with the Italian words scattered amongst their halting English. But, because I couldn't read my mother's writing, I grew bored and leafed quickly through to the centre page, which was bulkier than the rest. On one side my mother had glued two postcards. I noted with surprise that the first was of a naked woman with her mouth wide open. She was clutching at her breast and looked to me to be in pain. By her side was a man who held his hands to his face. Above them swooped a red angel who was whipping them with a sword. I stared at this postcard, shocked. There could be, I thought, no greater pain in the world than that on the woman's face. Underneath was a copy of the print in our living room but this time not confined by a white border and a frame but bled off to the edge. On the other page was a postcard of a beautiful woman holding a baby. Two people stood on either side of her and a little angel played a musical instrument at the lady's feet.

These two pages were by far the most interesting, and I was disappointed when the next page reverted to the same dense script as before. Despite my lack of understanding, I kept turning the pages, driven only by the knowledge that my mother had written these words. But when I turned to the last page, there was another postcard. This time it featured an elaborate oblong chest. The photograph had been taken from the lower front, that perspective foreshortening the lid and emphasising the woman painted on the central of the three front panels.

This woman stood – naked – on a drum carved with a low bas-relief and pointed her left forefinger at a mirror held in the crook of her right arm. She made no attempt to suck in the rounded belly that curved above her shadowed pubic region. Underworked muscles had caused fleshy pockets to form at the base of her buttocks. Her breasts were small and pointed like those of a girl-child. But despite the belly and breasts, she was still a woman. Her stance was assured and her face knowing. Three sexless putti mooched around the base of the drum. One, in a Roman toga, was holding a horn and leaning back against it. Another naked child rested on its forearms and leaned forward over the drum. In the foreground another little Roman strutted about while rolling an instrument between its hands. It surprised me that they seemed to be taking no notice of the naked woman above them standing in her marble arch between her mirror and a wide-open window.

Beneath the postcard, angled across the right-hand corner, there was a smudged inscription that read '*povera* Prudencia', followed by three exclamation marks. I peered closer and followed the even script with my index finger. The words were not like any I had come across at school. I gave up on the first word and counted the nine letters in the second, and like a toddler taking a first attempt at a word, I sounded it out loud – Pru-den-ci-a. I thought the last three letters were soft like a sigh. It sounded like a name. Could it be the name of the woman on the chest?

But the first word puzzled me. I crept down the hall to the living room where Lawrence kept his books in a glass bookshelf and pulled down the Italian-English dictionary. The definition next to '*povera*' read 'poor'. 'Poor Prudencia', I whispered.

I liked the name, just as I liked the handmade paper of the journal. But who was Prudencia? And why was she 'poor'? And was she the woman who stared out at me from the chest? I knew that 'poor' could have two meanings – either Prudencia had no money or something awful had happened to her. I wondered why either of these possibilities had concerned my mother. And why was her name followed by three exclamation marks? I sat for a long time idly tracing the faded indigo script with my finger. Then I wrapped the journal in a square of purple velvet my aunt had given me and carefully placed it in the wardrobe behind my jumpers.

3

Aunt Monica didn't return to Peterborough for three months. She rang me each week from Melbourne and our conversations followed the same comforting pattern. She asked me questions about school and, as I was in year five and the prospect of secondary school was not far away, I chatted about my fears and she reassured me. After which my aunt kept me up to date with her preparations for Italy. Despite these calls, I began to wonder if she might never visit us again. Lawrence didn't mention her absence or even appear to notice it, and there was something that prevented me from asking him about her. Summer slid into autumn, and Lawrence was working day and night on a commission for a sculpture. When I wasn't at school, I spent most of my time alone in the house while Lawrence worked in his studio. If I listened hard, I could hear the rhythmic thud of mallet on gouge, after which there was always an appraising silence. It was then that I held my breath. If I heard the scrape of sandpaper followed by a tuneless whistle, I knew things were going well. Lawrence only relaxed when he was working. Then his brow smoothed and the tension in the muscles of his forearms was released into action. And when his work flowed, I stopped worrying.

Our house was a weatherboard building, the rooms built and added to with little thought. It had once belonged to a fisherman who sold it to my parents in the mid-nineteen-sixties. Lawrence's studio couldn't be accessed from the house, only from the rickety veranda that ran its width.

At the beginning of grade three, Lawrence stopped walking to the bus stop with me and I took the sandy beach track alone into town. The track lay hidden between the road and the dunes, but I was never frightened. Each morning before I set off, I checked on Lawrence's progress, watching as his meticulous works evolved within its white walls and open louvred windows.

Lawrence kept the studio almost bare except for his current project, which stood on a large plinth in the centre of the room, so he could circle and scrutinise his work with ease. Even when he was preparing multiple exhibition pieces, he stored the finished works in a room inside the house in order, he said wryly, not to run the risk of plagiarising his own work. The only other objects in the studio were a table, on which lay an assortment of tools, and two chairs. The walls were also bare except for a giant print of Giambologna's bronze figure of Mercury. Lawrence regarded this as a perfect sculpture. He said that when he walked around it in the Bargello in Florence, it seemed to have no beginning and no end. It had choreographed his movements, and ever since, he had aimed for this spiralling perfection in his work.

It was a cool Saturday morning in early April, exactly twelve weeks since Aunt Monica's last visit. I pulled on the jeans and T-shirt I'd thrown on the floor the night before and went to the kitchen to find Lawrence before he started work for the day, but I was too late. On the table was a half-full mug of coffee and a plate littered with crumbs.

On the bus home from school the previous afternoon, Lucy had asked me to spend Saturday at her house, and I'd forgotten to ask Lawrence's permission the previous evening. He didn't like interruptions when he was in the studio, but I reasoned he couldn't have been long gone and I skipped around to the back of the house, navigated my way across the loose boards on the veranda and pushed open the creaking door. Lawrence looked up at the noise and walked over to me, brushing powder-fine sandpaper dust from his fingers.

I reached up and wiped a splotch from his nose, and he blinked as if he wasn't quite sure what was happening.

'Monica rang last night,' he said. 'After you went to bed. She's coming down today and driving back early tomorrow afternoon. So don't wander too far away because you're the one she wants to see. Apparently she's leaving for Italy next Friday.'

My heart leaped but I stood still and nodded my understanding. I made a mental note to phone Lucy.

Lawrence looked worried but then his gaze drifted back to the swan emerging from a large piece of Huon pine. Its neck stretched forward, running with the grain of the timber. The sides of its body were bulbous, the wings yet to emerge. I could see flight in the pale grain of the pine sweeping through its body.

Pride swelled in me and I said, 'It's just right, Dad.'

Lawrence signalled his acknowledgment with a wave of his hand, and I left him to it and went to the kitchen to get my own breakfast.

As I cracked an egg into the pan and slid bread into the toaster, I bit my lip and thought of my aunt's imminent departure.

Until now I had been able to pretend that she wasn't going to Italy, just as I had kept my mother's death at a safe distance until I saw her grave. But the marble slab and the journal had slammed home the reality of Allegra's death and now Aunt Monica's sudden return to say her goodbyes cemented her leaving. It was another body blow, and my world was rocking wildly. Just at that moment, the toaster popped up too soon, sending the bread flying to the floor. I picked it up, blew on it hard and slammed it back to toast to the level I wanted. Then I gulped down my breakfast and went back to my room.

I sat on my bed, buffeted by sadness and anger, after which there was a storm of tears. When I finally stopped crying, I felt empty, but then fear arose again from nowhere and I clutched my stomach. This fear was different from the panic I'd felt in the cemetery. That fear had circled and pounced but then vanished, leaving me shaken but much the same as I'd been before it hit. It had stayed outside me. This new fear invaded my body. My hands grew so cold that the tips of my fingers went numb. I licked my lips, which felt swollen, but I couldn't sit still and, as the morning had grown colder, I went to get a jumper from my wardrobe, pulling out one after the other and holding each against me. I'd grown over the summer, and everything was either too tight or too short. I reached further and pulled out a sloppy windcheater that had once been Lawrence's. The journal had lain beneath it and there was a thud as it hit the floor. I picked it up and ran my fingers thoughtfully over its leather cover and then sat cross-legged on the floor with the journal on my knees. I felt calmer, but the fear in my stomach remained. I knew I couldn't hold on to my aunt any more than I could give Allegra back her life. But perhaps I could try to reach – force – my mother to reveal herself through the pages of her journal. I needed to belong more than anything.

After a short while, I put the journal back in the wardrobe, having decided to look at it later in the day. I knew that it was safe from discovery. Marcie Gibbons was the only adult who came into my room. Once a week she helped with the housework, changed my sheets and tut-tutted at the state of my clothes. She worked quickly and thoroughly but was certainly not into cleaning out cupboards. And Lawrence rarely visited me there. When he did it was to stand at the door and issue vague directives, such as, 'You'd better tidy this place up' or 'How on earth can you find anything?' It was unspoken between us; he offered suggestions and, unless it was important, I took no notice. I had thought I'd eventually show the journal to Aunt Monica but now changed my mind. The journal was mine and I alone had to unlock its contents.

Just before midday I heard Lawrence greet my aunt at the front door and then their clipped footsteps on the polished boards as they headed towards the living room. I dawdled down the hallway and then followed them into the room. Lawrence looked relieved to see me. He mumbled a few words about 'leaving us alone' and 'having work to do' and left me to it.

'Iris!' Aunt Monica hugged me and then stood back, tilted her head to one side and held my hands. 'It's so good to see you again. I'm sorry to have been away for so long but I've had so much work to do, and then all the preparations for Italy ...' Her words trailed off as I half turned and craned my neck to see if Lawrence had gone left or right at the hallway. If left, I knew he was headed for the studio, and we would be alone. He would remain there for hours.

My aunt waited for me to turn back before saying, 'Let's go for a walk. Up to the crannies. I can tell you what's been happening. I'll go and put on something more suitable.' She waved a hand across her pale silk skirt and smiled. 'Meet me out the front in ten minutes?'

I nodded and went to get my shoes.

As we set off along the poplar walk, Aunt Monica chatted about her students, the marking she had to do before she left for Italy, and the reams of forms she had to fill out. I said nothing and was glad when the steep climb up to the cliffs stopped my aunt's chatter.

We arrived breathless and light-headed with exertion after the climb from the bay and stood looking seaward while our breathing steadied. In the distance a grey sea merged with a silvery sky, the horizon a charcoal line across its width. It was flecked with the small foam-topped waves we had always called seahorses, their bowed heads processing towards the shore in evenly spaced rows like miniature warriors.

I decided to let my aunt speak first and waited for what seemed like ages until she eventually tapped my shoulder and, when I turned, handed me a photograph. I stared at it. It was a stone house on what looked like a rather bare hill. There was a stone fence set squarely around the building, parts of which had tumbled into small heaps of rock.

Three cypress trees of equal height broke the otherwise stark ridgeline behind the house.

'Is this where you're going to live?' I said.

'Yes, and isn't it lovely? It's just outside a town called Montespertoli. Perhaps one day you'll come and visit me there?' She squeezed my arm. 'Just think what fun you could have exploring a new place.'

I searched the photograph for whatever seemed to make my aunt so happy, but I couldn't find anything better than our sea and the honeycombed cliffs of the Peterborough coast.

'It looks nice,' I said as I gave back the photograph. The faint line between Aunt Monica's brows deepened. 'Let's sit down over there.' I pointed to a grassy part of the cliff where we could dangle our legs over the edge in safety and said, 'I have things I want to ask you.'

My aunt's eyes widened but she followed me without speaking.

When we were settled, we again stared silently out to sea, captivated once more by the coastline's rugged beauty. Then I took a deep breath and the words I'd wondered if I'd have the courage to say tumbled out easily. 'I want you to tell me about my mother.'

Aunt Monica took a deep breath. 'Well, you already know that we were twins and' – she patted her dark hair – 'that for some strange reason she was gold-blond whereas I'm a brunette.'

I put my hand out to stop her and said impatiently, 'I know all that. But I want to know how she met Lawrence, and I want to know what she was like. I want to know' – I hesitated and then blurted out – 'how much she loved me.'

My aunt's mouth opened like a fish.

'I want to know, I want to know … everything!' I said desperately.

Aunt Monica looked at me and sighed. I had the feeling that she'd been waiting for these questions. 'Your mother and father met at a night club,' she finally said. 'It was really very simple. Lawrence said he fell in love with Allegra the first time he saw her. It was literally across a crowded room.' My aunt raised her eyebrows, but her smile was sad. 'Your mother's blond hair reached to her waist. But it wasn't that white blond that can look lifeless; it was flecked with gold and in the right light just the merest tint of red. Her face was straight from a Renaissance painting. Pale, clear skin. Oval blue eyes with dark brows and lashes, which is unusual for a blond.'

'Did she fall in love with Lawrence at the same time?'

'Yes. She said she did, and she once told me that your father had "brown velvet eyes".'

I thought of Lawrence's dark eyes. They had often looked sad or far away, but I'd never thought of them as being soft like velvet. 'What happened then?'

'They married and went to Florence for their honeymoon. That's where you were conceived.' Aunt Monica's voice thickened and she took my hand. Her own was cold and I could feel the bones and soft veins. 'Allegra even knew when. It was the night before they visited the Uffizi Galleries. Your mother said that the love of art was written on you while in the womb. When you were born, she said that she had delivered the world a great work of art. I think she believed art would play a part in your life.' She looked at me wryly. 'How can it be any different with your mother besotted by paintings and your father a sculptor? You know the print on the wall in the living room?' She waited until I nodded my confirmation. 'It's called *Primavera* and your mother loved it. I often think she could have stepped out of it herself. It was her kind of world. A world of myth and flowers, of beauty and mystery.' The muscles in my aunt's jaw and forehead contracted as if to gather her thoughts. When she spoke again, her voice had lost its softness and become businesslike. 'Iris, your mother's world was a dream world, a world of feelings. Real life was often too harsh for her. Always remember that feelings and reality must be carefully balanced.'

'I know that,' I said. My mind was working furiously. My mother's dream world of feelings hadn't done her much good. After all, she was dead. I'd seen her grave. On the afternoon of my visit to the cemetery, I'd learned that feelings could make you scared. And as I sat on my bedroom floor that morning, the fear had come again. Perhaps feelings had made my mother scared? Perhaps they had made her die? I put all this together and announced, 'When you dream, you die.'

Aunt Monica gasped. 'No, you mustn't say that.' She looked distressed and her fingers flexed around my own.

'Why not?' I said.

'It's all right to dream' – my aunt searched for the right words – 'but dreams must have boundaries. They're fragile but can grow very large indeed, a bit like clouds. Think about this. When the sky is covered with clouds, nothing is as clear as it is in bright sunlight. Similarly, when you spend your life in a dream world – a cloud world – the real world goes out of focus, goes under a cloud. It ceases to hold your interest in quite the same way.'

'You mean my mother wasn't interested in me and Lawrence?'

'No! Of course I don't mean that!'

Aunt Monica was struggling. 'Listen carefully and I'll give you an example,' she said. 'I've been told I live in a dream world. Me, with my saints and sinners. But my work has a framework that keeps it in order. I teach about the past, about how people lived and thought in other centuries. I compare and contrast ideas and write academic papers. I spend my work time in the past, but the rest of my life is lived in the here and now. My dreams have a focus, whereas Allegra, your mother ...'

I waited but she didn't seem to know how to continue. She looked winded. Fear again butted the bottom of my stomach, but I quickly summoned up first annoyance and then anger. My aunt could talk all she liked of dreams and feelings, but when asked to tell the truth about her own family, she had ended up speechless. Obviously, when it came to family life, truth was as fragile as a sandcastle: whole and beautiful until a wave came and it drowned.

The wind picked up, and I noticed that the seahorses were now bucking their way to shore. I pointed them out and Aunt Monica laughed. She lifted her hand high and let a thin stream of sand trickle to the ground. The strain eased.

'Why did we come to live here when you and my grandparents lived in the city?' I asked.

My aunt continued sifting grains through her fingers. 'When Allegra and Lawrence returned from their honeymoon, your father needed to work in a quiet place, and so they moved here. Your grandparents were upset because they thought it was too far away, but they visited you every month until your mother ...'

I watched her drift again and then return. 'You know, Iris, Allegra kept a journal, but Lawrence said he doesn't know what happened to it. It's such a shame. It'd be a wonderful thing for you to have. One day you would understand it.'

I looked down so my bright eyes wouldn't betray me and said, 'We should go home now. Lawrence will have got lunch ready. I think your house is lovely and I'd like to come and see you one day. When Lawrence doesn't need me.'

I got to my feet and pulled Aunt Monica up by the hands. She looked perplexed, I thought, but relieved.

After dinner that night I did my share of the washing up and went to my room. Half an hour later, my aunt tapped on my door, a quick rat-a-tat-tat that over the years had become our signal.

'Do you want to hear about my latest finds?' she said. She continued without waiting for my reply. 'I've found four new versions of Ursula's life. Amazing, really. That's what I find so rewarding about my work. Different stories from different people about a person they can't be sure even existed but who so enamours them that they are compelled to tell their life story – even make it up or elaborate what's already written if necessary. Shall I go on?'

The question was more by way of courtesy as my aunt knew I was always interested, but this time when she opened her mouth to begin her story, I sat up and yawned exaggeratedly. 'I'm really tired,' I said. 'Let's save it for next time.' I knew, however, that this side of her leaving there would be no next time.

Aunt Monica rose and bent over to kiss me, bringing with her the scent of spice. Her lips were soft and her breath light but warm. My heart fluttered and I fought the desire to keep her with me, but our afternoon conversation had wearied me. I was sick of saints and sinners and dream worlds. They were just words that led nowhere, certainly not to the place where I would find out more about my mother.

After she left, I got out the journal and flipped through it to a blank page near the back. I sat up in bed and reached over to the side table for my favourite blue pen. I wrote the word 'dream' followed by 'die'. I held the journal up in front of me and studied the words. Then I flicked back and forth through the pages of postcards and notes, muttering my words like a mantra, at first softly but gradually louder until I felt them echo in my eardrums and tears ran down my face. I wiped the tears away impatiently, sat up straight and squared my shoulders. I picked up the pen and began to fill the entire page with my two words. I wrote faster and faster, until the words lost all meaning and became just marks on a page. Somewhere in that writing, I convinced myself I would not be like my mother. I would not be a dreamer. If dreamers died and abandoned those they loved, I didn't want to be one. I reached the end of the page and stared at what I'd done and felt calmer. In order not to be something, I realised, you had first to understand it.

I decided then that one day I would travel to Italy to see the paintings in the journal in order to know my mother better. I would find her through things that were as concrete as her slab. In the meantime, I would translate her writing bit by bit. Filled with determination, I opened to the first page and looked closely at the script. I fished under my bed for the dictionary and translated a word here and there, but the overall meaning of sentences eluded me.

Frustrated, I again began leafing impatiently through the journal, wishing it would miraculously translate before my eyes. When I reached the double-page spread just before the centre postcards, my eye caught the word *Primavera*, but only because it was printed whereas everything else was in script. I stopped and pressed the pages down with the flat of my hand and searched backwards until I found the start of the paragraph. Using my index finger as a pointer, I worked my way through the sentences word by word. There were few other words I recognised, only Florence, Uffizi, Arno and *bella*. Lawrence had mentioned the beauty of the Uffizi Galleries in Florence and my aunt had, of course, spoken of it that afternoon. As for the River Arno, I had a teacher who was keen on world geography. *Bella*, I must have absorbed from my brief early encounters with my grandparents. It was one of those words that is almost onomatopoeic: it sounds like what it means. I attempted to translate a few other words but only came up with night, light, dream, building, and walk.

I remembered the afternoon conversation with Aunt Monica. It was logical that my mother would have written of her time in Italy, and the postcards made me suspect the journal was written at the time of her first visit. With a jolt, I reasoned that it was very possible that I had come to life at some time before, between, or after these paragraphs, perhaps sometime between a dream and a walk.

4

I tossed and turned but couldn't get to sleep that night. In the past, thoughts of my mother had been like mirages; tantalising and mysterious yet, despite being ungraspable, emanating the promise of comforting warmth. Recent events, however, had given her a shape and begun to fill it out with flesh and blood. First there'd been the visit to the cemetery and the cold reality of a mother lying beneath a marble slab. After that, the terse exchanges between Lawrence and Aunt Monica suggested all was not well. Then I'd seen the journal with its postcards provoke rare anger in Lawrence. All of this followed by Aunt Monica's revelations about her sister that afternoon on the Crannies. With each of these my mother materialised more clearly. She was no longer simply a woman in a photograph with a startling resemblance to a main figure in a famous painting. She was not just an impassive beauty. She was a woman with a hidden story, and I wanted to know that story. Each time I closed my eyes and felt sleep slip over me, I saw her beautiful face and jerked awake.

In the end I gave up and decided to go and look at the print of *Primavera* in our living room. The front porch lantern was still on and threw dim shadows through the opaque fanlight above the door, creating just enough light for me to creep carefully along the hallway. My aunt's door was ajar and her room was in darkness. She'd been tired from her early rise and the long drive to Peterborough and gone to bed early.

As it was late, I thought I might be alone with *Primavera*, but when I drew close to the room, I heard the music of Corelli and then saw the glow of a table lamp. Lawrence was slouched in his favourite wing chair toying with an empty glass.

I slipped into the room and sat on the rug near the foot of Lawrence's chair.

'Everything okay?' He bent over and I turned my face upwards. We looked into each other's eyes. One part of me wanted to slip from the gaze but another wanted to stay and so I held on. It was Lawrence who finally slid his gaze to the glass now upside down in his hand. 'You should be in bed,' he said.

'I had a bad dream. Can I go back when the music finishes?' I leaned against his legs and picked up the Corelli album cover from the floor. A bewigged, curly-haired man looked out to one side, a small smile playing around his lips as if he were watching an amusing episode just out of our line of sight. Several small violins patterned the album's edges, and I absently traced their low-relief curves with my fingers. The music rose and fell, notes spilling into our comfortable silence.

Minutes later I heard a click as the stylus lifted, and Lawrence playfully nudged the back of my head with his hand. 'Time to go,' he said.

'Lawrence?' I pointed to *Primavera* and tried to sound as though my question was unrehearsed. 'Where did that picture come from?'

There was a sharp intake of breath and then Lawrence stood up and walked over to the print before speaking. I felt like a traitor and was glad he couldn't see the heat rise in my cheeks.

'It came from Italy, from Florence, from the Uffizi Gallery,' he said.

'Did you bring it back here?'

Lawrence reached up and ran his finger along the rim of the brass frame before turning and answering my question with a perfunctory, 'Yes.'

'Why did you choose this one?'

'I didn't choose it,' he said, a little too quickly. 'I mean, we both chose it – your mother and me.' He was frowning and sounded like he'd been caught trying to hide something and been found out at the last minute. He rushed on. 'Mostly because it's so beautiful and had always seemed to me – to your mother – to be out of place in an art gallery.'

I hoped he would go on talking about my mother, and I waited for him to echo Aunt Monica's comment about *Primavera* being my mother's 'kind of world', or at least say more about the two of them in Florence. But he was silent, and to keep the conversation going I said, 'Why doesn't it belong in a gallery?' Beautiful I could understand, but not out of place.

Lawrence sighed. I got the impression he didn't want to continue the conversation, and this made me all the more determined, so I repeated, 'Why doesn't it belong?'

'Your mother wanted it to be on the wall in a home. She wanted people – us – to live with it every day, not just pass it in a gallery.' Lawrence again turned to the print and his voice changed. 'Allegra believed that paintings speak to us if they're given the chance. And for this to happen we must live with them and discover what they have to offer. She understood things ...' He stopped then, shut his eyes, and shook his head. When he opened them, they looked watery. When he tipped back his head, I recognised that simple method for stemming tears.

He sat down and patted the arm of his chair. I sat on its edge, swinging my feet. Lawrence's manner returned to that of a school master instructing his pupil as he continued, 'They think it was originally painted for the home of one of the Medicis. They were a powerful family who ruled Florence on and off for a few centuries. It's thought to have hung over a day bed or a chest, possibly in the main bedroom. In those days main bedrooms were used like our living rooms, as a place to show off your best things.' He looked at me and smiled. 'There's a big difference between a bedroom and a gallery with over forty rooms full of artworks. So, you see, it was always meant to be in a home.'

'So how did it end up in a gallery?'

'Heaven alone knows its provenance.'

I had no idea what this meant but thought if I asked too many more questions, he'd send me to bed. I desperately wanted more and, thankfully, he realised that I wouldn't understand what he'd said and hastened to explain. 'Provenance is the history of all the different places an artwork's been over time.'

My father stood up, put his hands in his pockets, and stood directly in front of the print with his feet apart to steady him. He looked more relaxed, and I could tell he was about to embark on one of his mini lectures. I wanted to hear more about him and my mother, but our conversation had veered in an entirely different direction. I sighed inwardly.

'You know, there are two main schools of thought about galleries,' he said. 'One suggests they are temples to the power of art. The other says that by removing art from its home, we dilute it – sort of take away the reason it was painted in the first place – and then preserve it in aspic.' My father's tone made it clear he adhered to the latter opinion.

'What's aspic?'

'A kind of jelly.'

This made sense to me. We often made jellies and set fruit into them. I thought of the fruit's journey from its leafy plant or tree into our gelatinous, brightly coloured mass but was pulled back to *Primavera* when Lawrence suddenly said, 'You know the woman in the centre is Venus, the goddess of love, don't you?'

'Of course,' I said. I'd lived around art for long enough to have picked up some key figures. 'And I know that the woman in the dress with the flowers is Flora. But what's the blue man's name, the one chasing the lady without any clothes?'

'He's Zephyrus. The lady is Chloris. And when he captured her' – Lawrence stopped and weighed his words – 'when he reached her, she was able to make flowers bloom. That's why she has them coming from her mouth. In the end, she turns into the goddess Flora.'

'So, Chloris is Flora,' I said slowly. 'They are the same people.'

'Yes,' my father said. Neither of us mentioned the likeness between my mother and Flora, although with the photo directly below, it could hardly have been more obvious. I thought the idea of painting one person twice on the same canvas rather interesting and was about to say so when my father continued, 'Flora was a popular subject for artists at the time Botticelli painted this picture. Until then most art had religious themes, but the world of old myth and legend became fashionable, and Flora was a goddess from old Roman times.' Lawrence looked at me. 'Over two thousand years ago, you know.'

He reached up and traced along the bottom of the print with his forefinger. He stopped at Flora's feet and pushed his finger hard against the surface so that its tip went bright red and his knuckles whitened. 'Legend says Flora gave aroma to wine, charm to youth, sweetness to honey, and fragrance to blossoms.'

I'd been listening intently, staring at Flora and coveting her ability to do such amazing things, but when I turned to express my delight to Lawrence I was stopped by the lost look on his face – that look of a small child confused by adult behaviour. I understood this feeling only too well. There was a long pause during which he dragged his finger away from Flora's feet and ran it down the wall, where it came to rest on the mantelpiece. He looked at me, clicked his tongue, bit his bottom lip, and raised his eyebrows at the same time, and then said, 'Any more questions?'

I couldn't restrain myself and asked, 'What are the names of the three naked ladies?'

My father sighed. 'The women aren't naked. Their dresses are made of a sheer fabric. Painting it to look see-through shows you just what a great artist Botticelli was. Anyway, they're called the Three Graces. Aglaea gives, Euphrosyne receives, and Thalia returns.'

'What funny names,' I said. 'What do they give, receive, and return?'

'We don't really know. It's all about art, about being ready for whatever comes. Spring brings birth; art is like birth. The painting's called *Primavera*, which means spring.'

I didn't tell him I already knew its name.

'Go back to bed,' Lawrence said. 'That's enough for one night.'

I stood on tiptoes to kiss my father's cheek and left him standing in front of the print.

I stood in the dim hallway, leaned against the wall, and picked my way through our conversation. Any mention of my mother or Flora had brought that faraway look I knew well. And I couldn't shake the image of the slow fall of my father's finger down the print. I thought it very strange that he hadn't mentioned the resemblance between my mother and Flora. Surely that must have been one of the reasons my parents bought the print.

In my mind, I saw my mother standing in front of the painting, and my father marvelling at the likeness. I saw him lean forward and kiss her while she pulled away and looked around to see if anyone was watching. I saw her rest her head on his shoulder, the two of them in silent contemplation.

But there had been no mention of any shared joy. The only time Lawrence seemed himself was when he was giving mechanical details of the painting. I knew he was at sea when it came to feelings, especially feelings about my mother. But surely talking about memories with your daughter would bring comfort? And why had Lawrence never mentioned the purchase of *Primavera* before? It was the sort of story usually shared in a family. It seemed to me that memories took Lawrence to a lonely place where no one could accompany him, even me. I thought again of the day in the cemetery just a few months earlier. I hadn't been able to reach him then, either. Something other than the death of my mother had happened between the time the print was bought and now. Whatever it was led him to this dark place and there, I realised, he had hidden something I needed to know.

Finally, I gave up and walked slowly back down the hallway. I passed Aunt Monica's room and was surprised to see that her door was now shut. Light slivered through the cracks between the door and the architraves. So, my aunt, too, was awake. It seemed no one was having a restful night. My aunt's room was also Lawrence's study. He kept all his art books there, so at least Aunt Monica would have plenty to read. It was also the one room in our house with a telephone. I went to walk on but, suddenly, I heard her voice. I pressed my ear to the crack. Aunt Monica was speaking to someone in what I knew was Italian. I couldn't understand what she was saying but her distress was clear. Her voice was strangled, the pitch higher than normal. I heard her mention Lawrence's name, then the word *cimitero*, followed by a twice repeated *povera Iris*. I started. It took only a second for me to recall my mother's writing in her journal: *povera* Prudencia beneath the postcard. And the similarity between *cimitero* and cemetery was obvious. As I pieced together my few fragments of knowledge, I felt uneasy. Why was my aunt telephoning so late at night?

Why was she upset? And why was there a need to mention *cimitero* – cemetery – and 'poor Iris' in the same sentence? Once again, I was left with a little pile of words that I couldn't understand. First from my mother's journal, and then from conversations I was not meant to hear. But, again, one thing was clear. The visit to the cemetery was about more than connecting me in a concrete way with my mother. But it seemed no one, however, was going to tell me what that was.

Before I went back to bed I sat on the floor and wrote down all I could remember about *Primavera* in my mother's journal, on the page opposite my earlier list of repeated words. I described the scene with its myriad colours, paying special attention to what Lawrence had told me about the characters. I imagined my mother carefully rolling up *Primavera* and slipping it into a cardboard cylinder. I saw her relief when she slid it out on their return home and found it coiled but not creased. I saw Lawrence frame it, and the two of them carefully position it on the wall.

I turned to the back page and traced Prudencia's name with my finger. Perhaps my mother knew this person. Perhaps they had something in common, something to do with dreams and death, spring and birth. I turned the pages back and forth, staring until words and images blurred and swam before my eyes. I stopped at the postcard of *Primavera* and poked at Flora with my finger. *Tell me*, I said. *Who are you?* I wasn't sure if I was asking the question of Flora or my mother. In my mind, the two had merged. *I know you're dead*, I continued. *But why do I have the feeling I have to find you?* Flora looked silently back at me. If she was as bountiful as Lawrence suggested, why did she look so distant? That peaches and cream complexion, secret half smile, and pale-grey, untroubled eyes which seemed to say, *You've had enough, now.* Then it struck me that my mother was like Flora in more than looks. She, too, had the power to bestow gifts: a mother's love, the warmth of a caress, a million ministrations that spoke of the powerful bond between mother and child. Yet – and this now seemed glaringly obvious – if you have the power to give, you also have the power to withhold.

I put down the journal and picked up my favourite book, *Five go down to the Sea* by Enid Blyton, expecting, as usual, to be transported within minutes to distant places. But the mysteries in my own life that demanded I seek answers now blocked my entrance to the restful world of imagination. I felt as if I was reading from a distance. I put down the book and thought of Aunt Monica's saints and sinners, feeling suddenly very wise. Once, I wouldn't have questioned a saint's uplift to some heavenly realm. I'd thrived on the miraculous in their stories, but things had changed. When my aunt left for Italy, there would be a hole too big to be filled with saints or sinners or characters from books. I gasped and shook my head. There would be a void just as big as that beneath my mother's slab.

Sometime that night I woke with the first of my nightmares. In it stiff violets sprouted from the bases of two tombs. The tombs' slabs were transparent and in one lay Prudencia and the other my mother. The women's long, fair hair spread out above them and flowers trailed from their mouths like Chloris. When the purple blooms hit the underside of the slabs, the flowers wilted and fell back into the earth. I woke gasping and tried to sit up, but my body wouldn't move and I rolled onto my stomach and buried my head in my pillow. Then I smelled violets again. But it was not like the other times when the scent was faint. This time its green notes cut my senses, and I inhaled until I couldn't hold any more breath. When I had to let go, the scent vanished, and I opened my eyes.

The following morning, Aunt Monica, Lawrence, and I ate a big breakfast of bacon and eggs, accompanied by my Lawrence's delicious fried bread, which was white bread spread with tomato sauce and fried sauce side down in butter until crisp, then topped with a liberal sprinkling of salt. This had been our indulgent habit when my aunt visited ever since I could remember.

Afterwards we drove to the Bay of Islands and walked the nearby wild coastline, clambering down to the beach where possible, and when forced to climb back to the road, peering over the cliffs at the spectacular rock formations jutting out of the ocean. Before Aunt Monica left just after midday, we sat on the shady front veranda and toasted her new venture with apple juice.

Lawrence and I stood and waved as she pulled out of our driveway in her bright green Volkswagen. Then Lawrence went into the house, and I ran beside her car until she reached the Great Ocean Road. I kept waving frantically until her little beetle disappeared from sight.

The following Friday, Lawrence and I drove down to Melbourne when Aunt Monica flew out to Italy. We parked in the airport carpark and made our way to the terminal. My aunt was waiting for us near the check-in counters. She embraced us jubilantly.

'I can't believe this is really happening,' she said. 'For so long I've wanted to live among old stones and frescoes and do my work from one of its wellsprings.'

I said nothing but let her talk on. She was excited and her cheeks were flushed. She kept brushing back hair from her face as we three wrestled with the luggage. She didn't notice my silence as I fought bubbling tears.

After the luggage was tagged, we threaded our way through crowds and queues to the international departure doors.

'Well, wish me luck,' Aunt Monica said. She reached towards me and, even though I wanted to hold back, for the first time since the day of the crannies, I rushed into her arms.

'You'll come back, won't you,' I sobbed.

'Of course I will!' Her eyes glistened and she held me so hard it hurt. Then she looked over her shoulder to where my father stood balancing the luggage, cupped my ear, and whispered, 'But I think you might come to me first.'

My father gave Aunt Monica a quick hug. Then we watched the stainless-steel doors glide shut behind her. I looked up and saw tears in Lawrence's eyes. I let him lead me to the car and we began the long trip back to Peterborough in silence.

Peterborough

Australia

1976–1990

5

After the events of the summer and autumn of 1976, my world returned to what it had always been. The years were marked by our annual visits to the cemetery where Lawrence picked out weeds from around the base of my mother's grave and said little. I pretended to help him and counted the weeds as I built them into a single small pile. When the grave was again pristine, and Lawrence began to sweep the marble surface with a dustpan and brush, I counted anything that appeared in multiples: the cows in the nearby paddock, the pencil pines ringing the cemetery's perimeter, the graves themselves. When he'd finished and stood brushing the dirt from his hands, I stood beside him, and we both stared at the slab. I murmured my old prayer and year by year perfected my memory of the wooden plaque.

It was always around this time that my dream returned. I would wake shaken and sweating, crushed by the weight of those two tombs and assaulted by the scent of violets. But by the following morning, the dream would have receded into memory. Apart from this yearly pilgrimage and my dreams, it was as if my mother had never existed.

In autumn the trees in the poplar walk turned from green to gold and then disappeared into the coastal winds, and each year I waited for spring, surprised at how the new leaves seasoned the winter grey like a sprinkling of herbs.

Our distance from a major centre meant that much time outside of school and work was spent travelling for shopping and medical or dental appointments. In primary school there was a yearly fete with a few stalls and overzealous parents. Lawrence always came with me, but he was awkward in company, his mind always on his latest sculpture. I knew that my family was different. Sometimes, I longed for a mother like my school friends, but I understood this was not the shape of my life and I made the best of it. Milestone followed milestone: birthdays and school celebrations, Easters and Christmases. My lessons launched me into the world with a reading ability well beyond my years but no sense of mathematics. The latter was not my teacher's fault. I simply couldn't work out the relevance of numbers. When I was twelve, I travelled further afield to high school, but little changed except that there was no fete and Lawrence's presence at school was limited to an annual parent information evening. I was not a pretty girl, so boys didn't take much interest in me, and I was left to study in peace. As I watched my friends and their affairs of the heart, I learned that to be plain had its advantages.

As I got older, much of the care of our household fell to me. I became the practical one, the one who checked that nothing in the fridge had gone mouldy, that we always had milk and bread, that bills were paid on time, and a man came once a month to mow the grass around our house. Lawrence gratefully let me assume these responsibilities and retreated deep into his studio.

Aunt Monica had not returned to Australia after her time in Italy. Her fluent Italian language and impressive doctorate, coupled with the nature of her research – saints and sinners were the very stuff of Italy – secured her a tenured position in a university near Florence. For me, this was just another in a long line of betrayals. In the end, I accepted her absence, much as I had accepted my mother's as a very young child. I'd been annoyed but returned quickly enough to the life I knew with Lawrence. I never questioned my quiet, cloistered life. It was all I knew. But every fortnight I waited excitedly for Aunt Monica's letters. They were the exclamation marks that punctuated my routine days.

My early numerous attempts at translating the journal gradually became less frequent until they stopped altogether, and the journal lay untouched under a pile of old magazines. I consigned my plans to visit the original paintings of the postcards to the imaginary black hole where I pushed all impossibilities. As for *Primavera*, I passed the print every day, but its impact shrank as my outside interests grew. It once again became a pretty enough picture on the wall of our living room.

In 1983 I topped my final year at secondary school, and in 1984 I enrolled in an arts degree at the University of Melbourne, majoring in art history, and moved to the city. How could I have done otherwise? My home life *was* art. I simply couldn't envision a future without its central presence.

On the day I was to leave Peterborough by the early afternoon bus to Melbourne, I stood at the side of my bed, contemplating the neat piles of clothing waiting to be packed into my suitcase. There were serviceable jeans, T-shirts, shirts, and jumpers, but I knew that they were not fashionable. I'd read enough about university life and politics to know that, once again, I'd be the plain and studious girl who watched from the sidelines.

That morning Lawrence and I had walked the Crannies one last time in companionable silence. When we reached our turning point, Lawrence flopped onto the sand and patted the space beside him. I sat down and for a while we watched waves roll in to shore, hesitate, and then sluice backwards.

'It'll be very different to all this,' Lawrence said, waving his arm vaguely across the view in front of us.

I raised my eyebrows and said, 'Really?'

He turned and looked at me. 'Be careful, Iris. University life is wonderful, but you'll find much to occupy you other than study.' He hesitated. 'I want you to enjoy yourself. Experience different things. But a lot of first experimentation goes on at university and some of it doesn't end well.'

Lawrence was floundering. I decided to help him out and said, 'I'll be careful. Sex, drugs, and all that. And besides ...' I pulled at one of my springy auburn curls and then let it go. It leapt back into place. Then I ran a finger over the spattering of freckles across my nose. '... I'm no oil painting. So I don't think you'll have too much to worry about.'

Lawrence looked at me seriously, a slight frown creasing his forehead. 'Don't put yourself down, my beautiful girl. It's always been a puzzle to me why young women are so harsh on themselves. Your mother ...' He stopped and I held my breath, waiting for more. But he stood up, brushed the sand from his jeans, and held out a hand to pull me up. He didn't seem aware of his unfinished sentence, and

I lacked the courage to ask further questions. Once again, Allegra was suspended between us. An enigmatic and unreachable figure who was always absent, yet always just a thought or word or action away.

An unexpected surge of anger had risen inside me then, but I held my tongue and my temper and moved to the water's edge where I stooped and picked up fan-like shells and threw them one by one into the sea.

When I finished packing, I sat my backpack on top of the case and opened the slim, rather useless, outer pocket. Then I went to the wardrobe and retrieved the velvet wrapping containing my mother's journal. I folded the whole thing tightly in a pale-yellow hand towel and slid it into the pocket. The journal couldn't be left in the cupboard at home. The possibility that it would be found was remote but still too much of a risk. I zipped the pocket and secured it with a small padlock, putting the key into a coin purse, which I placed at the bottom of the larger part of the backpack. Then I stood back and surveyed my work. For the first time, I felt the reverberating thrill of new adventure. I was really going to Melbourne as a university student. Everything would be different. My future lay before me, exciting and terrifying at the same time. I placed my hands on the suitcase, leaned forwards, and let out a squeak of pure excitement.

Moving to Melbourne was a shock. In Peterborough, there was plenty of space and time. If I needed to think something through, I went on a solitary walk and cleared my head. In Melbourne, my thoughts were never my own. People, events, and my study workload filled every second of the day – and sometimes night. I enjoyed myself but realised I was even more of a loner than I'd first thought. When the bustle got too much, I headed for the Royal Botanical Gardens and sat watching the ducks and the swans. I often longed for my seaside cliffs and the smell of salt, instead of traffic and exhaust fumes. And then there was the endless parade of strangers through my life. In Peterborough, there was no need to monitor my every reaction. It was simple. People knew me, and I knew them. In the city, new relationships were an almost daily occurrence. I learned to read people carefully in ways I'd never had to before. I learned to be wary.

Louise was my roommate throughout my four years at university. She helped me navigate my new environment and despite – or maybe because of – our different personalities, we became firm friends. Brought up in inner-city Fitzroy, Louise knew her way around Melbourne and its inhabitants. She'd only chosen to board on campus because her travel route was indirect and notched several hours out of her day. She was outgoing with a matching dress sense, and in my first months in the city, I relied on her to stop me looking as though I'd just stepped off the farm.

On the night of our end of university party, she surveyed both of us as we stood side by side in front of the pitted mirror.

'You look pretty good, Iris. In fact, positively sexy! A little different from four years ago, eh?' She hesitated, and I could see she was weighing up her next words. 'But try not to look so serious, so *wise*,' she finally said. 'Boys find it scary. It turns them off.'

'What do you want me to do?' I puffed out my cheeks and opened my eyes wide until I resembled a startled kewpie doll.

'You're a twit,' said Louise. 'There's no hope.' She rolled her eyes and shook her head.

Then she turned towards me and was suddenly serious. 'Honestly, Iris, you really do always look like you know more than anyone else. Just try to relax a bit.'

She moved back to the heap of clothes on the bed and turned over tops and T-shirts in the hope of further inspiration.

I continued staring at my reflection in the mirror. It squinted back, viewing the world with detachment. There were already fine lines between my brows.

In mid-November of 1987, I returned home from university with an honours degree in art history. I'd not been home in four months, kept nose to desk by the coming exams.

I travelled by bus via the Great Ocean Road. There was a bus line that took the quicker, inland route, but after the crowded city, I was hungry for the coastline with its vast stretches of water. I'd never learned to drive as for four years my life had been lived close to the campus. My friends and I frequented corner pubs within easy walking distance from our accommodation, and when we wanted to go further afield to see a film or go shopping, we took the tram to the city centre.

Summer was a few weeks away and a spring breeze blew crisp and dust free. I left my suitcase to be loaded into the hold and settled into a seat halfway down the bus. It was cramped and I pushed my backpack hard against the side wall to make room for my legs. My eyes lingered on the cloth badge of a winged angel head I had hand sewn there in my first year at university. Now it was grimy and frayed at the edges. At the time, I regarded it as my link to my Lawrence and Aunt Monica, and perhaps to my mother. A link to the worlds of saints and sinners and angels that underpinned my childhood.

In the useless side pocket, still in its towel wrapping, lay my mother's journal. I had not looked at it for four years, although occasionally I'd thought about it and then pushed the thoughts away. I must have believed this kept me safe from the feelings and dreams the journal evoked. I didn't understand that simple law of physics: that pushing against a static object empowers it and stokes the fires at its centre.

I felt someone watching me and looked up, only to meet the gaze of a man about my own age. His face was familiar. Perhaps from some class or event on campus? But I didn't want to talk to anyone. So I flicked open the book on my lap and tugged at my ear thoughtfully. I knew time had improved my looks, but my hair was still a wild tangle, although longer now. And the span of dark freckles across the bridge of my nose that rendered my face an optical illusion had, much to my relief, paled in recent years so that my features could be more clearly determined. But I knew that I was arresting rather than pretty.

As the bus wound through the city streets and out to the Geelong Road, my mood clouded along with the day. This stretch of road was bleak, flanked by spiky grasses, and peppered near Werribee by the stench from the sewerage farm. I ruminated on my future and a world that seemed spotlit under my tutor's praise was now altogether less bright. I had no idea what I was going to do. I was to attempt to find work armed with a fourth year thesis that concentrated on understanding Lorenzo Monaco's *Coronation of the Virgin* through its depiction of symbol and spiritual hierarchy. A subject that had satisfied me but was hardly designed to make me an attractive employment prospect. I liked the way the world of Lorenzo's Camaldolese monastery viewed its art through the eyes of spirituality. Everything had meaning and could be explained. The virgin's graceful hand with the palm opened upwards meant 'she who points the way'. What seemed the disproportionate sizes of many figures in the paintings was just a way of showing who was really important. Everything had purpose and my paragraphs had followed each other with pleasing logic. It was all much more manageable than the indecipherable contents of my mother's journal.

I had stayed on this early side of the Renaissance, not admitting to myself that the great rebirth frightened me. When I did allow myself to peek into it, I saw figures released from the certainties of the medieval world into the vortex of emotion that accompanied that great reawakening. When we had to research an area of the Renaissance for a third year paper, I concentrated on the Medici family as the world's first true art collectors. At least this topic was underpinned by chronology and facts. Since that summer of 1976, I had tried to draw a line between facts and feelings, between theory and intuition. I did my best to live life from moment to moment, without the burden of past and future, and I orchestrated everything, from daily activities to studies, to make sure this happened.

But as I sat in the overheated bus on the long journey to Peterborough, even the familiar and comforting lure of my gilded medieval world paled as we drove over pitted bitumen under a grey sky.

Before we reached Geelong, I was asleep. I woke in time to see the sign announcing the town of Torquay. Stunted papery tea tree nudged the roadsides, darker grey against the grey sky. The coast was out of sight, but as we rounded the next bend, the land sloped into a sage-green sea. There was a storm on the way, and the water was still. I had been relying on its blue to lift my mood and this opaque green had the opposite effect. I closed my eyes again and concentrated on trying to guess where we were by the camber of the road or the hook of a bend. I knew this route like the back of my hand and as a child had spent many a carsick hour rounding its curves.

For the rest of the journey, I drifted between sleeping and waking, only rousing when rain splattered the windows and wind buffeted the side of the bus. When the Twelve Apostles ruptured the ocean, I knew home was close. The bus left me at the side of the highway. I heaved my pack onto my back, collected my suitcase, and set off towards the coast so I could reach home via the poplar walk.

I saw him long before he saw me. My beloved Lawrence in gumboots and a rubber apron, straight from the evening milking at the dairy sheds next door. I knew he only tolerated this work, but it had always been our bread-and-butter money.

As I watched Lawrence, I felt the university year melt away: the pressure of timetables and exams, the flickering gazes of people focussed on careers, the clever banter that underpinned even the most mundane conversation. Here, surrounded by paddocks broken only by the low-slung milking shed and our own house, I breathed in the sea air and felt my head clear.

Lawrence reached the fence that separated our house lot from the farm. With a gaze sharpened by absence, I saw that he threaded his body between its wire struts with more care, that on straightening he pushed his wrists into the small of an arched back.

'Dad!' I called. But the wind threw my voice.

Hoisting my backpack, I hurried to catch up with Lawrence before he set off up the hill.

When I was closer, I called again, 'Dad!'

He turned. 'Iris! You're early. Welcome home. How was the trip?'

'Fine,' I said. 'Even though we travelled straight into a storm.'

There was a pause as we assessed each other. Lawrence looked older. He had more grey hairs, but he was still handsome, his features refined by age. I wondered what he thought of me.

'You're going to find it pretty quiet around here. After uni.' He waved an arm over the landscape and affected a rueful glance.

'I think I'm glad,' I said slowly. 'It's been a long year and the quiet will help me decide what to do now. You've been to the sheds?'

Lawrence smiled and pointed to his apron. 'Where else?'

I laughed. 'When I was a child you told me you used to lay your head against the cow's hot flanks while you fixed the teats on the udders. I've never forgotten that.'

'You know,' Lawrence said. 'For some reason I've always loved the cows. Not so much the milking, though. Cows are sweet creatures, watchful, their eyes always trusting despite the throb of hard metal.'

'Have you done much work?' I said.

We both knew I wasn't referring to the milking.

'Yes and no. A few small commissions: a trophy for the golf club, a crucifix for a church in Warrnambool, a feature piece for a local cheesemaker. But I can't seem to find the right shape for my pelican.'

I must have looked perplexed because he laughed and his eyes grazed the hills. I knew then that he was talking about a sculpture. For as long as I could remember, he had used the hills to help him avoid sharp edges in his work. He said nature was fluid and it was a human impulse to box things in. That if you wanted form, you should take it from nature's flow.

'Show this pelican to me,' I said. I tucked my arm into his and we walked slowly towards the house.

We went to the studio first and Lawrence told me of his difficulties with the pelican. The surfaces were coated with dust and sawdust. Suddenly he walked to the table against the far wall, picked up an envelope, and blew on it. He held it out to me.

'This might interest you,' he said.

He waited as I opened it.

It was a document from Alistair and Sons, our local real estate agents, an unsigned rental agreement with my name on it on premises in Warrnambool to be used as a shop and art gallery.

'Oh, Dad! We can't afford to do this!'

'But think of the possibilities, Iris. The tourist trade is solid here all year. And then there are the locals. They always need cards and presents and ...' Lawrence's litany of persuasive reasons grew and I listened without interrupting, fascinated in equal measure by the subject matter and my Lawrence's uncharacteristic enthusiasm for something outside of his sculpture.

'I don't know, Dad,' I eventually said. 'Of course, I have to work, but Louise and I had plans, and shops are a seven day a week proposition.' I wanted to go to the city regularly, and Louise had planned to spend time with me in Peterborough. But the future was weighing on me, and we had little money. I didn't want to be a burden to Lawrence. And my options were certainly limited.

Lawrence continued, 'I can help out with the buying and give you days off, and of course we'll reserve a section for real art.' He waited expectantly for my answer.

There was a childlike energy in Lawrence, and I loved him all the more for it. I was his daughter, he loved me, and he obviously wanted to help me.

'I guess I'll be able to come home each evening,' I said slowly. 'It's only a short drive. Of course, I'll have to get my driver's licence.'

Lawrence nodded. 'Yes, it'll be good to have you back.'

His eyes were bright and he looked absurdly pleased with himself. And so, of course, I gave in.

I didn't hear the warning bells. That would have required intuition, and I had worked too hard for what answers I had to pay heed to such things.

6

I called my shop and gallery Pelican and Lawrence's sculpture – having never met his artistic standards – lived in the front window on a wooden plinth, backed by a painted seascape of blue, white-tipped scalloped waves.

The lease for the business premises included three rooms, one behind the other. The shop itself faced onto the street, with the gallery directly behind it. At the back of the gallery, a wooden door led into the third room, which served as the storeroom and contained a tiny kitchenette.

Lawrence and I poured our hearts and souls into the interior décor. Lawrence constructed the Baltic pine plinths on which we set our most outstanding items for sale, as well as the three-tiered stands that lined the walls. I chose the white ceiling and powder-blue wall paints. And, after lengthy discussion, we agreed to sand and stain the old pine floorboards. It was dusty and time-consuming work, but the end result proved well worth the effort.

Once the fittings were complete, we carefully stocked the shop and gallery. In essence, the dividing line was clear. Crafts – jewellery, fabric and knitted items, and paper goods – along with pottery were clustered around the counter and on the front room tiers. We displayed paintings, sculptures, and installation pieces in the gallery.

Four months after first signing the lease, we stood in front of the sales counter and surveyed our work in silence.

Finally Lawrence looked at me, grimaced, and said, 'I suppose we must have an opening night?'

We looked at each other in mock horror.

'I suppose we must,' I said.

Even though we lived in Peterborough, and Warrnambool was a forty-minute drive from home, we opted for convention and held opening night at Pelican. We invited all the artists and craftspeople from whom we bought or consigned work and kept our fingers crossed that they would come. Most tended to live away from towns, in places where there was space and time to think. And most tended to be loners. I understood this completely. Lawrence had, of course, chosen Peterborough, for those very reasons. We also invited the Peterborough locals who were a part of our everyday life: the proprietors of our small groups of shops and the three families who formed our reclusive circle. Much to my delight, Louise travelled from Melbourne to be part of the celebrations.

We put on a small spread and hired a local blues band to add some cheer. It was nothing fancy, just sandwiches, biscuits, and dips, with a few canapés plated up by the delicatessen two doors down from Pelican to add a 'touch of class', as Lawrence wryly commented. After much deliberation, we decided to provide red and white wine, and sparkling mineral water.

The evening was wonderful. My opening night nerves quickly disappeared amongst the banter and the music and the discussions about artists' current and future projects. About halfway through I absented myself from the milieu and stood to one side, observing. A few minutes later

Louise sidled up, nudged me in the ribs, and said, 'You must be feeling pretty pleased with yourself. The shop and gallery look amazing.'

I thought for moment before saying, 'Yes, I am pleased.'

'You know,' Louise continued, 'I never thought you'd settle back in the country.'

I turned towards her. 'What did you think I'd do?'

'Oh, I don't know. Perhaps move to the city and teach. Or something like that.' She was jigging to the music and made an attempt to get me to do the same, but I shook my head, holding up my glass as an excuse.

At Louise's words, the full impact of what I'd undertaken hit me. The decorations and securing of stock had taken every spare moment and I'd given no thought to the future. Was this a short- or long-term venture? Did I see myself running a regional shop and gallery until I was old and grey like Mr Calder? I took a deep breath and redirected my thoughts. This was an evening for celebration. The future could wait.

Louise stayed with us that night and returned to Melbourne the following day. As she boarded the bus, she turned, rested her hand on my arm, and said, 'If you need a break come and see me? Okay?'

I nodded and gave her a quick hug before backing away as the driver threw the now idling bus into gear and headed off along the Great Ocean Road.

In the space of a one-day stay, Louise had inadvertently twice sown doubt in my mind. A different version of my opening night doubts flittered through my mind. Was this a good use of my art history degree? Had I closed off the possibility of adventure while I was still young? I shook my head to rid myself of my thoughts, but they refused to budge. So I pushed them to the back of my mind by running through the list of tasks that waited for me that day. By the time I returned to the house, my unease had settled, swamped by the sheer volume of work required to run a business.

I joined the shopkeepers' association, which sported the grandiose title of Warrnambool Proprietors' Alliance, but largely kept to myself. As I drove home to Peterborough each day, it was difficult to make and sustain real friendships. I did get to know a few young people from the association well enough to have the occasional lunch or quick drink before I headed home. But their lives were in Warrnambool and mine was with Lawrence. None of this, however, really worried me. In a way, life was an extension of how things had been for me as a child. Eventually, university receded into the distance, an exciting and noisy hiatus bridging childhood and the adult world.

The misgivings I'd experienced at the time of Pelican's opening faded as life assumed a routine, a pleasing regularity. Louise and I kept in contact, speaking on the phone each week. And she came to visit whenever she could get time away from the law firm where she claimed she was 'the most junior of the juniors'. It was always only for two or three days and included the weekend, so she rarely came to Pelican. When she was with me, we were happy to walk the Crannies, lie comatose on the warm, sandy beaches in summer, and pace them briskly in winter, rugged up in thick wool coats, beanies, and gloves.

Over the next few years, I catered mostly to the seasonal changes in the tourist trade that was my staple market.

Summer brought city families with spoilt children and a surprising sameness. The women bought necklaces and locally dyed silk scarves. The men lounged against the wall outside, hands in pockets, occasionally swiping at a child who overstepped the mark. In winter there were the grey nomads: sharp Sydneysiders, tanned and laconic northerners, restrained Melburnians. Most couples with caravans and a barely disguised relief at having someone to talk to apart from each other. Ironically, despite spending my childhood alone, I became adept at the pleasantries needed to keep people browsing and, hopefully, purchasing. An assorted local clientele filled the rest of the year when it was a present for mum, or a treat for themselves, or simply a wander to relieve everyday tedium.

Only about half of our customers gave more than a cursory glance to the gallery where I exhibited local artists whose work Lawrence and I thought had genuine merit.

Monica's letter arrived like a bright bird on a grisly day just before the start of the 1990 summer season. I was rummaging in the counter drawer where I kept tape and string for posting packages. I knew supplies were low but didn't realise I had run out, and I reached to the back of a drawer in the hope of finding something to use. I wanted to give Joe a parcel when he came with the morning mail delivery.

With a start, I felt the soft towel that held my mother's journal, and realised I'd not opened it in close to eight years. I'd left the wrapped journal in my backpack the whole time I was at university. There'd been no need to open it. Life was simply too busy and too interesting. When we were setting up Pelican, I used the backpack to bring stationery items from home. I'd felt the journal as I was emptying the contents into the drawer, opened the side pocket, pulled out the wrapped parcel, and pushed it to the very back of the drawer. Once again, I hadn't been tempted to open it. I'd been too preoccupied with Pelican.

Morning trade was patchy at this in-between time of year, so I put up a sign to say I would be back in five minutes and returned to my desk. Then I carefully unfolded the towel, pulled out the journal, and ran my fingers over the crimson cover. It was even softer than I remembered and was now crisscrossed with hairline cracks. I opened to the first page and frowned when the contents made no more sense than usual. In my first year at university, I'd toyed with the idea of learning my mother's language but had withdrawn at the last minute. So my Italian was limited to art history jargon: *sfumato, putti, chiaroscuro, mandorla* ...

I knew it was ridiculous, but the journal seemed alive under my fingers. I removed my hand and swallowed hard. Suddenly, I was spiralling back to my eleven-year-old self and the dreadful panic I'd felt at my mother's gravesite, to the void beyond her slab that left me breathless. I sat quite still, trying to breathe evenly so as to settle myself. Tears slid down my cheeks. I kept up this measured breathing, in and hold for the count of two before breathing out, until the panic subsided.

For a while, I couldn't move. As I should have expected, opening the journal was like touching a fireball. I could only let my feelings flare and then wait until they burned themselves out.

In the silence after I closed the journal, I felt sadder than I had for a long time. I stared at its crimson cover. No matter what I did, the past would always be trapped between its pages. My life had no clear centre that could be talked about and explained. The centre lay in the journal. And, ironically, each time I went near it, I got burnt.

It felt as if Lawrence had thrown the journal into the bin to free himself, but when I retrieved it, his anguish transferred to me. The journal put me in the dead centre of Lawrence's fractured world. In putting it aside for so long, it had also gathered strength and now hit with brute force.

My thoughts spiralled. It was all right for mothers to die, but they had no right to just vanish and then cause this pain. Lawrence – my family – should have kept Allegra alive in other ways. In afternoons spent musing over photo albums, in those annoying but sustaining refrains: *Your mother believed ... Your mother always said ... Your mother loved ... Your mother laughed at ...* In all those things I had never experienced.

My life was not the orderly series of days running Pelican and evenings with Lawrence that I willed it to be. My life had an absent mother at its heart.

I sat back in my office chair and let my hands fall into my lap. It had begun to rain, thick drops splashing onto the building's tin roof. Outside, the sky was grey. I thought back to the night I'd seen Lawrence throw the journal into the bin. I saw his uncharacteristic anger, the tense flick of his wrist as he threw the journal as if it were alive and dangerous.

Then, I gasped as it hit me that maybe the journal *was* alive and dangerous. I'd always thought discarding it was no more than Lawrence's way of ridding himself of the past. My mother was dead, so why keep something that kept the pain of her loss alive? Perhaps it was because I'd not opened the towel in so many years combined with the fact that I was now older and wiser, but the thought struck me that there might be more than loss or pique behind Lawrence's anger. It had been too strong, too visceral.

The minutes passed. The rain now spattered across the shop's front window.

I picked up a clean sheet of paper and a pen and began to write down words, emotions associated with Lawrence. It seemed whenever the journal came to the fore, I ended up with lists of words.

The list grew: sad, angry, scared, frustrated ...

I stopped and stared at the words in front of me.

Most of them made perfect sense. They were emotional responses to a sad situation and quite reasonable. But in themselves they didn't explain the need to be rid of the journal. Surely you would want to keep such a personal item, even if it meant having to hide it from yourself.

My racing thoughts stopped at the word 'hide'. I'd been focussed on Lawrence's feelings as the reason for his impetuous act and not considered that there might be a practical reason. Perhaps there was something in the journal that Lawrence wanted to hide from me. Was there some dark secret he didn't want me to know? Was there more to my mother's death than I had been told?

Emotions as a motivating force were one thing; secrets were something else altogether.

I gulped, tapped on the journal's scarred cover, and said, 'What are you hiding?'

It was impossible to speak with Lawrence about it, and Monica had told me as much as she could. Anyway, she was too far away now, our only link the thin sheets of parchment she used for her letters.

I was back to where I had been at eleven. If I wanted to know more, it would be up to me.

There was a rap on the glass door. I looked up and saw with relief that it was our regular mailman, Joe. He was squinting into the room with kind, wide eyes. His bicycle lay on the pavement outside. His satchel of mail was tucked under his arm.

I opened the door, at the same time turning around my closed sign. After the journal, I needed a longer break. Joe took off his boots and placed then side by side on the doormat. Then he hung his raincoat on the coat stand inside the door and came inside.

'I thought you were getting a motorbike,' I said. 'It'd be a lot quicker and you'd get less wet.'

'Don't really want one of those newfangled things. Too old for change. Anyway, the old rust bucket'– he indicated his bike – 'keeps me healthy.' He looked at me and pursed his lips. 'You look pale, love. Too much time indoors. Tell you what. I'll lend you Milly this evening and you can take her for a walk. Let her chase a few sea cucumbers.'

Joe was both our Warrnambool mailman and our closest Peterborough neighbour. He lived in a neat weatherboard house, which he repainted every four years the same shade of sky blue. His wife Nancy was the local jams and conserves queen. In the absence of children, they lavished affection on their poodle/shih-tzu cross, a curly haired creature with brown almond eyes. I called her supermodel Milly because of her abnormally long legs. Milly and I had known each other since she came to Joe and Nancy eight years earlier, a scruffy waif whose frenzied scratching at the pet shop window had won Joe's heart.

'Good move,' I said. 'I'll come around about seven o'clock. A long sea walk sounds just the thing! I was going to give you a parcel but, unfortunately, I've run out of packaging ...'

'No worries,' Joe said. 'I'm sure whoever it is can wait another day.' He reached into his bag and fanned out two letters. 'One of them's airmail. And a nice fat one it is, too. Probably Monica. Have you been busy?'

'Not really,' I said. 'But give it a week or so and the summer invasion will start.'

'Suppose it will,' agreed Joe.

'Coffee?' I said.

Joe grinned. 'Why do you think I took off my boots?'

I made coffee and we sat at the front counter and fell into the easy banter of friends. It was a relief to be away from the journal and let my nerves slowly settle.

Finally, Joe got up and looked at me quizzically. 'You do look peakish, Iris. Make sure you come this evening. Milly will be waiting. And I know Nancy has made a batch of your dad's favourite pickles.'

And with those few words, he was gone.

I picked up the letters and saw the airmail was from Monica. How coincidental that I had been thinking of my mother only to receive mail from her twin? But I was more than happy to be distracted by Monica's chatter and the cuttings and cards that fell like confetti into my lap. There were prayer cards with Monica's scribbled notes for my interest, leaflets from exhibitions she'd visited, and a couple of medals she thought I'd find amusing: a Mary Magdalene with hair reaching to her feet and a Saint George astride a gentle-looking dragon. I turned each over, savouring the way they bought my aunt close to me.

I scanned the first page. There were chatty details of her recent visitors. In between her teaching and serious research, Monica gave lectures on obscure and colourful saints in a deconsecrated chapel near her house. They attracted the devout and the unusual, the spiritually hungry and the merely curious. It didn't matter, she said. They were just people searching for a truth. She went on with news of her parents, my grandparents. I was sorry to read that my grandfather was unwell and not expected to live for much longer. But to me my grandparents were abstract people who sent two cards each year accompanied by cheques. One for my birthday and one for Christmas. I could not remember them playing any significant part in my life.

And then came her request:

> *Iris, my love, I have a special favour to ask*
> *of you. There was an exhibition in England*
> *called* A Perspective on the Domestic in
> the Renaissance. *I couldn't get there but*
> *have since heard, would you believe, that it*
> *has gone to Australia! There is a tapestry of*
> *Saint Ursula that I'm particularly interested*
> *in …*

There followed a series of dot points outlining the things that interested her about the tapestry and a request that I go to Melbourne and look at it for her. Lastly came her usual plea that I visit her in Montespertoli.

I put down the letter and stared into the distance. When Monica first went to Italy, the possibility of visiting her had been mentioned, but I'd been too young to give it any real thought. Italy had seemed as far away as the moon. Then school and university and the minutiae of everyday life had pushed any such thoughts well into the background. Now that I was entrenched in the business, travelling to Italy would require massive organisation. We would need someone to run Pelican on a daily basis. And whoever it was needed at least a passing knowledge of art with regards to aesthetics and methods of production. For the first time, I felt a little trapped in a web of my own making. Then I pulled myself together. For goodness sake, I had a degree and a flourishing business, and a father who loved me enough to set me on this path. One day, I'd go to Italy to see Monica. Perhaps I'd even visit the paintings in the journal as I'd promised myself when a child.

I folded up Monica's letter and dropped it into the cane basket I used to bring goods to Pelican. Then I rewrapped the journal and purposefully pushed it to the back of the drawer.

That evening Milly and I walked through twilight into early night. The water was calm and the only sound was the hiss of small waves as they rolled to shore. I'd settled after the events of the day but there was a lingering unease, which I put down to Monica's request rather than the aftereffects of finding the journal. I'd been back to

Melbourne a few times since my return from university, mainly for shopping, and recently for Pelican-related business and purchases. The trip to the city took hours and was no longer a novelty, but I could hardly refuse Monica, and I always enjoyed the change of scenery once the bus ride was over. I could also catch up with Louise and thought I'd ask her to come to the exhibition with me. I began to warm to the idea. It might be good to visit an exhibition with Louise again, like we used to do when we were at university. Later we could have coffee and cake and dissect what we had seen. I returned a happy Milly to Joe and Nancy, collected our pickles, and went home to talk to Lawrence.

'Why on earth do you want to go to see an exhibition about the Renaissance,' Lawrence said.

He was seated at the kitchen table folding brochures for Peter Charleston's upcoming exhibition into three and stacking them into a neat pile. Peter was one of our star suppliers. His gorgeous green-blue pottery with its signature logo was by far our best seller, and we eagerly awaited his regular visits to Pelican with his latest creations.

'For two reasons,' I countered. 'I studied art history, remember? And it's only a small request from Monica. She was so good to me when I was young.'

Lawrence looked sheepish. 'I'm sorry. It just seems such a waste of time with the approach of the summer season. We can't really afford time out so close to the Christmas rush. And Monica's probably seen more than enough tapestries, paintings, and sculptures of Saint Ursula to last a lifetime. Why don't you get a catalogue and send it to her?' Then he changed tack and waved a brochure in front of me. 'Pete's close to finishing his series of wave pottery and I was hoping we'd get to check it out this Sunday. It's the first time he's moved from pots to sculptural pieces, you know.'

'Monica's never asked me to do anything like this before,' I said. 'And I need a break away. Setting up Pelican has taken an awful lot of time and energy. I'll catch the early afternoon bus on Saturday after we close for the weekend and be back on Monday evening in time to open Tuesday morning.'

'I thought you were happy enough,' Lawrence said.

I sighed. 'It's got nothing to do with me being unhappy. It's just a favour for Monica. A two-day break's nothing. It'll be good to do something different.'

Lawrence turned back to the remaining brochures. I got the impression he was no longer listening to me.

Finally, he looked up and said, 'You go, Iris. I guess Pete will have to wait until next week.'

I was perplexed and felt guilty. I put the guilt down to my other reason for wanting to go to Melbourne, the one I hardly dared admit even to myself. The previous week I'd contacted my old university lecturer, Concetta Carino, and asked if she'd be willing to look at my mother's journal. I felt it was time I understood her words. I knew this came with risks. I might discover something I didn't want to know. Concetta said she'd be at the university over the weekend and would welcome some distraction in between hours of marking first-year essays. Concetta and I had always got on well, largely due to our shared love of

Lorenzo Monaco. We agreed that I'd drop the journal to her late on Saturday afternoon and then meet her again on Monday morning to discuss her findings. But, despite this, I sensed that for Lawrence my trip was no longer about simply doing a favour for Monica but had mutated into disloyalty towards him and Pelican. And as if this wasn't enough, I was beginning to suspect that there was more behind Lawrence's reasons for not wanting me to go. But I had no idea what that could be. He looked petulant and it was simply not like him to go to the trouble of putting obstacles in the path of something so unimportant.

'I'm going to go,' I said firmly. 'It'll be good see Louise. I haven't seen her that much since she came down for the opening.'

I sat down at the table and made a show of sorting out the accounts spread across the kitchen table. The air felt charged. Neither of us spoke.

Melbourne

Australia

1990

7

On Saturday afternoon I left the journal at the university with Concetta. She must have intuited how hard it was for me to leave it, perhaps sensed my hesitancy when I placed it in her hands. Without words she put the journal on her desk. Then she turned towards me and said, 'I understand. I'll take good care of it. It is precious beyond words. We'll talk more when I see you on Monday.'

I nodded dumbly, tears pooling in the corners of my eyes.

I didn't linger. I felt agitated. I needed to move and shift the anxiety that was settling around me like a fog. So I made my way to a small hotel in a laneway off Spencer Street. It was basic but comfortable. I spent a restless night and, after a sparse breakfast of tea and toast, headed to Flinders Street Station, where I waited for Louise under the clocks above the entrance.

After university, Louise had moved to an inner-city shared house and manoeuvred her way into a small, but up and coming, law firm. This hadn't surprised me. Louise had a sense of purpose and destination granted to few. At university she'd worked hard, partied exuberantly, and then moved seamlessly into her chosen field. Despite, or perhaps because of, it being a Sunday, the station was busy. People jostled past me and I felt awkward, slowed by the pace of life in a country town.

'Iris, I'm over here!'

I followed the voice and saw Louise striding towards me.

'Hey, it's great to see you,' she said.

As she flung her arms around my neck, I noticed her blond-streaked hair and edgy clothing. I blushed at the thought of my own jeans and striped shirt bought from the general store two shops down from Pelican.

'Yes, it's great that you could come,' I said.

She released me, checked her watch, and tucked her arm through mine.

'I've got the whole morning,' she said. 'That should be plenty of time to have a look at the exhibition and then catch up over lunch. It's a shame I've got to go to this family thing this afternoon or we could have spent the whole day together. Come on. Let's go.'

Before I could say more, we were off along Swanston Street in the direction of the Melete Gallery.

We arrived at the gallery just as the first drops of rain began to fall. The gallery had been built during my final year at university to house small exhibitions. I had been there once to look at illuminated manuscripts. At the time I thought its postmodern angles unsuited to the curve of the medieval mind responsible for these exquisite works. Fortunately, a sensitive curator had challenged these angles when setting up for *A Perspective on the Domestic in the Renaissance.*

When we entered the gallery, Louise whistled softly under her breath and said, 'Hey, this looks great.'

Swathes of crimson velvet softened the room's corners. Freestanding lamps had replaced the centre lighting. Parlour plants in carved wooden pots were scattered about the room. The effect was intimate – a true perspective on the domestic – and as it was the last Sunday of the exhibition, there was the extra bonus of few visitors.

'Will we meet at midday?' Louise said. It was our old pattern: separate at the entrance and meet at an allocated time to discuss our individual responses to the exhibition.

'That'll be fine,' I answered. I could return after lunch if I needed more time.

I worked my way along glass cases containing open Books of Hours and frayed samples of needlework. It was no surprise to find a lack of paintings. For most of the Renaissance, these were considered artisan and generally the work of men. This exhibition focussed on the minutiae of women's lives.

At first I took no notice of the dark tapestry in the corner, but when I drew closer, I realised that it was Monica's tapestry of Saint Ursula. Moths had eaten away at the threads and the colours were faded. I stood back a little to view the overall pattern and then moved in closer to study its worn condition. Then I pulled out my aunt's list of questions, settled on a nearby bench, and did my best to answer them.

Time passed quickly and when I looked at my watch I saw I had only twenty minutes before I was to meet Louise. Satisfied that I'd done my best, I put the notebook away and walked to the small sectioned-off area of the exhibition I had yet to see.

It was a replica of a bedroom, complete with canopied bed and brocade covers. A painting of a nude woman hung on a makeshift wall. She was lying on a couch and held a spray of acanthus leaves over her sex. The sign beside the painting explained that the woman's role was to inspire the couple to make beautiful babies.

What I guessed was a marriage chest stood at the foot of the bed. There had been a second-year elective subject that concentrated on Renaissance furniture as art, but I had decided against taking it. I remember glancing over the contents, which told of the importance of household paraphernalia and listed numerous items, including these *cassoni*, and having a fleeting vision of the postcard in my mother's journal with '*povera* Prudencia' written beneath it and opting instead for an elective on donor paintings. I enjoyed the way these solemn, usually wealthy, people had themselves inserted into art. Whether it was true piety or mere conceit was a moot point. My choice of subject was made solely on what interested me. Now, as I contemplated the chest, it struck me that its shape was similar to the one in my mother's journal.

The exhibition *cassa* was about half the size of a claw-foot bath, each knuckled foot splayed out on the ground. The bulbous sides were adorned with low-relief, gilded mythological figures and an excessive amount of foliage. The dense embellishment made it difficult to decipher who or what was being represented, but amidst the scrollwork and intertwined vines and leaves, a god figure emerged from a froth of water six times – frieze-like – around the body of the chest. The lid was flat except for a slightly recessed rectangle in the centre and it, too, was a maze of foliage. With a start, I remembered that the chest in my mother's journal also bore a water god – probably Neptune because of the trident – and that its decoration was similarly dense. I wished I had the journal with me so I could compare the two *cassoni*.

As I stood taking in the chest's detail, there was a noise beside me, and I turned to see a black-clad attendant fiddling with the lock on a glass case containing pieces of jewellery. She lifted the lid, and I watched as she repositioned a brooch and reordered some of the case's contents. As she lowered the glass, it slipped and there was a loud thud as wood hit wood. She looked at me, flushed, and said, 'I'm so sorry. It's these gloves, you see.' She held up her hands apologetically.

'Don't worry. It's fine,' I said. She looked stricken, so I prattled on in an attempt to make her feel better. 'This is a beautiful chest. Where did it come from? The sign' – I indicated the wall – 'only tells us that houses were without cupboards and chests were used as both furniture and storage.'

The attendant walked over and stood beside me. 'We're not completely sure,' she said. 'It's listed as Venetian because it lacks the painted panels so prevalent on Florentine chests, and it has been confidently placed in the sixteenth century because the stylistic differences between fifteenth and sixteenth century chests were marked.'

'What are the differences?'

Jacky – she was close enough now for me to see the name tag pinned to her blouse – looked at me curiously. 'Well, all I know is that early chests were more box-like whereas later chests had the sculptural quality of Roman tombs.'

'Was this due to the Renaissance and the rise of classicism?'

Jacky raised her eyebrows.

I blushed and stammered, 'I studied art history at uni.'

'Oh, I see,' Jacky said. 'I did wonder. Well, you're probably right. But I'm afraid that's about all I know. If you like, I'll ask Marie, the curator, to come over. She knows a bit about *cassoni* and it's not busy at the moment.'

Jacky disappeared and returned with a slim blond woman whose handshake was unexpectedly firm. 'Hello. I'm Maree Silvers. I hope I can help. Jacky said you were asking about the chest.'

'Yes. It's such a lovely thing. So overblown, and it looks too fragile to use.'

Marie smiled. 'I can tell you a few things,' she said. 'None of this is written on the sign because our exhibition centres on the domestic, and we didn't include any information that strayed too far from our purpose.'

'The attendant explained about the lack of painted panels and the difference in shape between fifteenth and sixteenth century chests,' I said.

'Yes, these are both important, but there are other clues that help to date and place the *cassa*.' I could see that Marie was enjoying herself. She wouldn't have had too many opportunities to air her knowledge once the opening ceremonies finished and the experts returned to their ivory towers. 'The gilded *pastiglia* decoration' – she indicated the low-relief embellishment – 'is one of these. Early chests were more often inspired by oriental design. Also Venetian *cassoni* often displayed marine motifs in keeping, of course, with a maritime republic.'

I thought again of the postcard and wondered why I'd never been curious about the chest. In all my years of study, I'd never given it more than a passing thought.

I'd never queried its age or where it came from, let alone wondered about the painted panel on the outside. I rationalised that this was because the panel was small and insignificant, and the fact that it was on something else rendered it secondary in importance. Now I knew the chest was probably sixteenth-century Venetian, despite the painted panel. Against my inner warning voice, and knowing I was fuelling the fire I'd spent much of my life trying to dampen, I decided to describe my panel to Marie and see if she knew anything about it. But I still couldn't bring myself to admit openly to its existence and heard myself say, 'I once saw a picture of a similar chest with a marine motif plus a small painted panel in the centre. I guess this would still have been Venetian?'

Marie thought for a moment and then asked the question I'd been hoping for. 'Can you describe the painting?'

I recalled what I could of the nude woman with the mirror and her retinue of cherubs and saw recognition flash across Marie's face.

'Oh, that sounds like Bellini's little *Allegory of Prudence* – or I should say a copy of the same. The original is on permanent exhibition at the Accademia Gallery in Venice. It wasn't unusual for copies of paintings to be made. Where did you see this chest?'

'Oh, I don't remember exactly. It must have been during my art history studies,' I said.

'What a pity,' Marie said. 'I'd have been interested.'

Marie and I stood for a few minutes looking at the *cassa* and then she touched my elbow to gain my attention. 'Well, I'll have to leave you to it. I've a university group in this afternoon and a heap of brochures to photocopy. It's the last lot for the exhibition I hope I've been of help.'

I thanked her and she turned and walked quickly away.

I looked thoughtfully at the marriage chest. There was nothing especially significant in the fact that my mother's chest was probably Venetian. But why had she had written '*povera* Prudencia' – poor Prudence – beneath a painted panel of *Allegory of Prudence*?

I turned to see if anyone was looking and then bent and ran my fingers along the edge of the chest. I desperately wanted to open its carved lid and look inside. Maybe there was something in the chest? Touch ignited memory and I saw quite clearly the page in the journal where Prudence stood on her drum. The nagging question returned. Despite its secondary role, why had I never been curious about the panel painting? Perhaps because the other paintings in the journal were by the big boys of art? Adam and Eve being herded from paradise by the angel was a Masaccio; *Primavera*, of course, was a Botticelli; and the sacred conversation around the *Madonna and Child with Saints* was a Bellini. These paintings flashed like neon lights in any art course. In comparison, *Prudence* was insignificant and would only have been of interest if you were examining Bellini in depth. It occurred to me that the three paintings were also separate entities, whereas the *Allegory of Prudence* was attached to and part of an existing object: the marriage chest.

I moved my fingers under the extended edge of the chest and tried to lift the lid slightly. I'd thought it would be heavy, but to my surprise it lifted easily. I stood rooted to the spot, the lid of the marriage chest raised a few centimetres, and glanced around furtively. No one was looking, so I turned and lifted the lid higher, just enough to see the inside. The chest was lined with what appeared to be faded purple velvet and smelled musky, rather than stale. There was nothing inside. It occurred to me that its owners must have been wealthy as velvet had been a premium fabric and purple an expensive dye. As I stared into the chest's dim recesses hoping for a revelation, the outside world faded away. Then I smelled a familiar scent. I frowned and sniffed. Something about the scent registered deeply. Then the room spun as I realised it was the scent of violets. Two images flashed through my brain: my mother's perfume bottle and Aunt Monica's gift of purple velvet. I gasped and gripped the lid with both hands to steady myself. The scent faded as quickly as it had come – and then was gone. I lowered the lid, stood up, and shook my head. This was ridiculous, I thought. My imagination was clearly getting the better of me.

I felt oddly defeated. It was as if the journal had been biding its time like a living thing until I grew old enough to follow its clues. The first two had come to me. *Primavera* had been under my nose since birth and now I'd come across the marriage chest with its *Allegory of Prudence* as a result of Monica's letter. It was as if I'd reached a halfway point. The other two postcards couldn't come to me, but I knew where they were. Adam and Eve were in the Brancacci Chapel in Florence and the *Sacred Conversation* was in the church of San Zaccaria in Venice. I recalled my childhood vows to go and see these artworks that had meant so much to my mother. Then, my only aim had been to see what my mother had loved. Now this simple desire was overlain with mystery. I was certain there was more to my mother's death than I'd been told. I had no idea what to look for or what I'd find. I only knew that I had to follow my instincts. For a moment, I felt the thrill of adventure, but then a warning voice rose unbidden. Despite all these clues gathering around me like storm clouds, did I really want to do this?

I looked towards the other side of the room where Louise was watching me through narrowed eyes. She beckoned me over to her.

'What was that all about?' she demanded. 'Why on earth did you lift the lid?'

'Wait 'til we've ordered lunch and then I'll fill you in,' I said.

We settled in a corner of the gallery café and ordered coffee and sandwiches. The cafe still had the same kitsch name, 'The Eatery'.

'Well?' Louise said.

I took a deep breath and began, 'When I was eleven, I saw Lawrence throw a book into the rubbish bin. I got it out and realised that it was my mother's journal.'

Louise whistled under her breath.

'No one knows I have it, but there are four postcards pasted in it. One is a picture of a marriage chest like the one in the exhibition, and my mother's written '*povera Prudencia*' below it. I spent hours as a child thinking that Prudencia was a person and wondering why she was poor.' I took a deep breath and told Louise the contents of my conversation with the curator. When I'd finished, she tilted her head to one side and said, 'And?'

'Well, the chest I was looking at brought back all the confusion I felt when I first found the journal, and now I'm left with the new and strange fact that my mother wrote "*povera* Prudencia" beneath a copy of a famous painting by Bellini of an allegory of Prudence.'

Louise nibbled at her sandwich before putting it down and absently tugging out a loose shred of lettuce. 'I wonder if your mother knew a Prudence? Perhaps the painting reminded her of someone?'

We looked at each other, unconvinced.

'It's really peculiar,' I continued miserably. 'I come here for Monica and look what I find. For years I've tried to get away from the journal, but now I've a peculiar feeling that I was meant to find the chest ...'

'Maybe your Prudencia doesn't want to be anonymous any longer,' Louise said.

'Maybe the scribble is just my mother's flight of fancy,' I countered, and then warming to the idea added, 'Maybe she saw it overseas, liked it, and bought the card. And felt sorry for the woman because, because, I don't know, because she isn't wearing any clothes.'

'You don't believe that any more than I do,' Louise mused. She arranged her shred of lettuce into a circle and when I didn't speak leaned her elbows on the table and cupped her chin in her palms. 'Iris, do you realise that you never say "mum"? That you always say "my mother".'

'I've never really thought about it,' I said slowly. 'I don't feel as if I ever had a mother and "mum" is such an intimate word. My mother is more like a, a' – I struggled for words – 'like a concept than a person.' Tears welled in my eyes and Louise put her hand on my arm. 'What do you know about your mother?' she said. 'I mean, what was she like?'

I shook my head and shrugged my shoulders. 'Nothing much. Lawrence won't talk about her. Monica told me a few things before she went to Italy. But I was young then, so it was really just practical stuff. She told me once that my mother was a dreamer and that this hadn't been good for her.'

Louise was listening intently. 'Don't you think it's time to find out more? You told me once that Monica's always at you to go and visit her. Why don't you go?'

'I'm not sure I want to know more about my mother. Anyway, I couldn't possibly leave Lawrence.'

'Oh for heaven's sake! You're not tied to him. Your father must have been pretty pleased to have you go home and settle down like a good girl. My folks really kicked up when I told them I was moving out of home.'

'But it's different for us. We only have each other, and Lawrence needs me,' I said.

'Pooh,' was Louise's reply. 'There's a big difference between need and want. Are you sure it's not the latter? If you ask me, I think he's trying to hold on to you.'

'I'll think about it,' I said in an effort to put an end to the discussion.

She looked satisfied. 'Good. I'll ring you in two weeks and see if you've made any progress.'

Despite my confusion, I grinned.

We finished our lunch, paid at the counter, and walked out into surprisingly bright sunlight. In typical Melbourne fashion, the grey sky and rain had given way to clear blue skies. Louise turned, hugged me tightly, and looked at her watch. 'I've got to rush but when, and not if, you decide to go to Italy, come and stay with me for a few days first, hey? Someone's got to put you on the plane.'

The next morning, I returned to the university. Concetta answered the door quickly and ushered me into her office and towards a chair beside her desk. It struck me just how lovely she was, with her tumble of black hair and slight figure dressed in simple, tailored navy pants and a white button-through shirt. I realised that I'd never seen her flustered or hurried. She'd navigated rowdy students with quiet poise and a disarming smile. Concetta sat back in her desk chair, gestured towards the journal sitting in front of her, and said, 'This was beautiful but so hard to read. Your mother was,' she hesitated, searching for the right words, 'a gentle soul, perhaps what could be called a free spirit.' She shrugged.

I waited.

Concetta put on her glasses, turned to the first page and said, 'I hardly know where to start.'

I raised my hands, palms upwards in that gesture of helplessness and said, 'Please. Anywhere.'

'Even though there are no specific dates, it appears that the journal covers a two-year period: the time before you were born and the first few months of your life.'

'Phew,' I said. 'This feels so real. Almost surreal.'

Concetta smiled and continued, 'The part before your birth is filled with details of your parents' honeymoon in Italy and then life in Peterborough. The honeymoon section describes the places they visited and the artworks they saw. Your mother's comments are in-depth and meticulous.

But then, after that there are long sections describing the moods of the sea. I have the impression that your mother spent much time on the beach sitting and observing.'

'Lawrence – my father – is a sculptor. I guess he was often working.'

Concetta nodded and said, 'If it's all right with you, I'll call your mother by her name – Allegra?'

'Of course,' I said.

Concetta continued, but this time guardedly. 'At times it reads as if your mother was lonely, that she was pining. Throughout all sections she mentions Italy frequently, and at one point says she is "*struggersi per la patria*" – this means pining for a homeland – and the art she grew up with and loved to revisit. There are many entries where she speaks of the power of art to speak to our innermost feeling and desires.' She looked at me curiously. 'Did Allegra study art?'

'I know she began, but didn't finish, an arts degree. I'm not sure which of the arts she studied. But my aunt once told me my mother was besotted by paintings.'

'She had a student's curiosity,' Concetta said. 'Possibly an unrealised artist's talent.'

'What makes you think that?'

'It's her use of words. For Allegra, the sea is never blue or grey, it is *azzurro* – azure, *ceruleo* – cerulean, or *indaco* – indigo. And the sand is never simply yellow or golden, it is *increspata* – rippled,' and here Concetta smiled, 'or it is *infinita* – infinite, or *granulosa* – gritty under foot. There is a depth to Allegra ...'

Then Concetta reached for the journal, and I noticed the sticky notes scattered throughout its pages. For an hour we worked our way through what she had deemed major entries. Particularly evocative descriptions of the Peterborough landscape were interspersed with details of the works of Fra Angelico, Piero della Francesca, Jacopo Pontormo, Raphael, Bronzino amongst many others, all vividly described and playfully graded on my mother's scale, which ranged from adequate to majestic.

About halfway through, Concetta suggested we take a short break. She went to the nearby staff room and brought back two cups of coffee.

'This is an apology for coffee, but we must take what we can get.'

Then I asked the question that had dawned on me while she was out of the room. 'Does my mother ever mention Lawrence?'

Concetta pursed her lips and then grimaced. 'Not often and only in passing. You know, Iris, the most notable aspect of Allegra is a solitariness which seems to have forged in her a rich interior life unsullied by outside influence.'

I looked down at my coffee cup and then directly at Concetta and said, 'Does my mother mention me?'

'Of course! Each month she describes her swelling belly and is always sure her baby will be a girl. The free spirit is again there in her use of mantras for a safe birth and crystals for positivity.'

'My parents were hippies,' I said.

Concetta suddenly looked serious. 'Iris, the journal changes after you were born. But first you must know that she described you as her great work of art.'

'My aunt told me that, too.'

'The entries then become methodical. There are precise details of feed and sleep times, references to fatigue and your father's attempts to walk baby Iris to sleep by taking her along the beach.'

'No more paintings?' I asked. 'What about the postcards?'

Concetta shook her head and said, 'Nothing more about art and no reference to the postcards. The entries get shorter and shorter until they are sometimes just one or two lines, or even words, long.' She paused, inhaled, and then continued, 'The last entry is puzzling. It is blurred – perhaps by water, maybe tears – but simply says. "I fear this is too hard".'

I blanched. This was the first time I'd heard my mother's words and thoughts without my aunt or even Lawrence as intermediary. It had been enlightening, moving, and in parts unexpected. But the last six words had shocked me. What had been too hard? Was it me?

Concetta must have intuited my thoughts as she reached forwards and placed her two hands on my shoulders, forcing me to look at her directly. 'You mustn't think Allegra was referring to you. It could have been any number of things ...'

I looked at her ruefully and said, 'Perhaps you're right, but I'm there, aren't I? Right in the middle of things.'

Concetta handed me the journal and said quietly, 'Whatever happened to Allegra, she loved you, Iris. Never forget that.'

On the trip home, I had plenty of time think. Louise's questions and the journal's revelations had cut through to the vacuum at the centre of my life. I wondered how long

I could go on without answers. I understood that there were mysteries in any life, but mine had too many. Why wouldn't Lawrence speak about his wife? Why were my grandparents remote and uncommunicative? Why had Monica never returned from Italy? And then the more recent events. Lawrence's lease of the shop and gallery. His resistance to my seeing the exhibition. His lack of interest in Monica once she had moved away. Was Louise right in thinking that Lawrence was trying to hold on to me? I shifted uncomfortably. Ever since the day of the gravesite and the journal, I had shaped my life around whatever certainties I could find. Now it seemed that a sixteenth-century marriage chest, and an unknown person called Prudencia who had first visited me through the pages of my mother's journal, were trying to break through my barriers. I was again that clumsy child piecing together mismatched fragments of a jigsaw puzzle. But there was one difference. I was older and knew that by myself I could not make the puzzle whole.

I sighed inwardly and a wave of lassitude spread through me. Whether I liked it or not, I did need to know my story. The more I'd tried to resist, the more pressing the need had become. For a moment I entertained the absurd idea that if I just kept controlling my breathing, like I did when I felt panic and hoped it would wash over me, that all would be well. But an inner – and wiser – part of me knew that it was impossible. Knowing that I didn't have a story only made its finding all the more urgent.

'I will go to Italy,' I said under my breath. Then I sat up straight, and my previous lassitude was replaced with a fierce, new determination.

Four weeks before Christmas, Lawrence and I sat on the veranda watching the sunset flare red and gold across the ocean. On the mosaic table between us lay an unexpected letter from Monica, telling us my grandfather had died and then, old and worn down by grief, my grandmother had died a month later.

'What were they like?' I said.

Lawrence was silent for a while before finally saying, 'They were good people, and devoted to your mother and Monica.'

Before I could stop myself, I said, 'But not to us.'

Lawrence wiped his right hand across his face and leaned into his palm. 'It was a hard time,' he said. 'They took comfort in their homeland. It's difficult to deny that to anyone.'

He didn't mention my mother. As usual, she remained in the background, a ghost presence. There was little more I could say, but when the evening drama passed, and the multicoloured horizon flattened to shades of grey and blue, I turned to Lawrence and said apprehensively, 'I've decided to go and visit Monica. I booked my plane ticket yesterday.'

Lawrence was now sitting forward in his deck chair with his legs apart, his elbows resting on his knees, and his fingers spread along and supporting his jawbone. At my words he slid his fingers together and rubbed his temples. His gaze didn't stray from the sea. 'Well this is a day for news. Why do you want to go? And why such a sudden decision?' He sounded weary and I sensed that he knew the real answer – that I was a girl in search of a family – but was waiting to hear what I would say.

'I just think it's time I travelled. Monica's always at me to go and visit her in Montespertoli. It must be quite some place to have held her all this time,' I said. 'And after uni I went straight into the shop. Even though I've loved it, I'd like some time away to do what others do – you know, see the world. Also, Monica will be missing her parents, so perhaps my visit will help her.'

He sighed, looked at me, and slumped back in the chair, flinging his arms out over its arms so that they hung loose. His eyes were darker and more opaque than I remembered.

'Well, you seem to have made up your mind. I guess I should have expected it.'

His answer surprised me, and I felt the childish scrabble of nervous energy that came any time I displeased Lawrence. I drew in my breath and held it, waited for the butterflies to settle, breathed normally again, and then resisted the temptation to further justify my decision by saying lightly, 'Perhaps a bit of wanderlust runs in the family. After all, you and my mother travelled when you were young.'

Lawrence didn't respond to this provocation but said, 'What about the shop?'

'Well, I thought I'd make it an early autumn visit.' It was a relief to be on safe ground. 'It's quieter then, and Annette can manage during the week. That's if you'll do the weekends.'

He nodded again. His hands now lay between his legs, his fingers interlocked and drumming on his knuckles. 'How long will you be gone?'

'About four months. I'll be back before you know it.'

'Yes, of course you will,' he said.

He looked at me searchingly before returning his gaze to the sea.

Florence

Italy

1991

8

After my decision to travel to Italy, Lawrence spent more time in his studio, and at night when we sat on the veranda, he said even less than before. I tried to concentrate on the fact that he had worked hard to shore up our lives in the absence of my mother, and that my decision to leave for a holiday in Italy must have let in a tidal wave of emotions linked to loss. It was, after all, a place he loved, and Italy was filled with memories of Allegra. I understood that all this must have frightened him, but I puzzled over what had happened to make him so fearful of change. There was the fact of my mother's death, but surely time must have loosened its stranglehold? I began to view my father's need for uninterrupted quiet with suspicion. In my childhood our solitary existence and the intimacy of our daily lives had represented love and stability; now they smacked of obsession and control. Because of this, the need to do what pleased Lawrence – which had been so strong in my childhood – was tempered by the knowledge that my father wanted to hold me back. The tight little knot of anger that pulsed like a raw wound whenever I opened my mother's journal spread to Lawrence. It was not only mothers that left you, but also fathers when you didn't do what they wanted.

This time I had to sidestep Lawrence's needs and consider my own. I needed to take this trip and see what my mother had cared about. I thought back to the *cassoni* in the Melbourne exhibition, its possible provenance, and the words '*povera* Prudencia'. The words must mean something. Perhaps Louise was right when she quipped that Prudencia might no longer want to be anonymous. I recalled the surge of purpose I'd felt that day. The way my cheeks had flushed and I'd felt heady with the knowledge of what I had to do. Then there were the three postcard paintings, chosen for some reason, and carefully set into my mother's journal. Often, when I closed my eyes, the postcards appeared, suspended and silent behind my eyelids. It now seemed obvious that where Lawrence was intent on shutting out the world, I was beginning to open up to it.

I flew from Australia in early March 1991. Like all first-time travellers, I was a jumble of nerves and excitement. I remember little about my departure except for the contrast between Lawrence's haggard face and Louise's beaming smile as they saw me through the international departure doors. But I do remember my heart light with adventure, and the plane flying high above Australia's red centre where I saw my world as if from the distance of God. I remember the inadequacy of my summer dress after we landed in the cold of an early Italian spring, and the blue-red blotches that dappled my bare legs. And the taxi ride into Rome with luggage that seemed now to be twice its weight.

I spent my first night in Italy in a hotel not far from the Spanish Steps. Unsteady but hungry after the long flight, I walked outside to buy something to eat and was assailed by the smell of coffee while well-dressed people hurried past me along the busy street. I bought coffee and a pastry with my carefully rehearsed Italian and then hurried back to my room. I was overwhelmed and tired, but sleep was elusive. Eventually, I drifted into a fractured doze. I woke late the next morning feeling groggy and disoriented. I'd only unpacked the bare essentials, so quickly threw everything together just in time to catch the midday train to Florence.

Monica had been overjoyed at my plans but devastated when my arrival coincided with a two-week conference she was to attend in Naples. She was keynote speaker, as well as guest at numerous sessions, and her attendance at the end-of-conference dinner was – illness or death excepted – obligatory. As a result, I would spend my first two weeks in Florence alone. In truth, this didn't concern me. It was a novelty to be so completely untethered to either Lawrence or the shop. Even my time away at university had been governed by looming exams and the rhythm of term breaks and annual holidays.

Even though I was in my mid-twenties, my only experience of city life had been my time at university in Melbourne. But, despite this, Florence was as real to me as if I'd been a constant visitor. Lawrence had acquainted me with the city's art from early childhood, feeding me information haphazardly over the years. I'd studied Renaissance art and history, and I knew Florence's galleries, churches, and streets. The city map was imprinted on my mind. Now, as the taxi threaded its way through the city's cobbled streets, my first impression was that Florence's antique buildings were undisturbed by the sharpness of modern architecture. Their scale was human, enveloping rather than built for provocation or as an architectural statement. I had booked an apartment for three weeks in the district of Oltrarno on the south side of the River Arno. Their week began on Saturday, and I arrived on Wednesday, so I was to spend three nights in a hotel on the north side, just opposite the church of Santissima Annunziata in the heart of the city. I'd decided not to stay with my aunt, as she would be away most of the day, and it was better for me to be where I could easily visit Florence's famous sites. I would, of course, spend time with her in Montespertoli.

My experience of holiday accommodation was limited to the occasional motel I'd stayed at with Lawrence as a child, and the hotel I'd used as a base when I visited Melbourne. Because money was always scarce, these were usually no more than a bed, somewhere to sit, and a television. If I was lucky, there'd be a kettle, tea bags, and coffee sachets, and perhaps some cellophane-wrapped biscuits. I'd booked the Hotel Grazia in Florence largely because of its position in the historic centre. At first, I'd hesitated because the price was above my budget, but the few photos shown to me by the travel agent were pretty, the yellow-ochre-washed building obviously centuries old, and I reasoned it was only for three nights. It would be fun to stay in a building older than colonised Australia! But nothing prepared me for my room with its velvet drapes and ornate bedhead painted ivory with clusters of stuccoed blush-pink roses around its gilded outer edges. The floorboards had the patina of age, that soft mix of honey to brown to black only possible by long wear, over which were two deep crimson rugs. The dining room also had velvet drapes, and Renaissance-inspired artworks were spread tastefully around the walls. As I sat down to dinner on my first evening, I instinctively straightened my back and spread my cloth napkin over my lap. The waiter served my meal with reverence, placing the plate in front of me with care and then politely asking if there was anything else the signorina would like. It was my first experience of what I would discover was commonplace in Italy. Everyday living was an art; even the small and ordinary afforded due dignity.

On my first morning, I rose early, dressed, and packed a tote bag with my wallet, passport, sunglasses, and the few toiletries I would need during the day. As I was about to leave the room, I hesitated before turning back and tucking my mother's journal into the tote. At seven in the morning, most of the tables in the dining room were empty and I settled near a window with my guidebook. A tepid sun washed mauve along the grey stone loggia of the adjacent foundling hospital. Opposite me, Santissima Annunziata was already drawing pilgrims to its painting of the Virgin, said to have been completed by an angel. It struck me that here this might really be possible. I fancied that a cross-section of the city's stone would reveal strata of angels with wings spanning the centuries, full blown in the Renaissance but with only the tip of a wing in the present day. One of my lecturers had said that religious belief grew in direct proportion to the emphasis placed on it, and that whether this confirmed its existence or merely emphasised human susceptibility was an open-ended debate. He had laughed and said the modern world was cynical and angels had no time for cynicism – that they would bide their time.

I was pulled back to reality by the arrival of a noisy group of four. I stared out the window and toyed with the day in front of me. There was Brunelleschi's great dome to climb and a plethora of museums and galleries to visit, but first I wanted to see the painting I had spent the best part of a year with: Lorenzo Monaco's *Coronation of the Virgin*. I knew it hung in the Uffizi Gallery and thought this might be the place to start. After the *Coronation*, I would visit *Primavera*, take in as much more of the Uffizi as possible, and then head for the Brancacci Chapel and one of the postcards in my mother's journal: the frescoes of Adam and Eve.

When I reached the Uffizi an hour later, I was unprepared for the queue that snaked as far as the River Arno. Thwarted, I retraced my steps to the cathedral piazza but it, too, was already swamped with tourists. Perhaps it was the effect of my recent travels or simply the magnitude of the Duomo that rose before me like a marble mountain, but I was suddenly overwhelmed. I turned left and wandered towards the Ponte Vecchio. I knew the Brancacci Chapel was on the other side of the Arno and after that I could follow the signs. The famous bridge was smaller than I imagined, and its shops of gold jewellery had obliterated past ages when blood-soaked remains from its butcheries and tanneries were heaved into the river. I didn't linger. I simply glanced at the view over the river and walked on in the direction of Santa Maria del Carmine.

The austere facade of the church surprised me. It looked unfinished, as if it had been hastily erected, its builders impatient to be off to more illustrious projects. I walked through to the cloister and, feeling more purposeful, joined the short queue for the Brancacci Chapel inside. It was near lunchtime and spitting with rain. We stood in silence, waiting for the signal to enter from a young woman in a close-fitting black suit. Under it she wore a white shirt, its collar points monogrammed with letters I couldn't make out. Her hair was swept up in a perfect chignon, showing a long unblemished neck, and her earrings glittered with what I assumed could only be diamonds. Like so many Italian women, she was beautiful in the classic Mediterranean manner I'd seen in films and advertisements, and she carried herself with easy elegance. I attempted to smooth my unruly hair, glanced down at my jeans and cotton sweater, and shrugged inwardly.

As I stood in the still of the cloister, however, I was pulled out of myself by the grace of its architecture. As a student I had read much about the past, but it had always seemed the terrain of conquerors and art movements. Year after year we skimmed the surface of history, dutifully recording moments of great change, which we then used as bookends for periods or eras, all the while paying little attention to the dramas and tragedies of the ordinary human life in between. But in this symmetrical cloister, I glimpsed a more intimate past. Behind the shuffling queue and officious guides, I could hear the swish of a Carmelite robe and the intoning of a chant.

My thoughts were interrupted when the young woman announced in heavily accented English in a loud monotone, 'Follow me please. Hold onto the rail and do not speak. We will now enter the chapel.'

The queue funnelled into single file behind her and entered the dim stairwell. Our guide motioned continuously with her right hand, pulling the little group forward like the Pied Piper, until we turned the corner and the Brancacci Chapel opened out in front of us.

The chapel was smaller than I'd expected and was located in the church's right transept, rather than straight off the nave. Our guide stopped the group just outside the chapel. We waited for her to speak but, instead, she opened her eyes wide and gestured inwards with a theatrical palms-up flourish and then turned her back and sat in a nearby pew. We spread hesitantly throughout the chapel: four pairs, one set of three, and four single tourists. There was a lot of pointing but very little whispering. Something about the way we'd been led up the stairs and into the chapel made speech seem irreverent. It was as though we'd been presented as offerings to the chapel's beauty, our own petty responses irrelevant – even out of order.

It was strange to finally be in the home of one of Allegra's postcards. They had been confined to the journal for so long that seeing one enlarged on the wall in front of me was like catching up with a person known only by photograph, who you must then deal with in all the magnitude of flesh and blood with its retinue of demands. I rummaged in my bag for the journal and stood with it unopened in my hand. When I did open it a few moments later, it fell obediently to the pages of the postcards. I looked from Allegra's miniature Adam and Eve to the almost life-size figures on the wall. The colours were different, the original clear and natural, against which the postcard appeared yellowish.

This was probably due either to discolouration over time, or maybe the postcard was simply of inferior quality.

I flipped the book closed with my thumb, dropped it back into the bag, and continued staring at Adam and Eve, willing them to speak and tell me why my mother had thought it necessary to paste them into her journal. I imagined her standing in my place, her long blond hair tied back with a black velvet bow, a loose floral top tucked into her jeans beneath which – if the chapel had been visited after the Uffizi – I lay curled inside her. At university there had been the usual discussion about Eve's responsibility for the pair's expulsion from the Garden of Eden, about Eve as the source of the Original Sin that has forever since dogged humankind. This was always followed by vociferous rejection, especially from the feminists, but despite all the ironic comment and nodding agreement that followed, I'd felt as if Eve's crime remained hanging over us, hovering like a phantom. Given that the fresco on the wall had the power to summon up these thoughts and responses, it was logical that an onlooker might feel compelled to buy a postcard. But had my mother bought hers for these reasons? She had been barely out of her teens when she interrupted her arts degree to marry my father. And from what Monica implied, she had been a dreamy hippie. It seemed to me unlikely that she would have been drawn to the fresco only for its place in art history or role in biblical narrative.

I waited for my old anger to surface and place Allegra firmly back in her role as a deserting mother, but this time it was frustration that bubbled inside me, followed closely by an unexpected incredulity at my own naivety. Why on earth was I here? Did I expect the fresco to step from the wall and tell me about Allegra? Whatever the fresco said to me was not necessarily what it would have said to my mother. She had been her own person and the workings of her mind – her thoughts – belonged to her. They were not mine to be discovered just because it was what I wanted. I was like a child who had been catapulted into one of her storybooks, only to discover that the characters she so desperately wanted to meet went on with their lives without even noticing she was there.

I was so absorbed in my own thoughts that I didn't realise one of the single men in the group had walked over and now stood quite close to me. He caught my glance and whispered, 'Marvellous, isn't it?' His voice was deep, the accent cultured, each syllable clearly enunciated.

I smiled politely and nodded, and we both turned to contemplate the fresco again. As he stared, now seemingly oblivious to the fact that he had spoken to me at all, I glanced at him furtively. He wore a silver-grey coat that reached just below his knees. The fabric had the sheen of fine quality wool. His trouser bottoms were level with his insteps, and his shoes were highly polished. He was standing with his legs apart, his hands plunged into his pockets. His collar was turned up and from his pale skin and steady gaze I guessed he was from a northern country. His face was too immobile to be Italian. He was frowning slightly and seemed to be looking beyond the painting. I wondered what he saw that I couldn't. I had about fifteen minutes to take in the other frescoes, but instead I stepped forward and stood beside him in the hope that whatever had so taken his fancy would also take mine. But nothing happened and I simply said, 'Yes, it is. This representation of human psychic pain is one of the first of its type in art history.'

He turned then and I couldn't decide whether his raised eyebrows signalled mild surprise or affected irony, but I did know that he was handsome. 'Are you studying art?' he said. 'It sounds as though you are.'

I blushed. 'Well I did, but I've finished now,' I said.

'Do we ever finish?' the man murmured more to himself than to me. Then he brightened and held out his hand. 'I should introduce myself. I'm Marcus Warren. And you are?'

I took his hand. 'Iris,' I said. 'Iris Maddison.'

'So, were you named after this city? Or was it just chance?'

It seemed out of place to tell a stranger that I'd been named after the floral emblem of the city in which I was conceived so I said lamely, 'My mother came here as a young woman and loved this city.'

Marcus nodded as if this was the most natural response in the world and then let go of my hand. 'Masaccio's work always silences me. What do you think of it?' He was staring at the fresco.

I looked up at Eve's hands, at her fingers spread loosely over her breasts and sex, glanced at Masolino's Adam and Eve on the opposite wall, and foraged amongst my store of art history jargon for a suitable response. 'You can see the difference between them,' I said. 'I mean, Masolino was still painting in the earlier International Gothic style whereas Masaccio heralded the Renaissance. Don't you agree?'

Marcus raised his eyebrows again and was silent for a time. Then he took a step forward and in that small step he slid into a different universe. 'I think,' he began, 'that if you listen hard enough, you might still hear Eve's wail as you walk back down the chapel steps.' He turned and looked at me thoughtfully through softly hooded eyes. 'I think that Eve is still wailing, and that she will wail forever.'

'You mean because she was driven out of the Garden of Eden?' I said. 'Because she ate from the tree of knowledge and her punishment was to see the world as it is?'

Marcus shrugged. 'Maybe she chose to eat it. Maybe she wanted to experience more.'

His thoughts were provocative, and I found myself saying thoughtfully, 'It's been touted through thousands of years of history that Eve was imprudent and should have resisted temptation.'

'Ah!' Marcus said triumphantly. 'Take this a step further and note it's his-story not her-story. Maybe Eve was a curious woman who made a decision and took the consequences. What would have happened to her had she done nothing?'

I warmed to his train of thought and added, 'She'd be alive but forever curious, I guess.'

'Exactly! Perhaps Eve was prudent and made a choice based on self-knowledge, and this choice carried the possibility of pain.'

Never in my wildest dreams would I have thought of all this. I couldn't think of anything to add so said lightly, 'Well, she certainly got pain. If I remember correctly, Eve's choice resulted in the pain of childbirth.'

Marcus smiled, more to himself than at me, and returned to the fresco.

I couldn't think of anything more to say. Marcus's comments were offbeat to say the least. Why on earth had he used the old-fashioned word 'wail' to describe Eve's cry? And who did he think was responsible for this pain that would never stop? But he didn't enlighten me further. We both remained where we were. He appeared unselfconscious about his outburst, and I was mute with embarrassment.

Only minutes later we were interrupted when our guide responded to a beep from an electronic device. 'It is time to leave now. Please complete your study of the frescoes.' She circled purposefully, a practiced hand at herding tourists. The bulk of the group moved obediently towards the exit, but Marcus remained staring at Adam and Eve. The guide tapped her foot and looked first at me and then at Marcus. 'Please,' she said. She indicated the way out, clearly assuming that we knew each other. She was frowning, probably thinking of the next party waiting at the foot of the stairs. I tugged at Marcus's coat.

Halfway down the stairway, I turned and glanced backwards, causing the guide who was following close behind me to cluck in frustration. For as I rounded the last corner and the dim light gave way to daylight, I could have sworn I heard the echo of Eve's wail.

When we reached the gift shop, I turned towards the exit and was surprised when Marcus came up behind me and plucked at my sleeve.

'Would you like to have a coffee or something? I'm here alone – and have been for six weeks – and it'd be great to have someone to talk to for a while.'

'Yes. Thanks. That would be good,'I said. I suppose there was some risk in taking an offer from a stranger, but

Marcus had been moved by art just as I had, and this made me feel safe. Added to that, he was respectably dressed and courteous, small practicalities that also suggested safety. And I was simply glad of the opportunity to talk.

Once outside, Marcus gestured towards the Arno. 'I know a little bar just up from the river. It's a bit away from the tourist run, so it's quieter.' When I hesitated, he looked at me and grinned. 'I promise it's not down a dark alley or anything.'

'Okay,' I said. 'That sounds good.' At the same time, I made a mental note to find an excuse to leave if I felt uncomfortable. 'You seem to know your way around here.'

He nodded. 'I've been coming here since I was a child. England's not far away, you know. It's a lot harder for you Australians. I guess that's where you're from? You haven't much of an accent, but what there is points to Australia.'

'Yes. I'm from a place called Peterborough in country Victoria,' I said. I had the feeling that I might as well have said Jupiter.

As it was mid-afternoon, the bar was empty except for an elderly man reading a newspaper in the corner. The bartender was leaning against the counter in earnest conversation with a heavily made-up woman. When Marcus ordered coffee, I saw her study his coat from under long lashes. As he led me to a table in the corner, I looked back and saw the two of them exchange glances. I was again conscious of my jeans and top and my worn, practical sneakers.

We sat down and Marcus leaned his elbows on the table and made a steeple with his forefingers. 'What brings you here?' he said.

'Oh, I suppose I'm just doing the usual pilgrimage to Europe.'

'Nothing more than that,' he said. 'I thought you might have family here or something. Your features and dark hair made me wonder.'

I stared at him. Despite my mother's heritage, I had never thought of myself as looking Italian. My freckles and riotous hair seemed incompatible with Italy. This was a land of flawless skin like my aunt's and hair that obeyed fashion. 'My aunt lives in Montespertoli,' I said. 'My mother's twin sister. I'm going to see her for the first time in years when she returns from a conference in Rome.' To thwart further questions, I said in as jovial a tone as I could muster, 'And what brings you here this time?'

'My work,' he said.

'What do you do?'

'Usually I make television documentaries.' Marcus sat back and sighed. 'Art history projects for schools, and the odd prime-time series for good measure. But this time I've run away from all that and am researching a project that's been interesting me for a long time. It's sort of grown alongside my work.'

'What's that?' I said.

'I'm fascinated by the story of women in art and history, particularly the Italian Renaissance, where I think there are some interesting puzzles.'

'Women?' I said.

'Well, I have a theory ... Or I suppose just a few unorthodox thoughts really ...' He paused, shrugged his shoulders, and raised his hands palms upward in a gesture of surrender. 'I don't expect it will be easy to get this one to air as it's an approach that's far removed from an art historian's, or even a general historian's.' Marcus absently stirred his coffee with a little silver spoon, stopping every so often to tap the spoon on the rim. I watched the spoon's travels for some time before reaching over, staying his hand, and saying, 'Penny for your thoughts.' He looked at me with that same expression I'd first seen in the Brancacci Chapel – the bemused air of someone who, for a brief and enjoyable period of time, had slid into a personal parallel universe and then been disconcertingly wrenched back to reality.

'Sorry,' he said. 'I was just thinking.'

'About what?'

'Are you sure this won't bore you?'

'How could I be bored by something that is clearly so absorbing to you?'

'It's women, you see,' he said slowly. 'If you study art closely, you will see the male and female divide in rather different ways. Men are usually portrayed with their symbols of power or learning; Saint Jerome and his books, the Apostle Peter with the keys to heaven, Charles the First on his horse, or even simply the impersonal face of the ever-democratic Venetian doge. Women, on the other hand, are seen as Madonnas or courtesans or seducers. Female power seems less of this external world and more as a conduit to internal, intuitive parts of ourselves – the vessel of divine feeling, the means to accessing our sexual natures. Many women in art, I think, embody what we can't touch – they speak to the longing in us.'

I must have looked surprised because he hurried to explain further. 'As I said, I doubt I'll ever get this one to

air as I'm not interested in proving every point I make –
which is what the people who employ me want. I want to
use art and emotion to tell a larger-than-life story and to
tackle unorthodox perspectives such as the one I've just
mentioned.'

'So, you're aiming at provocation rather than
hypothesis,' I said.

Marcus grinned. 'Perhaps a bit of both, but I've always
thought sweeping generalisations have their uses. They
can be argued against, agreed with, and so forth. Anyway,
I've given myself two months to see if I can pull it together
with some concentrated research. As I said, I've already
been here six weeks, so I need to get a move on. My old
professor, Max Colstram, has been kind enough to let
me apartment sit while he and his wife are in Germany.
Anyway, enough about me. How long are you in Florence?'

'Just three weeks. Then I'm going to Venice for a month
and back to stay with my aunt until I leave in early July.'

'Perhaps we could meet again?' he said. 'I'm going to
the Uffizi tomorrow. Would you like to meet me there?
Perhaps near the *Rape of the Sabine Women* in the Piazza
della Signoria early in the morning to avoid the crowds.
Around nine-ish? We could have lunch later if you like.'

I didn't hesitate. The *Coronation of the Virgin* and
Primavera were on my list and, besides, I liked the smell
of his aftershave and the way his hooded eyes lingered on
that play of freckles across the bridge of my nose.

That evening when I returned to my hotel, I went straight
to my room and sat on the edge of the bed with the journal
in my hands. I tapped my finger on the postcard of Adam

and Eve and tried to recall the sense of quest that had driven me to Florence. Instead, I saw Marcus and heard his strange comments and was again affronted by the way the fresco drew him into a space that left the rest of us on the outside – more like voyeurs than true art lovers – an ability both galling and intriguing. We'd been taught in our studies that Renaissance art brimmed with emotions that went to the core of what it meant to be human. This was why I'd avoided it. My own emotional life was fraught enough, without spending my days analysing the inner lives of others – especially dead people in frescoes and paintings. I'd always kept Adam and Eve firmly in a box labelled 'Example of Early Renaissance', comfortingly disconnected from any inward journey they might be said to express. But a stranger in a wool coat had casually opened the box and set the lid to one side. To him, Eve's cry was much more than part of a superb depiction of an early Renaissance biblical narrative. It was a woman wailing because of searing emotional pain. Now, no matter how hard I tried, I couldn't fit the lid on the box as precisely as before.

I laid back on the bed and stared at the ceiling; long shadows cut diagonally across it, bending unnaturally when they hit the cornice. I drew my knees to my chest in an upside-down foetal position and hugged them tightly and heard again the chill echo of Eve's wail. I shivered involuntarily, shook my head, and was glad when a more sensible part of me took hold. Marcus was clearly following a whim, I told myself. And this romantic city had enveloped me, too. Then I stopped and frowned. There was no denying it. Florence had touched my senses, highlighting feelings and sparking emotions, niggling away at the young woman who traded on certainty. The curious thing was that I couldn't say what these feelings and emotions actually were.

Marcus was unlike anyone I had ever met, interesting and handsome despite being dignified in an annoyingly aristocratic way. There was something of the English country squire about him, but I could enjoy his company, listen to what he had to say, and maybe even have a holiday romance. It would all lead to nothing, but as long as I took care, no harm would be done.

I laid my clothes for the morning out on the bed and studied them. I tossed aside jeans for my only pair of tailored pants and settled on a three-quarter-length herringbone tweed jacket and a lime green scarf, which flattered my skin. Satisfied, I walked over to the window. The sun had slipped behind the buildings, and the sky was the palest of blues and fringed by blurred city lights. I heard the tinkling music of a distant carousel and at eight o'clock smiled as I counted the peals from a nearby bell. Below my window a group of teenagers clattered past, talking at full volume. When they passed, there was unexpected silence, the piazza outside my window empty except for a flurry of pigeons at the base of the steps leading to the foundling hospital.

The next morning, I stood on the opposite side of the piazza and watched Marcus examine the *Rape of the Sabine Women* as he waited for me. He circled it slowly, running his eye up and down its length. Then he walked back a few metres and stood with his body aligned in front of the sculpture. I forgot the Uffizi and pushed my fist against my fluttering stomach. Feeling slightly foolish, I walked over to him and coughed to let him know I was there. He turned and said, 'Good morning. I hope you had a good night. Are you ready for the gallery?'

'I hope the queue's a bit better than yesterday,' I answered.

'We should be all right at this time of day. Shall we go?'

In a quaint, old-fashioned gesture, he held out a crooked elbow. I slid my arm into it, and he patted my wrist and smiled. He was wearing the same coat as the previous day and, just as I thought, its wool was as slippery as satin. We walked mostly in silence to the Uffizi. Occasionally Marcus pointed at a building or an architectural feature, and I followed his gaze and nodded. I had the impression that here in Florence epochs ground against each other like the earth's tectonic plates, their friction showering the sparks of brilliance that were everywhere in the city.

9

It was just after half past nine when we entered the Uffizi's internal courtyard on our way to the gallery entrance. As I'd hoped, the queue was short – about fifty people – and appeared to be moving steadily, with groups of around eight being let in after earnest conversations between ticket officers, who were presumably in contact with others stationed at the exit, monitoring the numbers leaving. We were inside within twenty minutes and negotiated the purchase of tickets and the checking of bags in silence, but when we arrived at the first room, Marcus paused and said, 'Do you have anything in particular you want to see?'

Tucked into one corner of my mind were the *Coronation* and *Primavera*, but I'd not thought it necessary to explain their importance to me to Marcus. I'd half decided to simply stop when we arrived at the two works, stay as long as I needed without being too obvious, and then move on. I could always come back alone another day if I wanted. But when Marcus spoke, I had been deep in thought, savouring the prospect of seeing these works I knew only from reproductions, and his question caught me unawares. Without thinking I said, 'I did my honours thesis on Lorenzo Monaco's *Coronation of the Virgin* so, of course, that's high on my list. It'll be wonderful to finally see it.'

'You've never seen it?' Marcus sounded incredulous. 'Yet you've written on it.'

'I'm from Australia. Remember? And my father didn't have any spare money to send me to Italy during my studies.' I recognised in Marcus's exclamation the persistent notion of Australia as some sort of cultural backwater and snapped, 'But even though our access to the Old Masters is limited, we're not culturally illiterate you know.'

He grimaced apologetically.

'The art history department organised a large-scale print and our library was astonishing.'

By this time, he was nodding, but I could see he had difficulty digesting the fact that I'd written on something I'd never seen.

I decided not to justify myself further and changed tack. 'My mother liked *Primavera*, so that's another on my list. After these two, I'm open to being overwhelmed.'

'Liked – in the past tense?'

'Allegra died when I was a child,' I said. 'I don't remember her much. My aunt told me about my mother's love of *Primavera*. There's a framed print on our living room wall.' I waited for the usual expressions of sympathy but instead Marcus bit his lower lip while nodding his head slowly.

We meandered through the first rooms filled with archaeological exhibits and then onto the fifth and sixth rooms with their displays of International Gothic art with its graceful, aristocratic elegance and luminous colour. My excitement grew. Lorenzo Monaco – my Lorenzo – belonged to this school of painting. Finally, I would see his work in person. When we arrived at the *Coronation*, Marcus stood back and let me look at it in silence.

It wasn't a large altarpiece but its seductive use of gold and ultramarine blue hypnotised my senses and what was absent in size was made up for in effects. The Coronation took place between two heavenly multitudes of haloed saints and the venerable learned and was surmounted by a small annunciation: the Virgin out-glamoured by an Archangel Gabriel with pastel, tesseral wings. It was a safe piece, a work made by the devoted for the devoted, imbued with a medieval code understood by both the learned and illiterate of the time, in much the same way we now use psychology to cast light on our modern, abstract shapes.

'What made you choose Lorenzo?' Marcus said.

'It was probably because of my saints and sinners childhood,' I said wryly.

Marcus looked puzzled and I added, 'Aunt Monica. Her university field of study centres on Medieval and Renaissance saints and angels – and sinners! As a child, they were quite real to me. We had no close neighbours and few visitors, so Monica's stories peopled my world. In some way, it was only natural that I'd go on to study art history.'

'Of course,' he said. 'That all makes sense. I guess she told you quite a few stories. Some of them must have been pretty hair raising for a small child.'

'I never felt frightened by her tales,' I said thoughtfully. 'Monica had a knack for putting things in perspective. She gave me the history, the wider picture, so to speak.'

His question as to my choice of Lorenzo Monaco had set me thinking and I continued, 'I know for a fact that religion wasn't behind my choice of Lorenzo. I don't remember my father ever once mentioning God. I've sort of drifted through life without making any decisions as to His existence or not. But, you know' – I half-turned and was surprised at the intensity in Marcus's gaze – 'in the face of Lorenzo's fervour, it's difficult to actually disbelieve. This sort of work has a spiritual pull that radiates from art created by a devotee. It has a certainty about it. If God does exist, he would be pleased by His creation's creation.'

'It's all to do with lack of real-life perspective,' Marcus said. 'Later Renaissance painters saw this as primitive – leftover from Byzantine art – but it's really quite logical to depict heavenly or other-worldly doings in non-human ways, on non-human planes.'

'To force our thoughts upwards to heaven – or perhaps even downwards to hell,' I said.

Marcus smiled at this. 'Despite all its beauty, I don't think this art makes you feel emotions that are linked to being human. It's above that. It's selling the end result of the journey to God rather than questioning the quality of the life we lead now.'

We stood for a while longer, before circling the room and moving towards the door.

After the *Coronation* we stopped and started our way through room after room of art until we reached the Botticellis. I noticed that Marcus didn't try to see every painting. In each room he singled out one work, studied it closely, and then stared out a window or stood near an entrance while I dizzied myself trying to take in every painting.

It was *Primavera*'s size that made me stop just inside the room and gasp out, 'It's huge!' In height and width the painting was far greater than a human, and the number and scale of the figures made me feel as though I'd walked into an intimate gathering and must somehow interact with these elusive and beautiful creatures from another time.

'I suppose it's a bit bigger than a living room print,' Marcus said.

'Yes. Of course, that's it,' I stammered. 'I don't know what I was expecting.' I stepped forward and stared into Flora's – my mother's – face and surprised myself by saying to Marcus, 'My mother looked like Flora. There's a photograph of my parents on our mantelpiece, just below the print. As a child I was fascinated by this double of my mother amidst all those flowers. To me, Allegra and Flora were one and the same.'

Marcus moved close to the painting, raising the ire of a guard who sauntered pointedly towards us, stopped a short distance away, and folded his arms. Marcus obediently stepped back and whispered, 'One school of thought says *Primavera* was painted for a Medici wedding chamber.'

I hesitated. I knew this type of painting was supposed to encourage the making of beautiful babies, but it seemed inappropriate to mention such things to a man I'd only just met.

But, once again, Marcus was unfazed and said, 'It was hoped that such paintings would allow for' – he paused, searching for the right words – 'a delicate – hopefully productive – ecstasy. Babies were prized but often died young, and an heir was crucial.'

This response silenced me. 'Delicate ecstasy' was such a sophisticated way to describe sex.

'Perhaps you could call it a painting with the capacity to steal reason,' I said awkwardly.

My thoughts flitted between our print and photograph and this enormous *Primavera*, and I felt unexpectedly lightheaded with a muted version of the childhood panic I'd first experienced all those years ago. Then, I had been unable to name it; now, I knew it stemmed from the terror that something would pierce the membrane that protected my memories of my mother. A painting – a woman – with the capacity to steal reason, indeed. I steadied my breathing and the light in the room – which for a moment had flickered alarmingly – returned to an even glow.

When we left the Uffizi three hours later, I was satiated with paintings and could think of nothing except food and drink.

Marcus took me to a restaurant tucked into a small street opposite the Pitti Palace. On seeing my companion, the waiter came up and took us through a series of ever-smaller rooms to a dining area away from through traffic.

'What do you like to eat?' he said.

'Anything except offal and seafood.' I studied the menu. My Italian was limited and the lists of foods in front of me might as well have been written in Chinese. I frowned and said, 'I think I'll just have to guess.'

'It's okay. Just tell me,' he said.

'Some sort of pasta with tomato and bacon would be good.'

I had learned yesterday that Marcus could order coffee and supposed he was proficient enough to order a meal, but I was taken aback when he signalled to the waiter and conducted an animated conversation in what appeared to be fluent Italian.

The waiter poured our wine and Marcus raised his glass. 'Here's to your holiday,' he said. 'Now, tell me what you thought of the Uffizi.'

'I don't think I'll remember very much,' I said truthfully.

He nodded. 'That's the trouble with art galleries. There's so much in one place it all gets jumbled. Sometimes paintings sort of die in a gallery – lose their reason for being.'

I must have looked surprised because he reached across the table and touched my arm. 'Are you all right?'

'Yes, yes,' I said. I wasn't going to tell him that his reflections had swept me back to my father's musings. 'It was just an interesting mental image. A gallery of dying paintings.'

But Marcus didn't laugh. 'Most of the paintings once had a role in life,' he said. 'They were objects of worship or enhanced civic or personal life. Now we've turned them into' – he searched for the right word – 'relics,' he chose triumphantly. 'The best we can say about galleries is that they are a temple to beauty.'

'Do you think the paintings still have any role?' I said.

'Oh yes, I think they can tell us a great deal about ourselves. For instance, I think the ones that draw us reflect us in some way, and then there's the common humanity at their heart.'

'And what does the Brancacci chapel say to you?'

'It challenges me to think about women through time, to try and track beyond Eve's wail to its source. Because it is a wail, you know, not a cry or a moan – and I refuse to call it anguish, which is far too abstract. It hits the viewer like a punch to the stomach and pierces the eardrums with a sound midway between weeping and screaming, and for my money that's a wail. I'm interested in how art calls us intuitively to some unexplored place and then leaves us breathless. That's what I want to document, you see.' Marcus sat back. He looked winded, as if someone had punched *him* in the stomach. Then he said ruefully, 'But it's probably all hubris.'

After lunch we walked back to the palace and bought tickets for the Boboli Gardens behind it. It was a soft afternoon, the sun covered by thin clouds. From the top of one of the garden's gravel walkways, I saw rows of cypresses recede into the hazy distance that heralds summer. Time had warped and the mores that governed my practical everyday life at home no longer seemed relevant. I'd stepped straight into my very own romance and it felt glorious.

Marcus was the first man I'd ever been with, in that his shoulders were broad, his stance on the earth solid, his features set firm. There was none of the loose-jawed, unset, and unsure look of young men on the cusp of manhood. Marcus knew what he was about and this excited me and made me feel I'd entered a serious phase of my life. In short, I felt grown up, my own self for the first time. When I was with him, thoughts of my family receded and I was no longer a daughter or niece, and the journal's power diminished and sometimes even temporarily disappeared. I fancied myself as a mysterious and seductive woman who had attracted a handsome stranger – a man at least ten years older who understood things about the world that were yet to be revealed to me. Up until now, boyfriends had played a minor role in my life. They were just someone to go out with, their fumbling advances accepted or rejected more on whim that anything else. I'd only slept with two of them and these had been forgettable experiences: awkward and messy and shot through with veiled embarrassment. Even though I thought my time with Marcus would be fleeting, I knew it would be none of these things, and even at this early stage, I understood that in some as yet unknown way it was a turning point for me as a woman.

As we looked over those green hillsides, Marcus put his arm around my shoulders and then his coat brushed the side of my leg as he turned and faced me. He kissed me, a slow assured kiss, and I thought for a minute that I had forgotten to breathe. As he stepped back from me, leaving his hands on my shoulders so that I couldn't easily look away, I recalled Monica telling me that I was conceived before my parents' visit to the Uffizi. How strange that I should begin a relationship near the place where I had come to life?

I breathed deeply, cupped Marcus's chin in my hands, and pulled him back to me, teasing him with the tip of my tongue before his eyes closed and he pressed hard against me.

And so, the shape of our next two weeks together was formed. Art, followed by refreshment, and then long walks taking in the layout of the city with Marcus as my guide.

It was an otherworldly time when sometimes I took more notice of his breath against my cheek as he spoke of the treasures that lined Florence's churches and palaces and galleries than the art works themselves.

Once he kissed the nape of my neck as we stood in front of Michelangelo's tomb in the church of Santa Croce. I was staring at a bust of the great artist which sat atop the tomb. Statues representing painting, sculpture, and architecture were arranged around the base, suitably forlorn at the world's loss. I felt first the warmth of Marcus's breath on my neck and then his lips brush against my skin from beneath my ear to the corner of my mouth. For that moment, I forgot where I was, conscious only of my tingling nerve-endings and a slow-burning passion that left me flushed and slightly unsteady. When I regained my composure, I looked up only to find him watching me, a twist of a smile on his face. 'Shall we have a look at Giotto's frescoes?' he said.

I nodded dumbly.

During that time Marcus didn't once ask me to go back to his hotel, and when he accompanied me to my accommodation, we usually drank coffee in a nearby bar or café before parting until the next day. I was surprised at this, as he was not lacking in confidence. He held his own in restaurants and galleries, and the impassive reserve of many of the shopkeepers didn't faze him. He accompanied me when I shifted to my ground floor apartment just down from Santa Maria del Carmine, but he didn't ask to stay. He carried my case and numerous shopping bags and drank tea with me before leaving me to settle in. Of course, I was too nervous to ask him to stay, even though by now I wanted to.

I'd arranged to visit Monica in the middle of my last week in Florence. Even though she was due to arrive back at the beginning of this third week, we'd decided to wait until she was free of obligations so that we could enjoy our time together without interruptions. She had to spend Monday and Tuesday at her university, reporting on all that had passed in Naples. On Wednesday I would take the bus to Montelupo and then a taxi to her home in Montespertoli.

On the Sunday before my visit, Marcus and I put in a solid afternoon's walking before gravitating to the Arno, where we sat in the sun in a neglected park near its banks and shared a block of chocolate. I'd decided to ask him if he would like to come with me when I visited Monica. A little voice told me I should go on my own the first time, but I'd enjoyed these weeks of independence, and having Marcus with me would buffer the re-entry to family, which I knew would bring mixed emotions. Of course I was excited at the prospect of seeing my aunt, but she *was* my aunt and therefore my elder, and I knew my role would always be that of the child. Deep in the pit of my stomach, the nugget of anger linked to abandonment sat ignored but ever present. Monica had left me all those years ago, just like all the other women in my family. I could sugarcoat the fact, but it was indisputable. I plucked up my courage and said, 'Would you like to come with me when I go to Montespertoli?'

'Sure,' he said. 'But don't you want to see your aunt by yourself?'

'Monica won't mind. And I'd enjoy company on the trip there.'

'Fine. What say I hire a car?'

'From what I've heard, Italians drive as if they're in the Grand Prix. Are you sure you don't mind driving?' I said. 'I was going to take public transport. Apparently it's a reasonably straight route to Monica's.'

Marcus shook his head. 'Even though Italians have a terrible reputation as drivers, it's just a matter of keeping your wits about you. I'll hire a car and pick you up at your apartment.'

Early Wednesday morning we headed out of the city and took the turn-off to Montelupo. I knew this town was renowned for its ceramics, and Marcus and I detoured briefly so as to see the displays outside its shops, vowing to return another day for a proper look. From there we drove the picturesque ridgeline to the town of Montespertoli. Monica's directions were perfect. Above her house was my stock image of Tuscany: gentle undulations, pencil-like cypresses, a regiment of vines marching diagonally across a neighbouring property. The house was as I remembered from the photograph of my childhood: a low rectangle of ochre stone. What the photo hadn't shown, or possibly I had been too young to notice, were the blue and yellow ceramic reliefs above the windows and the vibrant geraniums that frilled the garden beds.

Monica ran from the house as soon as she heard our car. I had not seen her since her quick visit to Australia when I was sixteen. She'd had a report to make at the university and a conference to attend. Lawrence and I met her in Melbourne for a brief lunch before she again left us waving goodbye while she jumped in a taxi and headed back to the airport.

Now, on a picture-perfect Tuscan day, I wound down the window and waved frantically.

Through tears I heard the familiar childhood greeting, '*Mia cara figliola!*'

I wrenched open the door and leaped from the car even before Marcus had fully stopped. 'Hardly a *bambina* anymore, Monica,' was all I could manage before we were in each other's arms. We were both laughing and crying.

Monica cupped my face in her hands. 'Let me look at you,' she said. 'I can hardly believe it.' Then she pressed her hands against either side of my neck, pinning me, so that she could look into my face. In that instance we were so close that not even time could come between us. The years concertinaed and we were walking my childhood together on the poplar walk. I didn't realise how much I had missed her. She hugged me again and we stayed in each other's arms for a long time.

I forgot about Marcus and when I did gather my wits enough to wonder where he was, I looked and saw that he was leaning against the car and watching us with what appeared to be delight. I thought our display might have embarrassed him.

'Monica, this is Marcus,' I said. 'We met the first week I was in Italy. He has been my guide and companion.'

To my surprise, my aunt hesitated and then held out her hand. 'I'm pleased to meet you,' she said. She pressed Marcus's hand between both her own and at the same time squinted at him quizzically before saying, 'You're Marcus Warren, aren't you?'

Marcus bowed and I looked from one to the other in surprise.

'I'm so very pleased to meet you,' she said.

'How do you know each other?'

Marcus laughed. 'We don't.'

'I know Marcus from his work in art history,' Monica explained. 'We have copies of some his documentaries. It's astonishing but rather wonderful to find the two of you together. How did all of this happen? Come into the house and tell me about it.'

She took us by the hands and led us towards the front door.

Inside it was pure Tuscan: white walls, dark beams, terracotta tiles. The effect could have been stark but was relieved by brightly coloured ceramics from Montelupo.

After Monica had shown us over the house and grounds, we sat on the outside terrace with its mismatched floor tiles and watched as evening fell. Above our heads was a loggia supported by thick, stone piers and covered with a dense wisteria vine drooping with early blue-purple flowers. Wisps of sweet scent softened the air. The cypresses in the distance now cast long shadows and fading light blurred the ridgeline.

Marcus pointed towards the trees and said, 'Chiaroscuro.'

'Yes, light and shade,' Monica agreed. 'There's something about this area that layers time through landscape, and through this, history comes to us gradually and seems less like the past and more like part of ourselves. Here I have' – she searched for the right word – 'a sense of continuity.'

Marcus nodded.

'You'll stay here, won't you?' I blurted out.

Monica looked straight at me. 'I know what you're thinking, Iris. I told you all those years ago that I'd return to Australia.' She hung her head and said, '*Mea culpa.*'

I felt again the flicker of betrayal and didn't answer. I stared straight ahead.

'You know, Iris' – in Monica's voice was the distant tone of the lecturer – 'people can't always do what they say they are going to. Things change. People change. I changed.'

'And what about my "continuity",' I said. 'It seems to me that for all the nods towards caring, most people make decisions with only themselves in mind.'

Marcus rose quietly. 'I'm going to check out the vines next door,' he said As he walked behind me, he ran his fingers across the back of my neck and my skin tingled. I reached up and caught the tips of his fingers with my own before he moved away. I looked at my aunt. She was watching us.

'Iris,' she said, 'I know, I mean, I don't really know but I can understand that losing your mother so young must have left a gaping hole.' She looked troubled and had paled. 'Remember she was my twin sister, too. I guess that when I left, it must have felt like more desertion, but I had a career that demanded I took certain steps and ...'

'... couldn't be interrupted by anything as mundane as an eleven-year-old girl,' I countered. Even as I spoke, I knew I was being childish. 'I'm sorry. I shouldn't have said that. It's not just both Allegra and you leaving. Our family is all about desertion. It's full of silences that pull you into quicksand and then guilt trips when you try to hoist yourself out. You should have seen Lawrence when I told him I was coming here. You'd have thought I was an executioner.'

'I guess it wouldn't have thrilled him,' Monica said.

I shook myself inwardly and in an attempt to redirect the conversation said, 'Anyway, as I've been walking around Florence, I've tried to keep in mind that Lawrence and my mother must have done the same. I've been trying to gather a sense of Allegra.'

I chose my words with care, avoiding any mention of the journal. Just then, I could have easily told her of its existence, but I needed to hold it close to me until I understood it well enough to let go. Despite my omissions, I thought it would please her to learn that I was following, however inadequately, in her sister's footsteps. Surely it was only natural to try and understand the woman who had given you birth.

But Monica's face drained further, and I saw her hands clench the arms of her chair. 'Be careful if you are going to follow ghosts,' she said. 'You never know where they might lead you. I mean, sometimes it's better to remember the good things and not chase shadows.'

10

Marcus and I left Monica's just on nightfall and parked the car on a high point of the ridge line to watch the sun settle behind the low hills. In the distance to our left, I could see faint yellow lights from a neighbouring farm. Except for the lack of sea, it was not unlike the view from our Peterborough veranda. As I looked over the rolling hills dotted with cone-shaped cypresses, I was reminded of my childhood poplars, and in my mind's eye saw Lawrence alone on our dark veranda, slunk in his deck chair, twilight a bruised slit on the horizon. I expected to feel elated after seeing Monica for the first time in ten years but instead I felt confused, torn by my love for my father and my aunt, and an irritation towards them that bordered on anger. What I'd always accepted as character traits were now sources of annoyance. Lawrence's neediness, which I'd accepted as inseparable from his love for me, now had a selfish edge, a dark side. Similarly, even though I knew Monica also loved me, her academic brilliance – the source of so many of my childhood bedtime stories – had claimed her in the end. I was deep in thought when Marcus said, 'You didn't say much during dinner.' I jumped and it took me a few moments to gather myself, but even then I didn't reply immediately. I continued staring out of the side window, my thoughts whirling. I was aware of Marcus sitting opposite me but felt no pressure to respond. The silence deepened and I registered him link his hands behind his neck and lean back into them. He was facing the windscreen and remained completely still, calm even. There was no hint of annoyance at my silence.

Monica's explanation for her decision not to return to Australia prickled at me, mainly because it made sense. I knew I was being childish and that – at twenty-five and unattached – it was unreasonable to expect to be the centre of any person's life. Monica had every right to do as she pleased. But knowing that my feelings were unreasonable only made things worse. Also, her warning about ghosts smacked of something I couldn't put my finger on, and she had made no effort to explain. Secrets? The supernatural? Perhaps it was simply a case of words reflecting an overactive imagination that spent too much time reading about the dramatic lives of long-dead saints and martyrs. Despite Monica's good food and wine, and now the Tuscan sunset, my mood had sunk into despondency. I had so many questions and so few avenues down which to find answers.

Marcus shifted so that his back leaned against the car door and he faced towards me. 'When did Monica come to live in Italy?' he said.

I sighed inwardly, relieved that the turn of his conversation required nothing more than an easy factual answer from me. 'I was eleven. So about fourteen years ago now.'

'And why?'

'To finish her book.'

'What was it about?'

'Saint Ursula.' I groaned. 'The very prolific Saint Ursula. I don't think there's a painting or story about her that I haven't been told every detail in detail. Where will I start? There's Memling's maiden Ursula with a bevy of miniature attendant virgins gathered under her cloak. She's the namesake for the Ursuline sisters, who use an iconic representation which portrays her as more like a middle-aged nun than a young bride-to-be. I think everyone has had a go. There is even a dramatic Poussin, which paints her like an escapee from Greek or Roman mythology. But, to my mind, the best is Carpaccio's delirious apotheosis at the end of the Saint Ursula cycle in Venice ...'

'Ah! Yes, I know it. The one with the retinue of virgins in attendance. How many actually were there?' Marcus said.

'Folklore has it at eleven thousand, but there is a theory that a mistranslation of the Latin abbreviation for eleven virgin-martyrs by the Bishop of Cologne saw Ursula and her ten virgin companions each be supplied with a thousand attendants. So eleven became eleven thousand.'

We both smiled. Despite my mood, it was a delightful legend and I said, 'I waited for Monica's stories in the same way other children waited for a new Enid Blyton. But now it all seems fatuous.' I sighed, shrugged my shoulders, and added, 'Because one day she simply took her stories and left, just like all the other women in my world.'

Marcus leaned over and reached for my hand. He raised his eyebrows again and pursed his lips as if I were a puzzle he needed to solve. I mused that despite only knowing him for a short time his touch held the assurance of long acquaintance. It was a strange but true fact that it is sometimes easier to be intimate with a stranger than one you love. Any thoughts and observations – even unpalatable ones – come from a viewpoint unhampered by the complexities of a shared past. And because the relationship is usually transitory, there is little risk of repercussions down the track. So, I let my clenched fingers relax into Marcus's warm hand.

'You expected her to go back to Australia, didn't you?' he said.

'She promised she would. I was a child. I still believed what people said. So why wouldn't I believe her? I'd lost my mother and at that time Monica was the only constant woman in my life. I know it was unreasonable but, yes, I felt betrayed.'

Marcus shook his head. 'I can see it must have hurt you when she didn't return.'

His reply jolted me simply because it was so unexpected. I thought he would have agreed that my response was childish, but instead he'd acknowledged my feelings without needing to point out my failings. We sat and watched the night lights wink across the low hills. Every so often Marcus absently stroked the knuckles of my hand with his fingers.

Marcus must have guessed that I didn't want to be alone because as we neared my apartment in Florence he said, 'The hire car company's not expecting me back until late tomorrow morning. It's safe enough to leave the car here at night. As long as you make sure there's nothing valuable to be seen.' It was his unspoken way of saying he'd stay the night.

We walked back to the apartment through cobbled streets, which by this time were empty apart from scattered groups of teenagers. The bars were closing, and

I felt the stone buildings close around me and heard my own echoing footsteps. Monica was right about one thing. History wrapped itself around you here. It held you as tightly as a mother should a child.

The key to my front door was large and ungainly and painted black and looked more like a kitchen implement than my definition of a key. It clattered loosely in the keyhole, the noise magnified by the night air. Next door, I saw my landlord's curtains shift. Just inside the door was a kitchenette with an oversize table and six chairs. There was no actual living room, and a short flight of stairs led to a single bedroom with an ensuite bathroom, into which was squashed a shower, basin, washing machine, and toilet.

'Obviously for visitors.' Marcus indicated towards the chairs as he squeezed between the table and the wall and sat down. 'Because this is definitely a one-person dwelling.'

I laughed, put on the kettle and began to wash my few mugs, which had piled up in the sink. When I turned around a few minutes later armed with clean mugs and a jar of coffee, I saw that Marcus was studying the postcards in my mother's journal. I had left it lying open there that morning.

My heart thudded in my chest: a thick, unsettling feeling that left me unsteady on my feet. It was the first time someone other than myself had seen the journal. A mix of emotions surged through me in quick succession. First a rush of anger at this intrusion into the heart of my life, followed by the realisation that the journal was now shared and discussion would inevitability follow, and then an unexpected relief that I no longer had to keep it secret.

'These postcards are years old,' he said. It was more question than observation. He twisted his mouth sideways and sat looking at me with his chin resting on entwined fingers, waiting for my answer.

'Yes, they are,' I agreed. The room was quiet except for the ceramic clock over the front door, which ticked so loudly it had to be dismantled each evening or it could be heard in the bedroom. I'd always been sensitive to noise, no doubt spoilt by the quiet of Peterborough.

'Where did you get them?' He picked the journal up and turned it towards the light. The desire to snatch it from his hand flared like a match but quickly burnt itself out and I sat heavily in the chair.

'They're my mother's,' I said.

'Your mother's?'

'Years ago, when I was a child,' I continued. 'I sound like an old storyteller. The only trouble is I don't have a complete story to tell.'

Marcus didn't smile at my feeble attempt to be light-hearted. Instead, he simply said, 'And?'

I told him about my father and the journal with its postcards, and Louise's insistence that I come to Italy. As I spoke about the journal, I felt its weight in the pit of my stomach; I felt its power to pull me down into dark places. My earlier frustration returned and as my tale petered to a close, I said miserably, 'You see, I don't know anything really, and I've a strange feeling there's a truth out there somewhere and I'm being prevented from knowing it. I thought that if I saw what interested my mother, I might get to know it – to know her.'

Marcus got up and made the coffee and set mine in front of me. We both sipped thoughtfully. Finally, he indicated the journal and said, 'Does Monica know about this?'

I shook my head.

'I see.' He ran his fingers lightly across the cover, pressed one forefinger hard on its centre, and said, 'So, this is the real reason you came to Italy.' He picked up the journal and turned the pages slowly. He didn't stop long enough to read any of the contents, which I knew would be easy for him. As far as I could tell, his Italian was near perfect. 'You've obviously had this translated?'

'Yes. I took it to a lecturer I got on well with at my old university in Melbourne. She told me it began around the time of my parent's honeymoon in Italy and ended a short time after my birth. The first part is full of details about my parents' time in Italy and the early days in Peterborough while my mother was pregnant. The second part is after my birth and details my mother's – it's hard to find the right word – perhaps bewilderment or overwhelm at the complexities of motherhood.'

'There's a big hint there,' Marcus said.

'What do you mean?'

'I obviously haven't read the journal, but your description of the last part suggests a postpartum problem. Maybe depression or something?'

'The translator said my mother seemed a gentle soul, a free spirit. I don't remember Lawrence saying that my mother was unwell. But then he's never spoken of her much at all.'

I took a sip of coffee, cradled the mug in the palms of my hands, and stared at a few undissolved granules floating on the surface. I wanted Marcus to speak first and wildly conjectured that perhaps he'd been sent to give me an answer to my questions, but a short silence grew into a longer one and eventually I sighed and said, 'That's why I went to the Brancacci Chapel. Lawrence, Monica, and the journal appear to be dead ends with regards to my mother. I wanted something to happen in the chapel. I wanted the fresco to step down from the wall and speak to me about Allegra.' Irritation fizzed in my stomach and spread until it reached my throat. When I spoke, my words were high pitched, harsh. 'But, actually, it was more like confronting another brick wall.'

'What did you feel when you looked at Adam and Eve?'

I'd been expecting sympathy, not a discussion on art. I frowned, thought for a moment, and then answered, 'Early Renaissance, Masaccio's genius, human figures ...'

'No, I don't want what you know; I want what you felt. You asked me the other day what I saw when I looked at the fresco. I told you what I felt. Now you tell me what you felt.'

'I don't know where this is going but I'll go along with you – for now.' I put the mug on the table with a purposeful thump and said, 'Adam and Eve are being chased out of the Garden of Eden by an angel. Eve looks straight ahead, distraught. Adam looks downwards, browbeaten. The landscape is barren and reflects their states of mind.' As I made each point, I clicked my thumb and middle finger for emphasis.

'That's all well and good but won't get you very far,' Marcus said. 'All that's knowledge. What about feelings? Does the fresco make you sad? Angry? Do you think Masaccio painted it with notions of the early Renaissance running through his brain? He was probably aware of the extent of his talent, but the Renaissance didn't even have a name then. Perhaps he was simply painting pain. Perhaps your mother looked at Adam and Eve and it spoke to some pain in her. Perhaps she knew what it was like to be cast out of paradise.'

I looked at Marcus, shook my head in wonderment, and said, 'My mother. Cast out of paradise. By an angel. Don't you think that's a bit fanciful?'

'No, not by an angel,' Marcus said. 'Maybe something less divine, but just as powerful. You mightn't like this, but I think your mother's choice of paintings tells us about more than her interest in Renaissance art. It tells us about her and how she felt.' His voice held gravitas, and this in turn held me.

I was dumbfounded. It had never occurred to me to look at my mother's postcards in this light. 'How am I supposed to know how she felt? I can't divine the past, nor am I a mind-reader.'

'That's just it,' Marcus said, again with that calm that soothed my mind and brought me back into my body. 'You don't have to know. You just have to feel. As I said before, if you only bring to the journal what you know, you'll just answer questions asked by others before you. To learn about your mother, you'll have to leave the road most travelled and look at art as more than art history.' He sat back in the chair and ran his fingers through his hair. 'It's impossible to look at Adam and Eve in the Brancacci Chapel and just think "psychic pain"! How textbook can you get? You'll have to try and feel what your mother felt. You'll have to' – there was a long pause – 'I think looking for your mother means putting to one side the sense of being the abandoned child.'

I felt a prickle of anger, but it dissipated as quickly as it had come. Hadn't I just mentioned betrayal and all the women who had left my life? What were they if not abandonment? I pointed first to the Botticelli below Adam and Eve and then to the Bellini opposite and said, 'What messages do you get from *Primavera* and the *Sacred Conversation?*' Then I sat back in my chair with my hands resting palms up on the table top and added, 'Abandoned child makes me sound about two years old.'

Marcus leaned forward and covered my hands with his own. He looked directly into my eyes. 'Iris, the abandoned child is an archetype. It's the part in all of us that feels hard done by but doesn't seem able or refuses to do anything to change a situation. We are all an abandoned child at one time or the other. I wasn't trying to be smart, just help you.' He hesitated, looked at the wall as if it could tell him what to say next, then redirected his gaze back to me. 'I guess I'm trying to say that you won't find your mother if you carry around an academic shield, no matter how brilliant and shiny. There is knowing and there is feeling. We need both to understand anything fully. But to feel is challenging – and often takes courage. These cards "meant" something to your mother.' He stopped and shifted awkwardly in his seat.

I wanted to tell Marcus it was presumptuous to tell me how to handle my own problems, but even though it rankled, I knew there was truth in what he said so I kept quiet.

Marcus looked crestfallen. 'I'm not telling you what to do, just opening a different door. I'm sorry if I spoke out of turn, but' – he looked at me as if he were a teacher wrestling with a dim student – 'when you try and find out about other people, you inevitably learn more about yourself first.'

'What do you mean?' My voice was strained.

'I'll explain but then let's take a rest from all this.' He took a deep breath and began. 'We see others in the light of what we think we know about them, but this limited knowledge often makes us draw conclusions that have no real depth. I mean, how can we ever really know another person?' He stopped, searched for the right words and then said carefully, 'Behind what we think we know about someone lies their shadow world, of which we understand nothing. The conclusions we draw answer questions we ourselves have formed and answered with limited knowledge. My studies of art history have made this clear to me.'

I tried to follow Marcus's reasoning, but it had been a long and emotional day, and my tiredness was escalating by the moment. 'I'm not sure I follow,' I said.

'If I look at a painting thinking only about its provenance or social relevance, that is, what I know about it, I miss the reason it was painted in the first place, and that is a different thing altogether.'

'And what's the reason?' I was curious now.

'More often than not, I believe it's feeling, emotion,' he said.

I waited for more.

When he spoke again, I had the peculiar feeling that he had walked into another room, leaving me struggling to catch his fading words. It was the same sensation I had felt in the Brancacci Chapel. 'No artist begins to paint thinking only about a work's usefulness,' he said.

'That's not true,' I blurted. 'What about all the art that uses conventions.' Lorenzo Monaco was uppermost in mind.

Marcus looked at me and then at the postcards. 'And behind the conventions?' There was the merest hint of scorn in his voice. 'Come on, Iris. Something must drive an artist to want to paint those conventions.'

'Perhaps money,' I said. 'Perhaps just love of God, of the church, or just plain old obedience.'

Marcus took no notice. He didn't even look up. 'We can only see into a person, into a painting, by feeling, and feeling exposes us. We have to move beyond – let go – of what we know so we can begin to understand.' He looked up. His eyes were bright, and there was a twist of a smile on his handsome face. 'And then we see just how inadequate our knowledge really was. And in that lie the lessons we learn about ourselves.'

'We are quite the psychologist, aren't we?' I said. 'By all this, are you telling me that my search is impossible?'

'No, as I said before, only that there is knowing and there is feeling, and we need both to understand anything.'

There was little I could say to this. Marcus's words echoed Monica's warnings about ghosts, and her warnings and his talk of feelings shared a territory pitted with emotional landmines. Foreboding flooded through me. Marcus had hit my raw nerve. I wanted to find out about Allegra, but I resisted anything that might make me feel too much. I'd trained myself to distrust those who said the way through fear was to explore it. At that moment it would have been easier to tell Marcus to mind his own business. But what he said made sense. I bit my lip. I was enjoying my time with him and wanted it to continue for as long as I was in Italy. There was no point arguing over something that had already consumed a large part of my life. I reached over and closed the journal with my index finger and threw my hands in the air in mock frustration, effectively closing the conversation. As the cover shut with a faint thwack, I caught sight of the postcard of Prudencia and quickly looked up to see if Marcus had also noticed it. But his coat must have slipped from the back of the chair, and he had bent to pick it up. I didn't mention this last postcard. I'd had enough for the time being.

Marcus rose from his seat, walked around the table and stood behind me. I smelled his aftershave – lemon tamed by the woody scent of cedar. I felt his thumbs press lightly against the side of my neck and his fingers slide up and through my hair. The tension in my neck dissolved. I leaned my head backward against the side of his leg and his fingers drifted across my lips Neither of us moved. I was aware only of the still room and the charge between us, and the startling sensation of tears sliding down my cheeks, which Marcus stopped with his thumbs before pulling me to my feet.

We walked up the short flight of stairs and into the bedroom. Marcus let go of my hand and moved to the window to close the shutters against the glare of the streetlight. He stood for a moment, looking out over the uneven terracotta rooftops, and I felt my throat catch. When he came back, there was a slight awkwardness as he stood close to me with his legs apart and cupped my chin in his hands, looking directly into my eyes. Then, not shifting his gaze, his fingers moved to the buttons of my shirt, and I let my hands lie by my side, aware only of the anticipation that fired my nerve ends. The fine linen fabric slipped from my shoulders to the ground without a sound. He ran his little finger along my collarbone from throat to shoulder, then opened his hand, slid it down my back, and held me as if we were about to waltz, all this in a motion as smooth as if I'd been made of silk. I followed his lead and leaned against him. He was warm and I felt dazed, even slightly drunk, despite the effects of the wine from dinner having worn off hours ago. But as we moved closer to the bed, I hesitated, drawn by the bright blade of streetlight thrown across the carpet where one shutter had refused to shut fully. I wasn't having doubts. I wanted this holiday romance. My hesitation centred around my quest, my search for my mother, and the realisation that in sharing Allegra's story my relationship with Marcus had become something more profound than an affair in an exotic location.

'Is everything okay?' Marcus said. 'Are you sure this is what you want?'

'Of course,' I said. 'It's just been a big day.'

Marcus studied my face and then again touched my lips with his fingertips. He left them there, not moving, for several seconds, and then slowly traced along their outline as if to smooth away my protective – small – smile. Then he leaned forward and kissed me. His lips were soft and warm, and I leaned against his chest. I felt the gentle thump of his heart against my cheek. The room closed around the two of us and, suddenly, all I wanted to do was forget.

11

The following morning, I woke and looked at Marcus sleeping beside me. I hugged my knees and my thoughts drifted back to an elderly man I'd seen walking in the loggia of the foundling hospital when I'd been staying at the hotel. He'd paced its length many times with slow, even steps while reading from a newspaper held at elbow height. His clothing was impeccable: dark knife-pleated trousers, green tweed jacket, white shirt, and plain darker green tie. He appeared the perfect continental gentleman, measured, unhurried, perhaps even a little austere, worlds apart from the laid-back Peterborough locals and the farmers straight from the paddocks with their muddy gumboots and laconic grins. Similarly, Marcus was the opposite of anyone I'd ever been with. His touch was light, and when we'd made love, he caressed rather than groped. I'd had the sensation of being coaxed out of myself so that my shell – my carapace – fell away, and the essence of me was laid bare, freed. Several times during the night, I'd woken and felt the warmth of Marcus's body beside me. Once, I placed the palm of my hand on his back as if to reassure myself that he was real. He stirred briefly but quickly fell back into a deep sleep. I removed my hand carefully so as not to disturb him further and eventually fell asleep. When I woke the world had seemed a brighter place.

Now I bent close enough until I could hear his breathing and studied him, looking for clues to his age. Perhaps late thirties? Only light stubble stippled his face and neck, despite his dark hair. His skin was taut but without clear muscle definition, the body of an academic rather than an athlete. I ran my hand across his stomach and pressed lightly. It was soft. He stirred, curled into a ball beside me, and opened his eyes.

'How old are you?' I said.

Marcus laughed. 'Good morning to you, too.'

'You've hardly told me anything about yourself, and you know things about me that I've never told to anyone.' I pushed my fingers into his stomach. 'Well?'

He rolled onto his back and stretched. I resisted the desire to lie down beside him. 'I'm thirty-eight. I've three sisters and two brothers-in-law, and between them they have two sons and a daughter.'

'You're lucky,' I said. 'It must be nice to have siblings. Being an only child means you're always at the centre of things.'

'I might be one of four, but I'm the only male, and that brings its own set of problems.'

'In what way?'

Marcus hoisted himself up onto his elbows. 'My father died when I was nineteen and deep into university life – not a good time for a conceited young man preoccupied with art, architecture, and literature. One who arrogantly had no patience with his father's stocks and shares and the maintenance of an English country house. I saw myself as a cut above money and work. I honestly believed it was possible to eschew all worldly goods and live the life of the mind.' He looked rueful.

The mention of a country house gelled with my earlier romantic impressions of aristocracy, and I envisaged a sprawling brick mansion of two or three storeys complete with oak panelling and the stuffed heads of deer mounted on the walls. The garden in front would, I imagined, be neatly hedged and contain a profusion of cottage plants pierced here and there by a blue delphinium spire. 'What did you do? Did you have to defer your studies?'

'No, fortunately my sister Catherine proved more adept at the stocks and shares part than me. So apart from weekend visits to help my mother organise the maintenance, I was left to carry on as usual. Even now, except for when I'm researching or travelling, I still go to the country every two weeks and, anyway, it's good to get away from London and the confines of my flat. It's beautiful country, so green, and the trees are massive, solid.'

This litany of family and responsibility was satisfying and anchored Marcus. Until then he had seemed free floating, a well-off male with unlimited access to the world's great treasures, and one who had probably never cooked a meal in his life. I saw him now as a young boy surrounded by girls, and then years later with one or more of their dishevelled toddlers pulling at his fine wool coat. And, after that, seeing to the mowing or gardening or roof problems, or whatever it was that constituted country house maintenance.

I waited to see if Marcus was going to tell me more, but he suddenly leaned over and kissed me quickly before leaping out of bed and reaching for his clothes. 'I'll go back to Max's and tidy up, and what say we extend the car hire and head for the Tuscan hills? If I get moving, I'll be back before midday.' He walked over to the window and flung open the shutters. Sunlight streamed into the room. 'It looks like a beautiful day, and we only have two left before you leave for the fabled city of Venezia.'

'And you leave for Rome,' I countered.

'I know where I'd rather be going.' Marcus stopped midway into pulling on his jeans and looked up at me. 'I mean it, you know. If I didn't have this appointment at the Vatican archives, I'd come with you – if you wanted me to. I haven't been back to La Serenissima for three years, and no sight on earth can rival mist descending over a winding canal with the looming façade of a centuries-old church in the background – all in the half dark, of course.'

I smiled at his flight of fancy and said, 'Perhaps we could meet there when you've finished your research in Rome?' I expected him to make some excuse as to why this wouldn't be possible, to say that he'd meet me when I returned to Florence, by which time it would be an easy step to invent a reason for being called back to England. Instead, Marcus looked up again – this time he was buttoning his shirt – and said, 'Yes, I'd like that. We could visit the Sacred Conversation in San Zaccaria. What say we make a date for dusk outside the church of the Frari this time next week?'

'Dusk outside the Frari,' I echoed. 'Sounds good to me.'

After Marcus left, I made breakfast and returned with it to the bedroom. My landlord had thoughtfully placed a wooden rocking chair at an angle to the window, from which I could see first only rooftops, but further into the distance narrow lanes and then the smoky shadows cast over the Arno by the buildings lining her banks – the colours all grey, mustard, terracotta, and cream – even the river herself – with the sky above a startling blue.

I sat on the sky-blue cushion dotted all over with bright yellow sunflowers, leaned backwards, and rocked slowly, the hot chocolate and almond-crusted croissant inert in my lap, and thought back to the previous evening's discussion. A hot flush of annoyance rose but quickly vanished. I hated to admit it, but some of what Marcus said made sense. Until now I had looked at – no, hit – the postcards with the full force of my art history armour, in the vain hope that it would inform me about the woman who had left me. I now saw that that was a dead end. There was no choice but to let myself feel. If I didn't, I would never discover what Allegra's postcards had to tell me. The skin on my scalp crawled and a dull headache spiralled upwards from the base of my neck. The postcards had taken on a life of their own. Marcus's comments had melded my mother with the cards, and I'd never see them in quite the same way again. My mother had entered the paintings, and whatever was going on in them was linked to the emotions inside her. It was a startling hypothesis but unstoppable once aired.

I sipped my chocolate, which had cooled, and pushed the thin skin gauzing its surface to one side with my tongue. Then I nibbled the croissant, acutely aware of the snap of almond flakes as I bit through them before my teeth sank into the pastry's soft centre. Small, golden flakes scattered over my dressing gown. A door had opened, and I'd been pushed through, and there was no going back. The thought that Masaccio's Eve was an embodiment of some unknown pain of my mother's intensified my headache, and despite attempts to focus on the view from the window and thus stop my thoughts from stacking one on top of the other, my mind drifted of its own accord to *Primavera* and the *Sacred Conversation*, and the alarming notion of what these precious works might also reveal. And then, of course, there was Prudencia. There was no clear reason why I'd been glad Marcus didn't see the final postcard in the journal, other than I was tired and impatient and, if I'm to be honest, rather keen for things between us to become more physical than cerebral. Nothing explained the relief I felt at keeping Prudencia to myself. Apart from Louise, Marcus was the only person who knew a little of my fractured story, yet I felt absurdly protective of the naked young woman whose life – if my mother was to be believed – had been blighted. Also, when our talk turned to Venice and the *Sacred Conversation*, I'd deliberately held back from telling him that I planned to give San Zaccaria only a cursory visit before moving on to search for what really interested me – an obscure and possibly non-existent marriage chest. I put my empty mug on the floor and rocked slowly. The sun was now warm through the window, and I drifted off to sleep until the Duomo's midday bells fractured my dream of the previous night and I sat up and rubbed my eyes. I had slept for half an hour. I quickly brushed my hair and wrapped a shawl around my shoulders over my nightgown. I went down the few stairs and sat at the table with a fresh cup of coffee. The room was still and warm. I pressed my feet down on the tiles and tilted my head back, aware that I was smiling.

True to his word, Marcus returned not long after the midday peals. He took the rainbow-coloured woven basket off its peg near the door and said, 'I'll go shopping for a picnic. Does bread, cheese, and olives sound okay? Do you have any favourites?'

'That sounds perfect!' I said. 'And no, no particular favourites. Surprise me! I'll shower and be ready by the time you get back.'

He walked over, kissed the back of my head, and said, 'I won't be long.'

I twisted around and linked my arms around his neck, pulling him towards me.

He laughed and said, 'If you don't let go, this picnic will be a nonstarter!'

Then he wriggled free and was gone.

Marcus returned half an hour later with coarse Tuscan bread, cheeses including provolone and a salty-sweet, full-bellied Taleggio, a mix of giant, green Sicilian olives and wrinkled, black olives from nearby Lazio, and a bottle of Chianti Classico. I heard him clattering in the kitchen, whistling a discordant tune, and when I went into the room, I leaned against the wall just inside the door. I watched as he riffled through my cupboards until he found an old thermos, which he filled with boiling water. Mugs, spoons, tea bags, sugar cubes in a plastic container, and tiny pyramids of long-life milk sat neatly on the bench. I kept silent, intrigued by his concentration, his habit of stopping and assessing each accomplished task. Finally, he stood back, started as he registered my presence, and said, 'Iris! I didn't realise you were here.'

I walked over and indicated the items on the bench. 'Tea? I guess at heart always the Englishman!'

Marcus picked up a teabag and shrugged. 'I guess I am. I love coffee but also tea in equal measure. And a picnic isn't a picnic without it. Childhood conditioning, I guess.'

'I get it. I've spent many an hour with Lawrence – my father – on our veranda drinking tea. Lawrence's is always scalding hot and black as ink.'

'Lawrence? Not Dad?'

'No, just Lawrence. It was always just the two of us, you see.' I struggled for the right words. 'We were alone. There was no need for formalities.'

Marcus looked at me questioningly, with his head to one side. But I had nothing more to say. I smiled and set to helping him load our provisions into a basket.

We drove through clogged city streets and then polluted, industrial outskirts, which in time gave way to vineyards tipped with green. After about twenty minutes, we turned off the autostrada and headed north into higher, more open country where the road zigzagged perilously. I was surprised at its wildness. Not wild, of course, by my Australian standards, but untamed enough after the dense cityscape.

We reached the town of Carmignano just as the shops were closing for their *riposo* and parked the car at the end of the town's main street. We found a bench set in a green alcove off the main piazza and attracted surprised glances as we spread our picnic on the seat between us.

'You do realise we're breaking the rules of decorum,' Marcus said.

'What do you mean?' I was balancing mugs on the slats of the bench, watched by a curious child. The girl, who must have been about four or five, held her mother's hand and did not take her eyes off us as she walked in a slow semi-circle, pulling her mother from side to side. I watched the woman sway with the child but continue to chat animatedly to her friend outside a store window crammed with everything from men's shirts to lingerie.

'Italians don't really have picnics in public places like this,' he said. 'It's a very English and Australian preoccupation.' He abruptly changed tack. 'After lunch, do you want to walk up to San Michele and have a look at Pontormo's painting of the Visitation?'

I groaned. 'Do we have to? It's not one I know much about and besides, I don't think I can bear any more art.'

'Just a quick look,' Marcus said. 'It's one I really like.'

I would have much rather gone for a walk along the dusty but picturesque road. The sun was bright and heavy. The food had been delicious, and I felt warm and sensuous and wanted nothing more than Marcus's company and the possibility that in some grassy field away from prying eyes we might continue from where we left off the previous night. At that moment the church held little interest. But we packed up the remains of our picnic and returned them to the car, after which Marcus took my hand and half-dragged me, protesting, along the street.

The church sat at an awkward angle on a corner of the main road and a narrow one-way street. We went inside and I blinked as my eyes adjusted to the dim light. I was surprised to see a number of people scattered throughout the pews. As our coins clinked into the tin box and the painting lit up in a blaze of greens and oranges, I looked around, half-expecting everyone to be staring at us, but no one took any notice. There was only the faint rhythm of prayer from a huddled group in a distant corner and the beguiling, musty smell common to Italy's old churches.

It was a divine painting. The Virgin Mary and her cousin Elizabeth embraced from within a flurry of brilliant garments – their pregnant bellies almost touching – watched by two other women who stood behind and stared straight over their heads. In the former, there was total engagement, and in the latter, a curious detachment. Marcus and I perched on the ends of two pews and silently fed our spare change into the slot. As the last allotted span of light faded, I glanced sideways at Marcus and was surprised at his depth of concentration. He'd disappeared again to some far-off place while I – in my usual way – sat methodically working through the painting's attributes to determine if it was a masterpiece: composition, ingenuity, use of colour, ticking them off my mental list like ingredients in a recipe. Suddenly, impatience rippled through me. What if I put all my knowledge aside and asked what these two women felt? I tossed the notion around, unsure exactly what to do. Tentatively, feeling a little silly, I asked Elizabeth if she was frightened at becoming a mother at an advanced age. Then I turned to Mary and asked the direct opposite. The vibrant greens and oranges of their gowns shimmered and merged. I was certain they would have been worried but also found solace in each other's company. This intimacy between Mary and Elizabeth brought unexpected tears to my eyes. Why had it been such an effort to see the obvious? Pontormo's brilliance lay in his ability to render the tenderness between two pregnant women through the medium of paint. These women could not have known that their children would change the course of world history. They were simply two expectant mothers overjoyed at meeting again. I felt exposed. At that moment, it was too much to delve into their exchange any further. But Marcus was right. Behind the attributes of artistry lay a deep well of feeling. A wave of heat spread through me and I rose quickly, knocking a small stack of hymn books onto the floor. Marcus bent to pick them up. I should have helped him, but I needed to be alone, so I hurried to the far side of the church and pretended to be preoccupied by a gaudy statue. Marcus didn't immediately follow me but waited a good ten minutes before joining me in my silent contemplation.

Before we left the church, we circled the walls, avoiding the praying women but stopping at a side altar in front of which was an honour-system piety stall and, nearby, a stand of votive candles. I bought a postcard of *The Visitation*, dropping my coins into the slot in the top of a wooden box. Then I turned and lit a candle. The flame faltered and flared. I leaned forward and sniffed. The candle's warmth had picked up the scent of a bunch of early blue-purple violets crowded into a vase on a pedestal above. They were there, of course, because they stood for faithfulness, and I grimaced at the irony of them being Allegra's favourite scent.

For the early part of our drive back to Florence, we watched as twilight turned on the first lights in the valley below. It was if land and sky had swapped places and we were looking down as the stars broke the darkness one by one.

I felt suspended again, just as I had when I saw my own country of Australia from the plane.

'It's a magic view, isn't it?' I breathed.

Marcus murmured in agreement and then asked, 'What did you think of *The Visitation?*'

'It's a lovely enough painting.' I picked my words carefully. 'But it is enigmatic. I read the description on the plaque beside it. It suggested the two women standing in the background were alter egos of Mary and Elizabeth. But perhaps they're just particularly straight-faced angels?' I sat back. I couldn't bring myself to tell Marcus about my experiment with feeling in the church yet. It was such new territory for me. So I said, 'Sometimes I get a bit annoyed when there's an obscure element like that.'

Marcus thought for a moment before saying, 'I think you're right about alter egos. Mary and Elizabeth are intimately engaged; the women behind them stare straight ahead and appear disengaged. But they are the same women, front on instead of in profile.'

'Oh,' I mouthed. I pulled out the postcard I'd bought and studied it. 'Of course! I should have noticed the facial similarities.'

'They're easily missed but unmistakable once you've noticed them. I think it's a powerful painting,' Marcus said. 'I think – I know – it has the capacity to change your life.'

I looked at him with surprise. 'How do you know?'

He glanced sideways at me. I think he wanted to catch my eye and make sure I was listening. 'I first went to Carmignano a few months after my father died. As I told you this morning, I wasn't really interested in taking over where Dad left off. But at that time no one in the family knew what to do. We were in that state of flux which happens when someone close dies. What has been a complete picture suddenly becomes a jigsaw missing a large piece, and all the other pieces don't fit the way they used to. I was filled with righteous indignation at my family's perceived belief that I would step into my father's shoes. In hindsight, the perception was all mine. So I took off and backpacked through Italy during the summer break.'

'How does Carmignano fit into this?'

'I'm getting to that. I thought the time away would clarify things for me. But I was young and, despite my indignation, bound to the notion that it was my duty to be' – there was a wry note in his voice – 'the man of the house. So I'd come to the decision to ditch my studies and do what I believed was expected of me.' Marcus was driving carefully with both hands on the steering wheel. The roads were busier now and he paused in his story as his glance darted from rear vision mirror to side mirror to road ahead as he weaved through a dense pocket of traffic that took no notice of road rules. When the road cleared, he continued, 'But for some reason I detoured on the way back to Florence and came across Carmignano, and as an art history student went to see *The Visitation*. I know this is going to sound mad or like some sort of an epiphany, but that painting saved me. When I left the church, I'd changed my mind.'

'A painting did that?' I was incredulous.

'Paintings can change anything,' he said. 'Pontormo's *Visitation* unstuck me; it freed me. It's something to do with those alter egos. They made me see that our shadow selves – the less exalted parts of us – are always nearby. But that they can change into something wonderful, like caterpillars into butterflies.'

'You're talking about the women standing behind Mary and Elizabeth?' I said.

'Yes,' Marcus said. 'I realised that Mary and Elizabeth willingly stepped outside accepted destinies. And I began to see that if I forced myself to take a preordained path, I would be like one of those alter egos and never fully embrace life.'

'I see,' I said.

Marcus nodded. 'Yes, I would stare into the future and never embrace what lay inside me. Mary and Elizabeth took big risks, you know. They opened themselves to joy, relief, and excitement. They embraced on many levels.'

I sucked in the sides of my cheeks and then let them go in a loud pop. In truth, I felt manipulated and a little annoyed. 'You took me to Carmignano on purpose, didn't you?' I said. My mind was whirring, and I was sure that if Marcus looked closely, he would be able to see my thoughts.

He didn't answer.

There was a charged pause and then Marcus said, 'I took you there to see a painting about two women who understood each other without words. Maybe this is possible for you and your mother. I've got you thinking, haven't I? When we get back, look at your mother's journal in a different light. Trust yourself. Feel. Read between the lines. Even imagine. Don't interpret something so precious using other people's platitudes, even if these are learned people. Don't you see? What your mother has left you is priceless.' He pulled the car over to the side of the road, sat back, and rubbed the back of his neck. I looked at him. He was a difficult man to stay angry with because he was so clearly disingenuous, a character trait guaranteed to disarm me. My thoughts slid sideways and I reflected on how his eyes deepened when he was thinking, and then they slipped even further to the saying about eyes being the mirror of the soul. Then Marcus leaned over and put his hands on my shoulders and looked into my eyes. His own eyes held no trace of triumph, no hint that he had expounded some wise philosophical lesson for which I should be grateful, just a look of genuine concern. 'It wasn't as calculated as you make it seem,' he said.

'You don't understand,' I whispered. I knew he did understand the dilemma I faced, and he was trying his best to help me find out about Allegra. But inside I was all confusion; my mother, Lawrence, and Monica were hiding things from me, and it was unfair. I was their daughter and niece and yet forced to fight my way through this maze of a journal, paintings, and a marriage chest to learn what should have been my birthright.

'Perhaps,' he said. 'It's not happening to me, but I can offer the little I know.' Then he shifted the conversation as he so often did when he felt it had run its course. 'Art is perfect for meditating on life,' he mused as he turned the key in the ignition and refastened his seat belt. 'We remove ourselves from the clamour and step into a small, contained world within a frame and for a time become part of something else. We take part in the picture by virtue of who we are, and each one of us is different.'

He pulled out into the stream of traffic heading towards Florence and put his foot down hard. 'You know I'm not sure if art galleries are the place for this, but in some of the little towns, you can feel as if a painting is yours alone. You can be flooded by it. That's what happens to me, at least in places like Carmignano.'

He turned his head briefly and smiled at me. We had reached the outskirts of the city and the roadsides were lined with brightly coloured fast food restaurants and petrol stations. In the distance, Brunelleschi's elegant dome rose high above the city buildings like some great force of nature It was dark when we reached the city centre. Along the route, buildings of the honey-coloured sandstone, which I now knew was called pietraforte, glowed under the streetlights. As the shops were near closing, there were few people on the streets, but couples and travellers still wandered along the banks of the Arno. I'd woken with Marcus beside me and in a single day we'd picnicked, seen and discussed art, and I'd made inroads into a new way of seeing and feeling that might help me find my mother. I leaned against the side window and hugged myself. With Marcus beside me I felt hopeful.

Marcus didn't drive to his parking spot of the previous night but wound his way through one-way streets to get close to the door of my apartment.

'Are you staying?' I said.

'No. You've got homework to do, and I've got to make a couple of phone calls. There are a few people I need to catch up with before I leave for Rome. I'll come around late tomorrow afternoon and help you get things ready for dinner. And I'll bring some of that wine Monica liked.'

I opened the door, mindful of every movement in a deliberate effort to avoid looking at Marcus. This was probably just the beginning of the end, I thought. I'd loved every moment I spent with him, but I'd been a fool to let a stranger so close. I would see him tomorrow and we would again exchange a few pleasantries about meeting in Venice – and that would be that.

Marcus opened his own door without haste and walked me to the apartment. He didn't explain his actions or suggest what my homework might be. He simply bent and kissed me slowly and, despite myself, I reached up and placed my hand on his cheek and spread my fingers. He pulled back slightly, looked at me, and then kissed me again quickly before returning to the car.

I went inside and sat at the table. I couldn't pinpoint exactly what it was about Marcus that so attracted me. The practical side of me ticked off a list on my fingers: good-looking, intelligent, similar interests, great conversation. But another – fledgling but intuitive – side of me knew it was more than that. I hated to admit it to myself, but behind his urbane facade Marcus, too, was an enigma, and I liked this about him. He was as much of an enigma as the painting we had seen that day in Carmignano, as much of an enigma as my mother's journal. When he touched me there was more than just a moment of desire or passion, there was a whole world, and I wanted to be part of it. His traits should make him indecisive or even anxious. But somehow, he sat comfortably in their midst, enjoying life without explanations, always looking for the larger story behind the little stories, and he was daring me to approach my mother in the same way.

I sat for a long time in the silent room. It was still and the lighting was dim. My thoughts slowly settled and eventually I picked up the journal and took it with me to the bedroom. I sat on my bed, took a deep breath, and thought back to my experiment in Carmignano. I'd tried to understand what Mary and Elizabeth felt but gone no further. I hadn't wanted to bring their feelings outside the frame; I was too scared to ask myself how the painting made me feel. I closed my eyes, steadied my breathing, and thought back to Marcus's words about trusting myself. Then I saw my father throw the journal into the bin and my resolve hardened. I opened the journal to the pages of the three postcards. I let my gaze linger on each postcard in turn. *Primavera* was all colour and joy. Even though, I thought wryly, it contained my mother's double. There was nothing threatening in *Primavera*. I had yet to see the real Bellini *Sacred Conversation*, but it looked serene. Mary and Jesus stared downwards in different directions, thoughtful expressions on their faces. The four saints were completely self-absorbed, engaged in their own thoughts. Only the little angel playing the lira da braccio, which I knew was a violin-like instrument, stared straight out at the viewer. This, too, seemed a safe painting. Then I looked at Adam and Eve and knew I had to let my mother speak to me. It felt as if someone had removed my clothing. All my life I had set about creating dogged certainties, building walls to hide behind. When I let the bricks tumble, I saw Eve's nakedness. I saw her anguish. I saw her closed eyes, too seared by trauma to look on the world. Pain zigzagged through me like a bolt of lightning, quickly followed by cold fear. Had my mother felt like Eve? And if she had, what on earth had happened to her? I walked to the window and stood with the journal in my hand angled into the light from the streetlamp. Just as my father had that night many years ago. I'd been told my mother died painlessly and quickly, so her anguish must be related to sometime earlier than her death. But Allegra and Lawrence had led a secluded existence. Surely Lawrence would have known if his wife experienced trauma. Why had he never spoken of it? I put the journal down and leaned against the bedhead. I hadn't found an answer, but I'd opened a world of possibilities. I knew I was acting on instinct and this was new to me. But for the first time, my mother felt like real flesh and blood, and a fledgling hope lightened the perpetual weight in my stomach.

The next morning, I walked the centre of the city to etch it on my memory. Even after three weeks its compact nature still surprised me. I was glad not to see Marcus until I had walked my thoughts into order, and I needed breathing space for when Monica came to say goodbye that evening.

I circumnavigated the main sites and ended outside the octagonal baptistery, where I unwittingly found myself recalling what I knew of it. Eight sides, one for each of the seven days of creation and the last for eternity. Inside the baptistery, mosaic tesserae winked out a code of salvation and damnation in a swirl of angels and devils. The crowds had built but I joined the queue anyway. It was an eclectic mix of well-heeled art lovers wearing their superior knowledge like a badge and excited tourists in serviceable shoes and jeans, too awed at where they were to feel self-conscious.

I felt something brush against me. I had been warned often enough about gypsies, and I started and pressed my arm hard against my shoulder bag. But it was only a little boy swooping what looked like a paper plane through the air. He was waiting with two men behind me at the end of the queue. I followed as he dipped his craft through wide arcs, all the while holding my gaze with solemn black eyes as if daring me to look away. I played his game and when he stilled his tatty missile, I clapped noiselessly with the tips of my fingers. Only then did he smile. I smiled back realising that the walk had settled me. I had also made a satisfying internal memory of Florence. I let myself slip into being a tourist and glanced back at the boy wanting to share one last secret smile, but he had dropped his plane and his face had clouded. He was staring to my left and biting his little fingernail. I turned to see what he was looking at. An old gypsy woman had set her basket of flowers against the baptistery wall, trapping those who waited in the entry queue.

'Buy a flower from an old lady,' she said. She caught my gaze and raised her voice, thrusting a fist full of roses into the air. Her dark eyes danced, daring me to buy, daring me to pity.

'Roses,' she whined. 'For love and desire' – she waved the bunch from side to side – 'for silence and secrecy.'

A stocky woman, dressed in jeans and a tight T-shirt, dropped out of the queue and sauntered over to the gypsy. 'I'll have some for the hotel bedroom,' she said. Her southern twang hung briefly in the air like the discordant notes of an off-key instrument. 'No need to give me change, honey.'

The gypsy's eyes followed the woman as she rejoined the queue with the roses pressed to her nose.

Then the old woman bent over her basket and picked up some irises. I saw her hesitate as she prepared her spiel and wondered what she would say about my namesake.

'Irises for the soul,' she sang. She looked at me and the world contracted until just the two of us stood in the packed square of Santa Maria del Fiore. 'And the symbol of this city.' She was in full flight and I felt pinned. I looked sheepishly at the men behind who nodded their understanding. They would mind my place until I returned with my unwanted flowers.

As she gave me my change, I smiled and for some inexplicable reason said, 'Actually, my name's Iris.'

She moved close and her breath was honeyed and sweet, at odds with her grainy skin and stained check dress. She drew a curve like an 's' on my cheek and I stood, mesmerised. 'Iris,' she said. Her fingernail dug into my flesh. 'So you were named after the goddess.'

I shook my head. 'My mother named me after this city.'

'After the goddess,' she repeated. 'The goddess who leads the souls of dead women to the Elysian Fields.'

I felt a slight chill, no more than an autumn breeze on a sunny day. When it passed it left its foretaste of change, a mere hint of winter.

As I walked away, I glanced back and saw that the gypsy hadn't moved. She was watching me intently, her index finger still raised from when she had traced the line on my cheek.

After that I didn't go into the baptistery. Instead I went back to my apartment and arranged the purple irises in a bulbous ceramic jug ringed by blue and yellow birds.

Marcus arrived just after five o'clock. He tapped on the door and came in without waiting. He sniffed. 'Something smells good.'

'Just pasta all'arrabbiata.' I said. 'Monica is marginally vegetarian, so I've erred on the side of caution. Anyway, I'm fond of tomato and chilli.'

'I think it's a specialty of Lazio,' Marcus added, as he let the armful of packages he was carrying spill onto the table.

There was no hint of the previous day's strain. 'This place is really well equipped for a holiday apartment,' I continued. 'There's a garlic crusher and even the plates match.' I gestured at the table, which I thought looked pleasingly rustic. Its oak surface was scored by use, suited to the weighty ceramic bowls with their uneven patternings.

Marcus indicated his parcels one by one. 'Vino, biscotti, *cioccolato*,' he said. 'There's even some pecorino, which will go well sprinkled over your sauce. Is there anything else I can get – or do?'

I shook my head.

'Then pass me a corkscrew and I'll pour us a drink.' He pushed a glass across the table and, when I turned to pick it up, he ducked his head to catch my gaze and said, 'Homework?'

I blushed, unsure of how much to say. 'It's all about Eve? Isn't it?' I finally said. But, still, for some reason known only to a secret part of myself, I again held back from mentioning Prudencia.

'Perhaps,' he said.

'And perhaps things will be clearer in Venice,' I said.

Marcus considered me for a moment. 'Perhaps,' he repeated. 'But throughout history Venice has always been a place of secrets and watery reflections. You never know what you might find.'

I wanted to quiz him further but there was a sudden knock on the door, and I hurried to open it.

Monica had arrived earlier than expected, and she'd obviously been shopping as she carried two large department store bags in one hand and some long-stemmed lilies in the other. She kissed my cheeks and brushed past me into the room. 'The wind is frightful this evening,' she exclaimed. 'I feel tousled inside and out!'

I smiled and followed my aunt into the sitting room. Monica placed her bags on the kitchen bench, along with the lilies. Then she glanced around. 'This is very nice. Just what you need. Are you planning to return here after Venice?'

'You know,' I said. 'I haven't thought that far ahead. I suppose I ...'

Monica frowned. 'I'd book it if I were you. The tourist season's not far away and it'll be frantic around here all too soon. But now, if you don't mind, I'll go and tidy up.'

I pointed in the direction of the bathroom and Monica disappeared upstairs. Marcus and I exchanged glances. My aunt was a force of nature, full of life and energy. She returned a few minutes later with her hair neatly combed behind a wide black velvet band and with her carmine lipstick refreshed. I turned back to stir the sauce on the stove and toss a salad, while she and Marcus sat at the table sipping wine.

After dinner, I prepared coffee and a cheese platter, and as I arranged wafer-thin crisps along a narrow serving dish, I listened to Monica and Marcus. I knew my aunt was burrowing for insight into what had jetted Marcus to his current pre-eminence and glanced over to them. Monica's face was alight with interest as she queried his different ways of observing a painting or artwork. Marcus was playing seesaw with a fork, rocking it slowly backwards and forwards from tip to tines and said, 'I think there are three ways of looking at art. There is the point of view at the time in which it was painted.'

'You mean its symbolism to the contemporary viewer,' Monica interrupted.

He nodded. 'Sort of ... Then there is the historical perspective. You know. The big picture with its eras and characteristics. High Renaissance and bodily perfection. Mannerism and distorted figures. You know what I mean.'

'And the third?' Monica sounded intrigued, but I knew we were back in the Brancacci Chapel and whatever Marcus came out with next was bound to parallel his peculiar comment on Eve's wail.

'The third. Well. That's what I'm interested in, you see.' He paused. I could sense him gathering the loose threads of his thoughts. 'I see a painting as a dot point on a line that reaches back into history and forward into eternity.'

'What's the difference between that and historical perspective?'

'Depth and vision,' he announced. 'Feeling and emotion.'

Marcus didn't wait for Monica to quiz him further but rose to help me serve the coffee. I watched while he poured as if there was no more important task in the world and wondered why he thought he had a take on the world of art that had so far eluded thinkers and critics? There was nothing of the egoist in him; he was too open to others for that. Nor was he a fantasist. He didn't embellish his achievements in order to make himself seem important. Marcus was simply grounded, lucky enough to be comfortable in his own skin.

Back at the table, the conversation turned to debate over the best open-air market in Florence and how to get high quality gold jewellery at a good price. I contributed but my mind kept drifting. Monica and Marcus must have noticed, but they said nothing and talked on. Both knew I was on a quest and each had had their say. Now they were leaving me to find my own direction. I might have felt patronised, but I still had my own secret, and this made me feel smug. Within the maze of Venetian *calli*, I was certain I'd find my chest with its *Allegory of Prudence*. It didn't occur to me that I had no idea what I would do after that.

Venice

Italy

1991

12

At the precise moment I boarded the *motonave* for the short trip between the mainland terminal at Fusina and the Venetian quayside of Zattere, an icy gust blew in from the sea. Sleet stung my face and daggers of silver light fractured the still lagoon in front of me. The low mist stirred like a large, heavy beast on the rise. I hurriedly stowed my luggage in the area provided, sat in the nearest window seat where I could keep watch on it, and wiped the entire fogged pane with my gloved hand. I tried to push away the feeling that this return to wintry weather was unlucky.

I peered out the window. There was so much water. It sloshed repeatedly against the sides of the *motonave* and then slunk back into the lagoon. Clusters of banded tree trunks served for marker buoys, and small deserted islands replete with crumbling ruins rose from nowhere and then disappeared in our wake. The very air felt liquid, the water as enveloping as the womb. I shivered involuntarily. The *motonave* occasionally thrust sideways or backwards, throwing us passengers around like dolls. It was an uncomfortable ride. I had risen early but, even though I was now anchored in my seat in a humid cabin, I wasn't sleepy. The whole experience was otherworldly. I'd heard people speak of Venetians as being different to those who lived on the land, but this had always seemed more flight of fancy than fact. Now I began to understand.

Being surrounded by water did make you feel as though you were cocooned in an alternate world. I was excited, intrigued. I felt the romance of a city built on water even through the enveloping mist.

For most of the journey, I stared out of my window in a trance. Monica had warned me about Venice's nearby industrial wasteland of Mestre, but even so I was taken aback when billowing smokestacks and the jagged outlines of factories loomed to my left. And when, quite suddenly, a disembodied stone tower pierced the mist and reached skyward, I caught my breath. This city's twice removed, I thought. Built first on water and then on air. I stared as the tower faded and the lagoon narrowed into the wide Giudecca Canal, its banks a cluttered mass of tumbling stone buildings and orange and yellow cranes. They seemed out of time and place, an untidy edge to a fantastical world. I averted my gaze and peered behind me hoping to glimpse again the ethereal tower. But it remained hidden. Low dwellings, shops, and restaurants flanked the canal, and as we neared its intersection with the Canal Grande, I gasped as the colonnaded churches of the Gesuati and Il Redentore slid into view.

I'd always associated Venice with wintry weather – with fog and floods and the swelling of tides. In my imagination the city wore red velvet and rich brocade, pulled tight against the sea. Its watery foundations forewarned of masquerade. Perhaps after all, I thought wryly, not everything need be seen through Monica's Tuscan alfresco haze.

When we docked at Zattere, I sheltered for a while in the pontoon, away from the strengthening wind and rain.

I knew my accommodation was nearby but, on impulse, I waited and boarded the next vaporetto to San Marco. My suitcase wasn't too heavy and the urge to see the heart of Venice was strong. It was a short ride, but nothing had prepared me for what I saw on arrival. To my right, the pink, fairytale Ducal Palace sat lightly, the onion domes of Saint Mark's great Basilica rising high behind it. Nearby stood the two twelfth-century pillars on which dedications to Saint Mark and Saint Theodore perched high like stylite monks. In the distance was a tall campanile. Their sudden mirage-like appearance after what felt like hours on rough water was disorienting, the usual transition of water into sand into vegetation usurped by a collision of sea and solid architectural matter, the eye tricked by this confounding of the natural order. I walked in the direction of the basilica. There was bustle around me, but it wasn't crowded. There was so much to look at I kept stopping and starting until suddenly I reached the Piazza San Marco and gasped. It was huge. I'd read that Napoleon called Piazza San Marco the world's most beautiful drawing room, but now I could see why. It stretched into the distance, framed by an arcade in which I glimpsed shops and restaurants. People were moving swiftly because of the rain, not stopping to linger or talk. Even the pigeons flitted haphazardly, flapping noisily. For a time I stared dumbstruck, until the cold forced my attention back to the business of finding my accommodation, Pensione Carlotta. I pulled out my map of Venice and the directions I'd been given over the phone. My pensione was some distance away and on the opposite side of the Canal Grande. The Accademia Gallery was close to it and high on my list of places to visit. But the gallery would have to wait. At that moment my main concern was to satisfy the basic need to escape the weather and get warm and dry. I headed back to the San Marco vaporetti stop, waited for the next vaporetto to Zattere, and then travelled across the choppy lagoon. My suitcase bumping noisily over the old stones, I threaded my way through winding *calli* to Pensione Carlotta.

I again woke early, excited by the thought of what the day might hold, but then drifted back into an uneasy, dream-filled doze. By the time I entered the dining room, breakfast had been cleared away. A waitress was laying tables for lunch, and she looked up as I stalled in the doorway. She must have felt sorry for me because she walked over and in halting English directed me to a nearby cafe. I took her advice and pored over my map while I drank coffee and ate a toasted ham and cheese sandwich and pondered what to do first. Monica had given me the address of her favourite bookshop, which she said had an impressive Venetian art history section. She was certain the knowledgeable proprietor would be the one to know about my *cassa*. I'd circled the shop in green pen, so this at least was a place to start, but finding it proved to be an entire morning's work. Like most people, I was hard-wired to a grid system of streets with clearly discernible points of reference, which Venice's curves took no notice of whatsoever. For me, Venice seemed a feminine city; a city to be approached intuitively. Venice – perhaps because of her famous watery foundations – appeared to court mysteries. I found that *calli* led to places far removed from where I'd thought I was headed, and more than once I found myself back where

I'd started. It was no surprise that practical people found themselves lost in this city. Our modern life – with its grids and planes and telephones and computers – wasn't equipped for a terrain of mists and moving waters. Maybe over centuries we'd lost this ability as we imperceptibly altered our brain's pathways towards finding the answers rather than the questions. With a beautiful and easy grace, Venice defied all attempts to map her and went on her own labyrinthine way and, like countless others before me, I got lost but fell under her spell.

I found the bookshop just as they were closing for *riposo* and, feeling both frustrated and pleased, I meandered around the surrounding district – being careful not to lose my bearings – until the businesses reopened for the evening. I could have headed for a tourist information centre, but a bookshop specialising in art history seemed a more likely place to find a reference to my obscure *cassa*.

The shop faced a narrow canal, and directly in front of the entrance was a shallow-stepped bridge with thick stone balustrades on either side. The bookshop was sandwiched between a business selling papier-mâché masks and a brilliantly lit shop full of colourful Murano glassware. I'd noticed that most of the shops were small and appeared to carry limited stock. But their window displays were elegant and intimate, subtly seductive. My bookshop was small, and volumes were stacked in alphabetical order on shelves that ran from floor to ceiling. In a corner to the left of the front window was a cluster of small tables of varying heights and sizes, on which ornate cast-iron stands displayed large format art books open at reproductions of the city's most famous works. I paused and stared at a book open at a double-page spread of Tintoretto's *Crucifixion*, mesmerised by his lightning brushstrokes. Next to it a smaller book showcased Carpaccio's medieval fantasies, Saint George spearing a fierce dragon with the remains of the beast's victims scattered around him. As I lingered, I felt as if I'd come home, and an unaccustomed peace washed over me. Is this what it's like to live amongst the world's greatest artworks, I thought? Being surrounded by the sublime – even in books – seemed to settle me, define my place in the grand scheme. I took the journal from my bag, opened it and smiled politely while I pointed to the postcard of the chest with its *Allegory of Prudence*. The sales assistant held out her hand and took the journal. She peered closely at the chest and tapped at it with her finger. 'You want to see the Bellini?' She spoke with a strong American twang, curiously at odds with her dark hair, aquiline nose, and classic Italian dress. 'This allegory is in the Accademia Gallery. I will give you directions. Wait while I get a map.' She sighed audibly, most likely assessing me as another tourist who did not have a clue about her city's heritage, and bent to open a drawer near her right hand.

'No,' I said loudly. The saleswoman looked up, surprised. 'I want to see this chest – *cassa*,' I said. 'Do you know where I can find it?'

'You want to see this *cassa*?' She was clearly confused. 'But the painting is not a Bellini ...'

'Yes, I know that, but can you tell me where the chest is?'

I clenched my teeth and waited. I'd gambled on the possibility of the chest's actual existence but knew the dice could fall either way. The assistant would either tell me she knew of no such item, which would send me out onto the streets to widen my search, or else her knowledge might extend to artefacts beyond the city's main drawcards.

'This *cassa* is of no great importance' – she shrugged her shoulders – 'but it is in the convent of Santa Celestina, on the Fondamente Nuove. The convent has recently been opened to paying guests, but you can request to visit the museum inside. It's an ugly place, but the cloister is superb.' Her voice lifted at this latter fact as if, after all, there might be some reason for my visit. But as she handed me back the journal and bent to the drawer below the counter, her expression again became blank and her manner off-hand. She visibly gave up on me. I knew my request was unusual. I was within minutes of an original work by a great master, but I wanted to see an obscure chest with its painted copy.

'I will give you the address and phone number,' she said as she scribbled the details on a piece of freckled, handmade paper and pushed it across the counter.

I thanked her and, out of politeness, bought two postcards and a bookmark and hurried out on to the street.

I phoned Santa Celestina from a nearby public phone. When another woman answered – and also spoke English – I took this as a sign and booked myself a room for the remainder of my time in Venice. I also phoned Monica's house and Marcus's hotel in Rome. Both were out so I left messages telling them the address of my new lodgings. Then I returned to the *pensione*, made my clumsy apologies, and packed my belongings.

It took me over an hour to walk to the Fondamente Nuove, a long stretch of concrete quayside that flanked the far side of the lagoon and looked towards the islands of Murano, Burano, and Torcello. The cemetery island of San Michele in Isola with its green-black cypresses and surrounding stone walls filled the near distance. I stopped twice to fortify myself with espresso, which I drank standing up in smoky cafes with marble counters and enticing displays of *pasticcini* and biscotti. It was now late afternoon. I was tired and my feet were sore from pounding the city's cobblestones. My legs ached. According to the shop assistant's directions and my impossible map, Santa Celestina was nearby. I dragged my case behind me and bumped it one step at a time over a small bridge, wondering how the elderly and mothers with prams managed.

Santa Celestina was marked on my map with a tiny Latin cross and the single word *convento*. I paused at the foot of the bridge and scanned the buildings to my left, pausing where I thought the convent might be. This location was occupied by a long, low dwelling with a pale ochre façade and no external ornamental features, other than a single doorway with wide, white surrounds. I was a little disappointed, even though I'd learned that the outside of Italian buildings often belied the inside. The marriage chest's convent home appeared quite humble.

The building stretched for about one hundred metres along the quayside. I walked up, pushed at the door, and it opened easily. There was no signage to suggest the public were welcome and, disconcerted, I stood on the doorstep wondering whether to knock or call out. I needn't have worried as within seconds a woman's voice called out, '*Avanti, prego! E chiuda la porta, per favore.*'

Flustered at not being able to understand what was said, I decided to take the words as a signal to enter and followed the voice into a partitioned-off area on the left of a long central corridor. A woman looked up from her newspaper as I entered. She said nothing, just took off her glasses and waited.

'Is it all right if I speak English?' I wanted to appear polite but was uncomfortably aware that I only sounded patronising.

'Of course,' she said, as if to do anything else would be an insult to her intelligence.

'I'm Iris Maddison,' I continued. 'I've a room booked for two weeks from today.'

The woman put her glasses back on and lifted what I presumed was the reservations book from a nearby shelf.

'Name,' she snapped.

'Iris Maddison,' I repeated.

She turned the pages back and forth, running her finger down the columns, until I began to fear there had been a mistake in my booking. Finally she stood up, plucked a key from a rack, and hoisted a large leather carryall onto her shoulder.

'Follow me,' she said.

I followed her out into the corridor. We passed more partitioned areas until we finally reached an elongated room that smelled of new paint. A television screen flickered in a far corner.

'Wait, please,' the woman said.

I examined the room while she spoke to a man lounging in one of the armchairs. The arrangement was unusual as it was divided by a wall, the lower third of which was solid brick and the remainder glass. The larger section in which I stood occupied about three-quarters of the space. There was something familiar about the shape that I couldn't grasp at first, but it quickly dawned on me that this room must once have been the nuns' parlour and that windows had replaced the grilles behind which the nuns had sat in the narrower section while they talked and gossiped with their visitors. There was an elaborate cornice around the entire room, which was laced with foliage and fruit into which ovals were set at regular intervals. These *mandorla* – I remembered Marcus had called them by that name during one of our many excursions in Florence – were alternately stuccoed in high relief with stiff, swaddled babies and Madonnas with bowed heads.

The woman returned and led me to a swing half-door in a far corner through which we entered the narrow side of the room. Her silence began to annoy me. To my mind, she lacked front of house skills, and her acquired continental reserve came across as surly. Surely a few pleasantries wouldn't have hurt. At the end of this corridor-like section, she opened another door and I gasped. She stopped and I glanced over to her. Her mouth was twisted in a half-smile, and she exuded resignation as she waited for me – in the same way she had probably waited for countless others – to recover from what lay in front of me.

We were standing in an open cloister. Pairs of twisted marble capitals alternated with Corinthian columns inlaid with geometric mosaics of gold crosses and stars. Benign medieval gargoyles decorated the tops of the columns. The watery afternoon sun glanced off the mosaic tesserae in a series of flashes that hurt my eyes as I looked around.

It was a surreal place, a mix of the Arab love of patterning and Venetian architectural form. A water well sculpted with swags of lilies marked a square central garden, which was divided into quarters. I noticed that the thick roots of old, chopped-down trees protruded from parts of the lawn.

When she deemed sufficient time had passed, my guide indicated our direction with a flourish and said, 'Across here, please.' She led me diagonally across the cloister and then down another corridor, off which ran sequentially numbered rooms.

'*Trenta*,' she announced. She unlocked the door, ushered me inside, and fumbled in her bag for a plan of the building, which she unfolded on the tabletop. 'Your room is number thirty' – she stabbed her finger at the leaflet – 'and breakfast is served in the refectory.' She poked at a different spot on the page. Then she pulled out another pamphlet. 'This tells you about the convent museum. If you wish to visit, it is on the other side of the cloister. The directions are inside.' She glanced at her watch and frowned. 'The bathroom is down the hall, and you may pay for your accommodation in the morning.'

With those few words, she was gone.

My room was a surprise. I was expecting it to be pokey, perhaps an original cell redecorated for the modern tourist with cream paint and nondescript furniture. Instead, it was huge, with heavy mahogany woodwork, mushroom-pink walls, and a white ceiling in the centre of which was a gilt-edged ceiling rose. The furniture was beautifully Baroque, all curlicues and flourishes. There was a burgundy, padded-satin quilt on the bed. The only concessions to modernity were the suitably ornate bedside lamp, the basin in one corner, and the small television suspended from its bracket on the wall opposite the bed. I set down my luggage, laid on the bed, and stared at the rose above my head until I fell asleep. When I woke it was dark. I smiled inwardly. Travelling was tiring. I seemed to spend so much energy getting from place to place that sleeping on arrival was becoming the norm.

Around seven o'clock I ventured out for pizza and coffee from a nearby trattoria. Although cold and dark, I ate at a little table overlooking the lagoon. There was an iciness in the air that crept beneath the thick wool of my coat and settled on my skin. The sensation I'd felt on my arrival in San Marco returned. Venice was a city where water and stone collided. A place of fluid and solid; both naturally cold and strong willed. The wind had died down, and I was rugged up in a coat, scarf, and hat. I watched scurrying crowds board and disembark from the frequent vaporetti, which banged against their rusted pontoons and heaved away with an escalating throttle. In between, the quayside was quiet. I realised that the absence of cars allowed forgotten sounds to rise to the surface: the click of footsteps, the coughs of passers-by, the whirring of my own thoughts. I had the odd sensation of having shifted down a gear. My mind ranged over the events of the previous weeks and I wondered if Marcus would come as he had promised, but then my thoughts turned to the marriage chest with its *Allegory of Prudence*. I felt ambiguity about reaching an end, the journey being always more alluring. I sighed and got to my feet, deciding to check the museum's opening hours on my way back to my room.

Just before midday the next day, I waited at the door of the museum and was surprised when the woman from reception came towards me. This time she was wearing a nametag printed with Dottoressa Clementina Canosa, a suitable title and an austere enough name. She nodded to me and opened the heavy panelled door. I followed her inside and waited patiently while she unlocked the tin box that served as a till and then took my entrance fee. I made to walk into the museum proper, but she coughed discreetly and said, '*Mi scusi.*' I turned back, bewildered, feeling like a chastised child, but the Dottoressa wasn't looking at me. She was staring at some point in the middle distance, while she tapped at a large open book on the desk beside here. 'Sign here, please.' I signed the guest book as directed. She nodded in acknowledgement, and I walked inside.

It was a small museum, a warren of linked rooms that drew the visitor inwards, but through which it would be necessary to pass again on the return journey. Each room segued into the next through doors which abutted the rooms' outer walls. By this I guessed that the museum ran down one side of the building. The first room was an eclectic mix of paintings and carefully grouped items of clerical garb. Its obvious drawcard was the fine display of old manuscripts propped up in glass cases. In the far corner a woman was bent over one of these cases. She straightened when I drew closer, nodded to Clementina, and smiled at me. She wore a sedate knee-length grey dress, a navy cardigan, and flat navy court shoes. Her only ornament was a gold cross, which was pinned to her collar. I realised that years of studying Renaissance history and art had skewed my reality. I still expected Venetian nuns to be garbed head-to-toe in black, their faces pinched by guimpe and wimple. Instead, greeting me was this upright sister of indeterminate age – I guessed perhaps sixty but no more than sixty-five – with kind, bright eyes that immediately lessened my loneliness. I relaxed for the first time since my moment of solace outside the Florentine Baptistery and wandered around the room, examining its diverse contents. But this brief interlude didn't last. The desire to find the marriage chest took hold and I moved quickly into the second room, glanced around briefly, and then hurried onto the next.

I found the *cassa* in the seventh room, centred against the far wall. I stood silently in the doorway, staring at the ornate marriage chest with its bold central paintings. A shiver ran through me. It felt like a portent. I didn't move until the physical sensation passed, but the sense of foreboding remained. I walked slowly across the room and stood in front of the *cassa*. This time there was no replica of a bedroom to tease my imagination. There was only what I guessed from my limited language was a brief explanation of the Cardinal Virtue of Prudence on the wall above. I stared at the plaque, not knowing what to do. Was this the end of my journey? I tried to place Allegra in the space in which I was standing, and I found myself foolishly reaching out my hand as if some filament of her might lie in this place where perhaps she had once stood. But there was nothing and I dropped my arm and looked down at the painting of Prudence on the chest.

There she was – Prudence, naked on her drum and holding a mirror in her hand. I wondered who Bellini had used as his model for the original. I knew that female models were scarce in the Renaissance and that, when closely examined, female nudes often bore traces of the artist's memory or desire. Perhaps this might explain the odd combination of girl and woman. The three cherubs below her were a delight, oddly louche in their half-nakedness, but in an appealing, babyish way. It struck me that they, too, combined opposing traits. In their case, innocence and knowledge.

Then I heard footsteps on the tiled floor. They stopped just behind me, and I turned to see the nun looking at me with her head to one side.

'*Memoria, docilitas, solertia, providentia,*' she said. At my bemused expression she laughed and held out her hand and spoke in English with only the barest musical accent. 'I'm Ursula. I live here, in the convent wing.'

I gasped at the irony of her name being Ursula. Obviously trying to guess the reason for my response, she said hurriedly, 'I'm sorry. Please excuse my Latin outburst. I'm particularly fond of this *cassa* and it is rare indeed that anyone gives it more than a passing glance.'

'No, please,' I said. 'It's my fault. It's the name Ursula. My aunt, you see ...'

Sister Ursula smiled, encouraging me to continue.

'... Well, she did her doctorate on Saint Ursula. That saint's followed me all my life, in stories, paintings, and tapestries. And now it seems' – I wound to a close – 'in person.'

We both laughed.

'Anyway, I'm Iris Maddison,' I said.

'I'm pleased to meet you,' Ursula said. 'And what's your aunt's name?'

'Monica Caroldo.'

'Monica Caroldo.' She repeated the name slowly, pursed her lips, and looked puzzled, and then light dawned and she said, 'The Monica Caroldo?' I detected respect in her voice and nodded.

'Of course, I've read her work,' Ursula exclaimed. 'I remember when it was published. A large part of it centres on an interpretation of Carpaccio's cycle of Saint Ursula in the Accademia here in Venice.'

I nodded again and turned back to Prudence. I didn't want to talk about Monica. 'What's the meaning of your Latin words?'

Sister Ursula took a step closer to the chest. 'You know about the Cardinal Virtues?'

'I know that there are four.' I ticked them off on my fingers. 'Prudence, Temperance, Justice, and Fortitude.'

'Yes,' said Ursula. 'Those are the four theological virtues. There are now others of a more secular nature, if a virtue can ever be called secular' – she raised her arms, the palms of her hands upturned – 'but in the time of this *cassa*, the four theological virtues reigned supreme. Each virtue has many parts, and in the case of Prudence the most important of these are ...' She indicated the plaque.

'... Your Latin words,' I guessed.

'Exactly,' Ursula said. She moved closer again to the chest and ran her hand along its edge. I wanted to do the same. Instead, I waited silently for her to continue. 'A prudent person learns the lessons of the past, which is the meaning of *memoria*. She takes advice – *docilitas*, is able to make skilled assessments – *solertia*, and uses foresight with intelligence – *providentia*.' Ursula squatted on the floor beside the chest and pointed to the painting. 'Of course, this is a copy of Bellini's *Allegory of Prudence*, but a good one nevertheless. The original's in the Accademia.'

'Yes, I know,' I said.

'You know of the painting?' Ursula sounded surprised. 'Not many people bother with Bellini's little panel paintings.'

'I should explain,' I said. 'I studied art history in Melbourne and' – here I resorted to an untruth – 'have always liked Bellini.' Having told one lie, it was suddenly easy to pour out others, and I heard myself say, 'I once went to an exhibition in Melbourne that featured a beautiful marriage chest, and this piqued my interest in *cassoni* in general.' I didn't mention my mother's postcards.

'The *cassa* must have had quite an impact.'

I smiled, more to myself than to Ursula, and said lamely, 'Yes, it did.'

If she thought my answer inadequate, Ursula didn't show it. Instead, she said, 'Well, I for one think your instincts were sound. This *cassa* has a little history all of its own.' She bent down and lifted the lid with her left hand, at the same time placing her right forefinger on her lips in a gesture of conspiracy. She leaned the lid carefully against the wall. Then she kneeled and pulled me down beside her.

'Look,' she said. 'In the back, right corner.'

I leaned forward and saw the word Prudencia embroidered in gold script on the inside satin lining, and in that moment – and in those minute, even stitches – Prudencia came to life. My mother's scribbles had always pointed to the possibility of her existence, and at times I had treated her as a real person, but I knew that lack of proof left this as just a tantalising conjecture. Now Ursula's words and actions had given Prudencia flesh and blood and to find answers for Allegra's interest in her suddenly seemed more important than ever, especially the reason for '*povera* Prudencia'? Maybe I wasn't nearing the end of my quest after all. I thought back to the day in the Curdies River Cemetery and Monica's metaphor of a grave being the doorway to other worlds. I smelled the early violets that grew around the grave, and I realised that my mother's death was taking me somewhere. I heard Marcus telling me to trust my feelings, but even so my own voice sounded far away as I asked, 'This Prudencia was a real person?'

'Oh yes,' Ursula said. 'But our Prudencia – she was a sister in this convent – did not live up to her name. She was hardly what one could call prudent. We know from our archives that this chest belonged to her. It is listed as having come with Prudencia when she entered the convent in 1567. It was probably to be her marriage chest and would have been given to her as a child. She was from a poor noble family and was only seven years old when her mother brought her here.'

I gasped. I knew that girls were sent to convents at a young age to avoid dowry payments, but this seemed inhuman.

'Seems wrong, doesn't it?' Ursula said. 'But you have to remember that those were different times. Anyway, as I said, Prudencia was a spirited girl, in more ways than one. She fell in love with a young Jewish trader and had a child – a daughter. You can imagine the chaos that caused in the convent.' Ursula sighed. 'Many girls were trapped, you see. There was no such thing as choice. Religion and life were intertwined. You know, there were immense numbers of convents in Venice in the sixteenth century and that doesn't include outlying islands. I suppose to admit you didn't want to be a nun was like slapping God in the face. And who could live with that?'

We both studied the chest and then Ursula said, 'If you're interested, I can show you pages from Prudencia's diary. They're never sent on exhibition because we have too few such documents. Manuscripts, you see, are my special interest.'

The feelings I had wrestled with all my life when dealing with Allegra's journal returned with force and my cheeks burned. So, I was to be confronted with another set of cryptic words written no doubt to soothe the writer but sure to confound anyone who looked at them. I turned my head away so Ursula could not see what I guessed were scarlet patches and waited a few moments before saying in as casual a voice as I could muster, 'Sure, that'd be fascinating. I'm here for two weeks so I can come whenever it's convenient for you.'

'Come now!' she said. 'One set of pages is on display in Room One.' She turned towards the door and indicated for me to follow. She seemed pleased with our discussion. I guessed that not many people took an interest in an out-of-the-way convent in a less frequented part of Venice. Also, given the number of large-scale attractions in the city, I was certain that not many people bothered with an insignificant marriage chest – however pretty. Or, for that matter, a young sixteenth-century nun.

When we reached the first room, Ursula went straight to the far wall and bent over a case. She looked up to see if I was following and her face shone with pleasure. I'd seen this look before on my father when he contemplated a loved piece of work. She beckoned to me, and I went and stood beside her. In front of us was a small open book, no more than thirty centimetres by fifteen centimetres. It was filled with dense Latin script, but the writing was faded and smudged and would take patience to decipher.

'This page was written early in Prudencia's convent life, not long after she was given to the anchoress,' Ursula whispered. 'You can tell she was very young.' She traced a spiral down the glass with her finger. 'Poor little thing. It was the anchoress who taught her to write Otherwise, this wouldn't exist.'

'An anchoress brought honour to a convent, didn't she?' I said.

'Yes, she was literally interred in a room in a ceremony similar to a Mass for the Dead, and her prayers were' – Ursula searched for the right words – 'a divine channel, a sort of light at the heart of the convent. During the Counter-Reformation when the church was re-establishing itself after Luther, the abbess brought an anchoress here as evidence of our, what will I call it' – she gave an embarrassed laugh – 'of our more serious nature.'

'Can you tell me what it says?' I said. 'My Latin's a bit dismal.'

'Of course.'

Before Ursula could begin, there was a sudden click of heels and then a waft of perfume, and Clementina appeared behind us. She pointed to her watch and then indicated the few people circling the room. I could see that an official-looking man in a clerical collar was trying to catch her attention.

'I have a lunchtime appointment,' she said. 'Otherwise, I wouldn't interrupt you.'

'Yes,' Ursula exclaimed. 'The desk.' She turned to me. 'I'm sorry. I have to take Clementina's place while she's away. Could we continue our talk sometime? I'm always here. Just drop by whenever it suits you.'

I looked down at Prudencia's childlike handwriting. There were marked breaks in the words. I imagined a young girl, new to the art of script, lifting her pen in thought before beginning again. There were few loops and only the occasional tied letter. There were also few sentences, mostly lists of words just like, I realised, the list I had scrawled in my mother's journal when I was eleven years old and first felt its weight in my hands. I wondered if all children started with lists of words, in between which lie empty spaces that only time can fill.

The truth washed over me like a wave. Prudencia is filling in the empty spaces, I thought. My mother left me a skeleton, a clue, and I had to travel across the world and down four hundred years to find her. The old surge of anger returned without warning, and I felt the next breaths scrape the sides of my windpipe. I drew another deep breath, held it for a moment, and then let go. Even when I could breathe without pain, the thought would not go away. *If you love me, why did you leave me?* Then came an overwhelming resolve. *I'll make you tell me.*

In an instance of serendipity, there was an unexpected phone call to my room from Clementina that evening, who informed me that a man was waiting on the other end of the phone in her office and she would switch him through. I waited for the click and then heard Marcus's voice repeatedly saying, 'Hello'. My heart really did skip a beat, an unaccustomed response from me, and I said lightly, 'Hello to you, too. How's Rome?'

There was a pause, and I could picture Marcus weighing up how best to move the conversation.

'Just as always,' he said. 'Magnificent but ridiculously hectic, but I found out what I needed to know and spent some time in the Vatican Museum, which is always a bonus. Now, tell me what you think of Venezia.'

'I haven't seen much of it yet. But the little I have is breathtakingly beautiful. It's' – I paused, searching for words – 'so old, so full of atmosphere. But it's not busy where I'm staying.'

'You're on the Fondamente Nuove, aren't you?'

'Yes,' I said. 'I decided to move because ...' I remembered that Marcus knew nothing of this part of my quest and my voice faltered. The day's discoveries and my own seesawing emotions had tired me, and the sheer effort of a telephone conversation brought me close to tears. I'd always found phone calls a chore. I needed to see faces. It was impossible to discuss anything properly – especially important things – without seeing your partner's face. It always seemed to me that so much of what is said is based on the subtle changes we observe, consciously or unconsciously, in the person in front of us.

It was Marcus who broke the silence. 'Iris. Is something wrong?'

His concern made me swallow hard in order to keep my voice steady. There was silence on his end as he waited for me to gather my thoughts. Even though Prudencia was proving to be a beginning rather than an end, I was still reluctant to expose her to the world, and so my initial reaction was to pull back from mentioning my discoveries, even to him. But then something gave way. Perhaps it was the beginning of resignation, the knowledge that life takes us on journeys we neither ask for nor want, and I said, 'There's a part of my story that I didn't tell even you. I came here to follow up on it. You see, there's more than just *Primavera*, Adam and Eve and the Bellini *Madonna and Child* in my mother's journal. There's one other postcard.'

There was an intake of breath on the other end of the line and then, 'Why aren't I surprised? What is it?'

'It's not just the postcard,' I said. 'It's something that's written beside it. I've discovered that there was a real person with the same name as the woman on the postcard and ...'

'Iris, who is on the card?'

'Well, it's a marriage chest with a copy of Bellini's *Allegory of Prudence* on the front.'

'And what's written beside it?'

'My mother scrawled "*povera* Prudencia" across the opposite page.'

'"*Povera* Prudencia",' Marcus repeated. 'Poor Prudencia. Poor Prudence.'

'I've no idea what it means,' I said. 'I always wondered why my mother felt sorry for Prudence. After all, I thought it was just a painting. Now I've discovered that Prudencia was real. She was a nun in this convent in the sixteenth century. My mother didn't feel sorry for Prudencia in a painting, she felt sorry for Prudencia as a person.'

There was a long pause as each of us absorbed my words.

'It sounds ridiculous,' I said. 'But this discovery adds layers to my travels with my mother's postcards. The thoughts about Adam and Eve were interesting conjecture, but that was all. There might be truth in them, but I'd never really know what it was. Now I've discovered that "*povera* Prudencia" was my mother's reaction to the plight of a real human being, to something that happened in this person's life. If I can find out what it was, it might tell me my mother's feelings about what was happening to her. Maybe it has something to do with pregnancy.' I stopped. The room contracted around me. My thoughts slowed, circling around the fact that Allegra would have been pregnant with me. My throat tightened. 'Maybe it has something to do with how she felt when she was carrying me? I know there is something about Prudencia I need to discover.'

'Just like there was something about Eve?'

'Just like Eve. But, as I said, just a bit more tangible.'

'I'm flying from here to Venice early the day after tomorrow,' Marcus said. 'What say I take the vaporetto as far as the Rialto Bridge and then phone you to come and meet me?'

I thought for a moment, mentally scanning what little I knew of Venice's street plan – or lack of it. 'That sounds good,' I said. 'I'll meet you at the foot of the bridge, on the San Marco side.'

There was a pause on the other end of the phone, then, 'I've missed you, you know.'

I felt Marcus's soft wool coat and then his hands on my bare shoulders and his eyes – kind and deep – not afraid to look into mine, and for the first time since I was eleven years old, I felt what is was like to really miss someone. This tenderness for another was new and wonderful, but also fragile. A frisson of fear struck as I remembered that everyone I'd felt tenderness for had eventually left me. Even Lawrence – the person I thought I could rely on – was proving to be a closed book. Would Marcus eventually disappear as well?

13

I didn't return to the museum the next day but decided to take the vaporetto to see the lagoon islands. I'd loved the trip from Fusina to Venice and thought I might recapture a little of the magic by heading to the outlying islands of Murano, Burano, and Torcello. I also needed space to let my thoughts catch up with the events of recent weeks. In truth, I was tired. My time in Florence with Marcus had been wonderful but busy and, at times, emotional. I had seen unknown and splendid artworks and been confronted by unexpected personal revelations. It had also been delightful to see Monica, but her cryptic words had left me disturbed. Venice itself was a treasure trove, but it was also full of tourists. The rumble of wheeled suitcases underscored a multitude of accents from cultivated French to the American drawl. Time out on the water with nothing to do but observe seemed exactly what I needed.

It was a hazy morning, the sun obscured by cloud, and the lagoon lay grey and still. The vaporetto was surprisingly empty, and free of crowds it was easier to imagine Venice as she would once have been: a silent, stone city rising out of the lagoon, people scurrying along the twisting *calli* or rowing small boats on the water. As it jerked along, I thought how much nicer it would be to glide by gondola through the haze or mist that seemed such constants here. Instead, each time I took one of the ugly daily transport vehicles, I had to push my way through jostling crowds simply to board. After a few long trips standing upright for the entire journey, I learned to forget good manners, ignore withering glances, and charge, blinkered, in the direction of any spare seat.

When we stopped at Murano, I almost got off, lured by the glass-sellers plying their goods near the quayside, but instead I sat back down. We docked at the lace island of Burano where I again resisted the urge to explore and then headed towards Torcello. By this time there were only three of us left. The bustle of Venice was far behind us and there was an unaccustomed quiet. I felt my thoughts begin to settle and focussed on the square Torcello campanile as it loomed towards us, rising high in an otherwise flat horizon. I knew the name Torcello had several origin stories, the earliest that it was named after Torcellum, a defensive gate of the nearby Roman town of Altinum, now Altino. But I preferred the more romantic *torre e cielo*: tower and sky.

My thoughts turned to the previous evening's phone conversation. It had been a relief to tell Marcus what I had carried alone since I was eleven. I had, of course, confided in Louise, but even though I had her to thank for pushing me to go to Italy, she was now on the other side of the world. In a way, Marcus had picked up where she left off. Although I'd known him for just under a month, I trusted him because he had no stake in the outcome of my story other than pleasing me. It was ironic. Families were supposed to be the people you turned to when you needed security and answers, but neither Louise nor Marcus were blood relations. My family – my childhood – had been all about disappearances. There was the mother whose violet scent was like a vapour trail through my life. The father who slipped away when I tried to hold him long enough to feel my way to the truth. The aunt who lived in a world of saints and sinners and viewed life from her ivory tower. And, finally, the grandparents whose special occasion cards had stopped at my twenty-first birthday, as if by reaching what they thought of as the age of consent set them free of me. Now I realised that I had to trust someone if I was to continue with my search, and what better person than the one who in such a short time had helped me to see and feel things in a different way. I wondered if by clinging to Marcus in this way I was being self-serving. Then I smiled to myself. Marcus, I was sure, wouldn't mind be used in this way. Once again, I realised that I missed him, that I actually longed for his reassurance, his touch.

When the vaporetto docked on Torcello, I took the path across the island towards the thousand-year-old cathedral of Santa Maria Assunta. I knew the island was the original lagoon settlement, at one point home to thirty thousand people, but my guidebook told me there were now only a dozen or so residents. There was an aura of abandonment, a quiet so intense I felt as if I might hear whispers from the past. I crossed the Devil's Bridge and soon reached the cathedral complex. Just as I'd expected, Santa Maria Assunta was a revelation. In the apse the Madonna mosaic gleamed like a beacon in a sea of gold high above the altar. On the rear wall the Last Judgement warned departing worshippers of their fate should they sin. I circled the interior, revelling in its sacred silence before reluctantly going outside.

I sat to one side of what had been the baptistery in front of the Basilica and again reflected on the postcard paintings. I recalled a lecturer telling his hall of restless students that 'physical distance could facilitate visions'. Unfortunately, this overblown language often buried the gems in his statements. He was talking about art, of course, and how to be at a remove sharpened the gaze. At a distance the mind often tried to piece together an artistic puzzle, discovering things invisible when in front of the work itself. His long-winded point was if the student then went back to the work, all might come clear. I smiled to myself and mentally added Marcus's words about feelings. In this quiet place I understood that the time had come for me to piece together my puzzle. The empty spaces in my life were no longer bearable. I remembered reading that the art critic John Ruskin called Torcello the Mother of Venice therefore making it, I decided, a fitting place to sit and think about my mother. Slowly, I recalled each painting, musing on whether Allegra had chosen them for something other than their artistic value. Then I began to search for links.

Before I realised it, an hour had passed, and I had only a short time to cross the island to catch the vaporetto back to Venice. As we chugged away from the island, I settled back in my seat, watching first the choppy waters of the lagoon and then Venice herself as she grew larger on the horizon. The afternoon hadn't given me answers, but I felt steadier, ready to cope with what came next. I knew without doubt that there would be surprises.

Marcus arrived late the next afternoon. I had booked a room for him at Santa Celestina and noticed Clementina eye us curiously when she handed him the keys, a significant reaction from the dour Dottoressa. I waited while he unpacked a few belongings into the top drawer of his chest, and then we headed out to eat at my trattoria at the edge of the lagoon.

Marcus ordered wine, but I was already light-headed from what I was about to say so I opted for tea instead. When our drinks were on the table and the meal ordered, I pulled the journal out of my bag and laid it down in front of him.

'I've thought a lot about what you said on the way back from Carmignano,' I began.

Marcus looked up from the menu he was perusing, surprised at the quick turn of my conversation.

'You know, when you told me to stop being the art historian and start being a person.'

'I didn't put it quite like that,' he said.

I let his protest slip by. 'Well, I sat on Torcello yesterday and wondered how my mother felt about her postcard paintings.'

'Go on.' Marcus's voice was guarded, as if he was unsure whether I was serious or being patronising. This was the first time I'd seen him wary. He always seemed so in control of his thoughts and ideas. I realised that by taking on board what he suggested and applying it to my own situation, I was stepping into his territory.

'I'm not trying to be smart.' I stumbled over my words, not wanting Marcus to think me rude. 'But try to recall what you said about Eve's wail that day in the Brancacci Chapel.' I gave him a few moments to think.

'I said something about still being able to hear it, didn't I?'

'Yes. And, well, I remembered that one of my early reactions when looking at the fresco was of how my mother left Lawrence and me. How she sort of cast us out of our family paradise. But by the time you and I spoke, I was strictly in art historian mode.'

'That was the "representation of human psychic pain" phrase.' Marcus's voice was deadpan.

I didn't rise to the bait. 'When we returned from Monica's, I tried to see Eve as my mother might have seen her.'

Marcus leaned towards me over the table.

'No, not quite as Allegra saw her' – I corrected myself – 'but as she felt when she saw her, and I think she saw a weeping woman with her eyes covered, running from what looks like a desert landscape.' I'd spoken the last sentence on a running breath and continued on, my voice now constricted and husky. 'I think she saw herself.'

I sat back in my chair, winded. I don't know what I wanted Marcus to say, but I think the child in me wanted congratulations, and I was a little disappointed when he only said, 'Is there more?'

'Just one thing. I think – feel – that Prudencia can tell me what it is.'

I sat back and drummed my fingers on the edge of the table. I felt like an explorer who had been convinced the world was flat but suddenly found herself falling forward as it curved beneath her. The Brancacci Chapel fresco was not only the story of the first woman to leave paradise and feel the isolation but also a harbinger for coming centuries. It was the story of many women writ small, and it set my head reeling backwards in time to places I could only imagine and forward to women – and this fact hit me hard – like my mother.

'What about the *Madonna and Child with Saints?*' Marcus said.

'I can't even think of that Bellini yet.' I gave an exaggerated sigh. Maybe when I've learned more about Prudencia.'

We walked back to the convent and stood for a while near the door to my room. The hallway was dim. There was no central overhead lighting, and the corridor relied on the glow from a diamond-patterned, stained-glass window at one end. This window overlooked the convent chapel on the lower level, and the light that burned constantly in the sister's place of prayer threw blurred pink and green shadows from the window along the floor of the hallway where we stood. It was quiet. There were no other guests in our wing, unless you counted the almost life-size statue of Santa Celestina herself, which occupied a niche set into the wall between our two rooms. Marcus pulled me to him and when he bent to kiss me goodnight I wanted nothing more than to pull him inside. Instead, I sniffed and said, 'No lemon this time?'

He looked confused.

I buried my head in the lapels of his coat and sniffed again. I was shorter by a head and when I lifted my face, I was at eye level to his throat. I bent forward and rubbed my cheek against him and said, 'Nutmeg or cloves, I think.'

'Spot on,' he said. 'There was a wonderful herbalist not far from my hotel in Rome.'

We stayed in each other's arms for a long time, hardly moving.

'I missed you,' Marcus said.

There were those words again. 'How could you?' I said and tugged playfully at his collar, drawing his face towards mine. 'We've only known each other for four weeks. You hardly know me.'

'You think so,' he said. He tilted his head sideways in order to look into my eyes. For a moment time stopped, suspended by the magnetic force surrounding us, until I blushed and buried my face in the soft wool of his coat. Eventually, he straightened and held me at arm's length in order to once again hold my gaze. He smoothed back my hair with both hands and then let them slip to my shoulders. Longing like a cool stream ran from my throat to my stomach and I blushed. This longing was different to that I'd experienced with the other boyfriends in my life. That had been more desire than longing and was easily satisfied with physical intimacy, which may or may not have developed into sex. The longing I now felt burrowed into the needy part of me I'd kept closed and wanted to make a deeper connection. No wonder I was confused. It was physics again: resistance versus surrender, the unpalatable fact that real intimacy involved giving up of part of yourself.

'Tomorrow, we'll search for Prudencia, eh?' Marcus said. He kissed me and then walked down the corridor to his room, straight-backed, dark hair licking his coat collar, every inch the erudite, urbane Englishman.

The museum was empty when we entered early the following afternoon. I went to pay the Dottoressa, but she waived me away and turned to Marcus, her hand outstretched as she said, 'Ten lire, please.'

Marcus paid, signed the book as directed, and we went straight to the case that held Prudencia's pages. Ursula was already there, fiddling with the leather binding of a small book with gloved hands.

'Ursula,' I said. 'This is Marcus Warren. He's a friend of mine.'

Marcus held out his hand. Ursula looked at him quizzically as if there was something about him she recognised, but she only shook his hand and nodded to him in polite acknowledgement.

'So this is the diary.' Marcus leaned forward to study the script.

'You read Latin?' Ursula queried.

'I'm an art historian and, yes, Latin and I are old friends. Six years at grammar school and then Oxford saw to that.'

'Marcus makes art history documentaries,' I blurted out.

'Marcus Warren?' Ursula thought for a moment. 'Ah, yes, I know of you. You did that lovely series called *Art in situ*, didn't you?' Marcus nodded. 'Very brave of you to say what many of us think about art and museums.' She turned to me. 'You move in illustrious circles. First Monica Caroldo, and now Marcus Warren.'

Marcus grinned. 'Not so sure about the illustrious.' He bent back over the case.

Ursula tapped on the case's glass lid and said, 'I turned the page yesterday.'

I hadn't yet looked at the diary and now bent over and scrutinised the new pages closely. There was something familiar about the words. It was not that I could understand much of it but there was something ... I frowned, leaned closer, and then fumbled in my bag for Allegra's journal. I pulled it out, leafed through the pages, and pointed triumphantly at a section of Allegra's writing that had been scrawled, obviously in haste, across the page.

'What is it?' Marcus said.

At first I couldn't speak but only pointed at the diary and then the journal.

Ursula and Marcus drew close, and, despite my confusion, I caught the almost imperceptible shake of Marcus's head that signalled for Ursula to wait for me to explain. She drew back far enough to give us privacy but still stayed close.

'I know that Prudencia's diary is in Latin and my mother wrote in Italian. But look' – I stabbed at the scrawled script – 'I've always thought the journal was just my mother's ramblings. In fact, that's what I was told. But it seems these words, at least, were actual transcriptions from Prudencia's diary.' I turned to Marcus. 'Tell me, please, what do they say?'

Marcus took the journal and began to translate haltingly, his eyes flickering between journal and diary.

> *As I write, I can hear my child's delighted gurgle, the sound from deep in her throat that tells me I touch her heart. Soon they will come for her, and I will not see her again. It is the way of this place to take daughters from their mothers and mothers from their daughters.*

Prudencia's plaintive words from so long ago were palpable, heavy with a sadness that briefly stilled the three of us until Ursula exclaimed, 'That's exactly what's written in the diary.'

Marcus continued with the final few words.

Sadness envelops me like a pall.

He looked up at me when he had finished. 'I wonder what she means about mothers and daughters and separation. You know, Prudencia really might be able to tell you more.'

'What you've just read are lines from a letter Prudencia wrote to her father,' Ursula mused. 'For some reason she repeated them in her diary, and now your mother repeats them in her journal.' She touched my sleeve and said, 'I should leave you, I think. You have much to talk about.'

'No, stay. I owe you some sort of explanation.'

Ursula listened intently while I told her the bare facts about Allegra's journal. I told of my parents' honeymoon in Florence and how I had followed my mother's postcard trail to Prudencia's chest in Santa Celestina's museum. I was nervous and shifted from foot to foot, but my gaze didn't move from the diary in its case. Finally, I drew my story to a close and looked at Ursula. She appeared composed but there was a glint in her eyes. 'I have a couple of questions,' she said. 'Didn't you wonder if there was more to your mother's journal than mere record or introspection?' She didn't wait for my reply. 'From my experience, people write about their lives in diaries because they believe there's something others need to know. Oh, I know that I work with old manuscripts, and it could be said I'm out of touch, but my work only confirms my belief. Prudencia wrote long before Freud and Jung, and she wrote for any number of reasons, but I suspect one of them was for an audience.'

'I suppose the notion of private writing that explores our psychological depths and is meant never to be seen is a recent phenomenon,' Marcus added.

'Exactly!' Ursula shrugged her shoulders, laughed, and said, 'People in the past didn't have the leisure time for such luxuries, nor often the ability. Nowadays, we're encouraged to use private writings to ask ourselves questions which are supposedly answered as we spiral inwards, are in effect lived out in our psyches. I don't entirely hold with this.'

Marcus cradled his elbow in his left hand and leaned his chin into his right palm, pressing hard. I was reminded of a Rodin sculpture, posed for thinking. 'I guess you're saying stories have an outward physical trajectory which embraces other people,' he said. 'And we make of this what we will.'

I hadn't expected this lengthy discussion and didn't know what to say. I'd told Ursula the facts, but I hadn't mentioned the years I'd spent with the journal locked away in case it once again unleashed my unwanted anger. I hadn't mentioned my father's silences or Monica's belief that a story or a fable could answer all life's questions. So I simply mumbled, 'I was young. As I said, later I'd had it translated but, like most children, I suppose I concentrated on what appealed to me – the postcards.'

'And by the time you grew up, this had become habit,' Marcus added.

'I guess so.'

'Now for my second question,' Ursula said. 'Do you know when your mother visited here?'

'It was before I was born. My parents came here on their honeymoon in 1965. Apparently, I was conceived in Florence.' Embarrassed by the intimacy of this detail, I quickly added, 'That's what Monica told me anyway.'

Ursula was deep in thought 'Many years ago, I came here as a young doctoral candidate to work on the archives,' she finally said. 'My special interest is in the intimate lives of my long-dead fellow sisters. During my time amongst these letters and documents, I've welcomed many people to the convent. Around the date you mention, we started a guest book – like the one you wrote in the first day you were here. I wonder ...'

I was already ahead of her and jumped in. 'Do you still have them all?'

'Come with me,' she said.

We followed her through a rear door into a crammed storage room. Ursula glanced along a high shelf and then turned and opened an oblong cupboard built into the opposite wall. She pulled out a small stepladder. Marcus took it from her, and she nodded her thanks and indicated a large leather box. He climbed up, lifted it down carefully, and placed it on a small table. Ursula opened the lid and then rubbed her hands to remove the dust. 'I'm afraid these don't get the same attention as the manuscripts,' she said ruefully.

She pulled the books out one by one, making a pile to the left of the box. 'Each book contains several years,' she explained. 'What year did you say you were born in?'

'1965.'

'Late or early in the year?'

'June.'

'So we want 1964.'

She pulled out two more books and then placed them next to the right of the box. 'Here it is! 1964 to 1970.' She put her hands on the cover and looked at me. 'Let's see. If you were born in June, you were probably conceived in October or November. What was your mother's name?'

'Allegra Maddison,' I said. 'And my father is Lawrence.'

She leafed through the book and stopped at the page headed with the word Ottobre. The three of us bent over the book. Marcus was the first to point to my parent's names – Allegra and Lawrence Maddison – halfway down the page. I took a deep breath and steadied myself against the edge of the table, but to my surprise Ursula kept turning the pages, running her finger down each column of names. She stopped suddenly and stepped back, shaking her head. 'I remember a woman who came here each year from Vicenza. She stopped coming after – oh, it's hard to tell – maybe five or six years. She was fascinated by Prudencia's story, too. But she doesn't seem to have written her name. I thought it might have been your mother.'

'My mother died in 1967,' I said flatly.

A door banged in some far part of the convent, its echo reverberating through to the room in which we stood. Footsteps followed soon after and then raised voices.

Ursula shut the guest book and glanced at her watch.

'It's my mistake then,' she said. 'Memories get muddled and it was a long time ago. Many people have come to peruse the archives over the years.'

She took my hands and pressed them between her palms. 'What a journey you're on. I must go now and prepare the convent roster for next week. The people belonging to those footsteps you heard a few moments ago will be waiting for me in our meeting room. It's almost closing time, but stay here as long as you like, and take no notice of Clementina.' she glanced in the Dottoressa's direction. 'She's not as fierce as she makes out. I'll tell her you're doing research. Just shut the door when you leave. I'll lock it later.'

Ursula let go of my hand, gathered up her gloves and the few loose papers scattered over the top of the nearby bench, and left us alone in the storeroom. Freed from her palms, my warm hands quickly cooled and I tucked them under my armpits, stared at the guest book, and bit hard on my lower lip. I felt no anger at my mother's unexpected appearance in this decades-old convent guest book, only a wash of inevitability, as if I were a puppet and high above me a master puppeteer had doused me with tepid water.

14

After our discussion with Ursula, I decided it was time to visit Bellini's little panel painting of Prudence in the Accademia. It seemed necessary to see the original of a painting that had become a focal point in my life, and a visit to the gallery was on my agenda anyway. Marcus and I arrived early, and even though we were well placed in the queue and our wait wouldn't be long, there was no shelter from the freezing wind. I felt the first drops of rain and looked anxiously at the storm clouds. 'Do you think we'll make it?'

Marcus angled his umbrella to avoid it turning inside out. 'We'll give it quarter of an hour and then perhaps come back later,' he suggested.

We were about to give up when the main doors opened. Luckily, we were in the first group to be ushered inside. We bought our tickets and headed upstairs where we spent the first ten minutes huddled over the radiators to get warm.

Marcus glanced around him and said, 'You should feel at home here.'

'Don't be smart.' I flicked his shoulder with my finger. He caught it and kissed its tip. Then he slid his arm around my shoulder, and we contemplated the artworks in the room.

The triptychs and polyptychs radiated the gold of Byzantium, many of them contemporaries of my Lorenzo

Monaco. In my student days this would have been heaven. It would have taken me days to decipher even some of the symbolic meanings sprinkled liberally throughout the paintings. I spent the best part of an hour wandering from piece to piece, registering at the same time that something in me had shifted. I had learned in the space of a few short weeks not to depend on answers and by default to accept the unknown into my life. I'd clearly recognised that even in my studies I had played with certainties instead of ambiguities. My bent towards pre-Renaissance art had pandered to this particular quirk in my character. I'd also acknowledged that all this was an attempt to quell the enigma of the journal that burned at the centre of my being. But now, I thought fancifully, I was learning to walk through fire, just like so many of the holy figures who peopled this room. I tore myself away from a particularly poignant Saint Francis and walked over to where Marcus was squatting in front of Veneziano's *Annunciation*. He looked up when he sensed me behind him.

'Doing an inventory of saints,' I said lightly. Marcus grinned. An impressive array of saints, hermit saints and prophets flanked the Virgin and the Archangel Gabriel.

'Sort of,' he said. 'I just happen to think this one is meant to be seen from a kneeling position. And, you know, Venice is said to have been founded on the Feast of the Annunciation.'

We both contemplated the work in front of us. After a short time, I reached for Marcus's hand, and he let me pull him to his feet. 'Let's look for Prudence,' I said.

'Finished already?'

'Yes, let's see where they've put her.'

Prudence hung on a wall with four other allegorical panel paintings. Although not true miniatures, they had a miniaturist's grasp of detail and the subtleties of colour. There was lightness, almost playfulness, about them, as if the master was enjoying himself when he painted them.

'Why do you think a copy of this Bellini was put on the chest?' I said.

Marcus considered the painting. 'I don't think that's so unusual. After all, Prudence is known as the Mother of all the Virtues.'

I flinched. It seemed as if everything I touched had something to do with mothers.

'What does interest me,' Marcus continued, 'is whether the original was on the chest, and if and when it was replaced.'

'Is that possible?'

Marcus shrugged. 'Possible yes, probable no. Giovanni Bellini died in 1516. When did your Prudencia enter the convent?'

'Ursula said 1567.'

'So it's unlikely then. Bellini was well dead. It's more likely just a copy by someone who admired it. And, like so many other art treasures, its provenance is lost to time. Prudence was a common sight in the Renaissance' – Marcus waved in the direction of the wall – 'as was Justice, Temperance and the others.'

'Why?'

'Hard to be certain,' Marcus said. 'But I've read it had something to do with the Venetian distaste for showiness.'

'That's hard to believe. What about all those rooms of gold?' I knew about the *camere dorate* where gold trimmings and furnishings were placed to dazzle visitors.

'Yes, but it was a delicate balance. They did have sumptuary laws and at times families were fined for flouting these, but painted images of virtues sort of sobered the people – kept them focussed on higher causes.'

I thought back to Ursula's Latin words and repeated what I could remember to Marcus. Then I said, 'So, what does Prudence actually mean?'

'Good grief. As far as I know, Prudence is theological deep water. The lay notion – at least my lay notion – is that she holds a mirror in order to see herself as others see her. To her, clarity of vision is of primary importance. I always imagine her walking around an idea and considering it from all angles, asking questions as she goes.' Marcus walked closer to the painting on the wall, talking as if he were Prudence speaking. 'Now, I have to make a decision. But before I do, what can history teach me? What does my intuition tell me might happen? Is there anyone around who can help me? And how will I apply all this to the problem at hand in order to make a good decision? Prudence is' – he emphasised – 'painfully prudent.'

'We could ask Ursula,' I said.

'I think there are a lot of things we need to ask Ursula about Prudencia if you are to find out much more. But' – Marcus stretched his arms up and then linked them behind his head and then stretched even further – 'will she know the answers?'

When we returned to Santa Celestina, we asked Ursula if she would like to come with us to the trattoria beside the lagoon that evening. If she was surprised, she didn't show it. She smiled and thanked us and agreed to meet after the museum closed at eight o'clock.

The lagoon was still after the morning's storm, the sky threaded with thin strips of pink and grey cloud. It was icily cold, so we chose to sit inside the restaurant at a table near the window. We ordered seafood and wine and sat for a long time chatting companionably about Venice and the convent and its history. Ursula was easy company and seemed to enjoy the break from her usual routine. I relaxed, and at one point when I heard Ursula and Marcus begin to debate the knotty problem of the accurate attribution of artworks, I let my thoughts drift. Through the window I could see the island of San Michele in Isola. I could see no sign of graves, only the rusticated facade of the church of the same name. I knew the island was the resting place of several famous people, including Ezra Pound and Igor Stravinsky, and of course to generations of Venetians who no doubt guarded their island jealously and perhaps looked askance at the strangers who wanted to lie there. I thought it seemed peaceful from this distance, a space set aside for – I wasn't sure what. I was so rapt in my thoughts that it took a moment to register Marcus's voice.

I turned and saw them both smiling at me.

'Where were you?' Marcus said.

'I was thinking about the island.' I pointed in the direction of San Michele.

'That,' Ursula said, 'is a good place for us to start.'

I looked at her inquiringly.

'Well, my guess is that you want to know about Prudencia,' she said. 'And San Michele is where her story ends. You see, the archives hint that she is buried there.

It's not impossible, as the church of San Michele in Isola was built in the mid-fifteenth century and the monastery was an active place of learning. But it is unlikely because burials as they happen today didn't begin on the island until the nineteenth century.' Ursula paused and then said ruefully, 'History doesn't move in straight lines in Venice. It's like the *calli*. It zigzags here and there, and following the twists and turns takes a particular mindset. There is, however, a grave in the convent garden without any inscription other than a date and the letter P, and this date corresponds to the time of Prudencia's death. So, we think this is more likely to be where she is buried. It's not surprising that there isn't a name. She was a nun, after all, and the sisters at the time could see no reason to tie themselves to this earthly life with words. They believed they'd gone to a better place. We only know the date because of the way she died.'

'How and why was that?' I interrupted.

'The poor thing died of plague.'

'How awful!'

'Awful, yes, but not uncommon in those times. And, as for why, there was a superstition that the bones of plague victims should not be later exhumed and placed in the ossuary as was usual. Victims were identified simply by date and the first letter of their Christian name and left where they lay, whereas the other sisters could be anywhere.' Ursula opened her eyes wide and looked about her, as if the bones of long-dead nuns could lie even under her feet.

'You said Prudencia had a child,' Marcus said.

'Yes, the convent chronicles are useful because they tell of her time with the anchoress, which singled her out from the other nuns. Otherwise, her story would probably have been lost. They also tell of her misdemeanours, which were infamous. I told you, she was a spirited young woman and caused the abbess quite a bit of concern.'

'I think you'd better backtrack,' Marcus suddenly said. 'I can usually zigzag through history quite well but when it comes to people I do need some sort of chronology.'

Ursula ticked off the facts of Prudencia's life on her fingers. 'As I've already told Iris, she came to the convent in 1567 with the marriage chest, which would have contained all her belongings. She was given to the convent's anchoress as a sort of servant and the anchoress taught her to read and write.' Ursula smiled. 'Ironically, this brought about her downfall. But I won't deviate now. I'll stick to the tale. Anyway, she had an affair with a Jewish trader, and they had a child. And this is where it gets interesting. Prudencia and the anchoress successfully hid the pregnancy and – I'm sure you know about the famous baby chute at the Pietà – well, we also had a chute at Santa Celestina and when the child was born, they placed her in it …'

'… and collected her at the other end,' Marcus guessed.

Ursula nodded. 'Many babies were disposed of like this, and no one would have found out except for Prudencia's diary and her conscience.'

'You mean the lines about mothers and daughters being separated,' I said.

'That and more,' Ursula said. 'Prudencia told her confessor. The confessor told his mistress, and the mistress told the abbess, and the child was taken from Prudencia. Prudencia died of plague not long after that and the anchoress took the little girl to Vicenza. The child's father, Ari, was banished from Venice for ten years for having had a relationship with a nun.'

I sighed. 'Poor Prudencia.' Immediately, what I'd said dawned on me and I gasped out loud and repeated, 'Poor Prudencia' and then, '"*Povera* Prudencia".' I looked at Marcus who was nodding his head slowly and smiling at the same time, clearly recognising this echo.

Ursula looked at us with raised eyebrows and said, 'Did I miss something?'

Then I remembered that I hadn't mentioned '*povera* Prudencia' when I told her about the journal. At that point they were just words in some way connected to a figure in a painting, whereas my emphasis in the conversation had been self-absorbed, concerned only with how the journal had derailed my life since I'd discovered it as a child. 'My mother wrote "*povera* Prudencia" near the postcard of Bellini's *Allegory of Prudence*,' I explained. 'She must have somehow heard the story and felt sorry for her. Really, it's impossible not to.'

'There's more to "*povera* Prudencia" than you think,' Ursula said.

Marcus rolled his eyes and said, 'Zigzags again, eh?'

We all laughed and Ursula continued, 'It's a sad but rather lovely story. From what has been pieced together from the archives, when Prudencia ran away from the convent with Ari, they hired a boatman to row them to Torcello – most probably with the intention of island-hopping to the mainland. Prudencia dressed in men's clothing, and as far as the boatman was concerned, they were just two lads out for a lark ...'

'A Renaissance joyride,' Marcus quipped.

'Yes, if you like, exactly that. Anyway, when they were about to leave Torcello, a storm blew up, and we guess the boat must have been in danger of overturning because Prudencia called out, "*Povera* Prudencia". The boatman realised what was going on and refused to take them any further, and Prudencia was returned – pregnant – to the convent.'

Marcus shook his head and gasped. 'Of course! I understand. How incredible! Caught out by grammar.'

'Yes,' said Ursula. 'It really was a case of "*povera* Prudencia" in more ways than one.'

I looked blankly at Marcus and then turned to Ursula. 'I don't understand.'

'Povera is a female adjective. It would have identified Prudencia as a woman,' she said.

There was a long silence as we absorbed the impact these two words must have had on Prudencia. Marcus sipped his wine thoughtfully while I again stared out the window, this time at nothing in particular. Ursula retrieved her bag from the floor beside her. She flipped through a thin pile of leaflets and envelopes and pulled out a handwritten document protected by an acid-free cover. I could clearly see the company logo printed neatly in the bottom right corner. She cleared a space in the centre of the table and laid the document down gently. 'This was found stitched into the lining of the *cassa*,' she said. 'One day when I was doing my doctoral research, I decided to examine Prudencia's handiwork. It's strange. There was no reason for me to do this, but when I smoothed it down with the flat of my hand, I felt a rise beneath it. I traced the edge of the rise with my finger, and it was square – letter-size. I received permission to unpick the lining and I found this.' Ursula pointed to the sheet in front of her. 'It's a letter Prudencia wrote to her father.'

Marcus and I leaned forwards in order to see the letter clearly. The writing was archaic, sloping, with long slim loops and flourishes in unexpected places.

Ursula looked at us. Her kind, brown eyes were troubled. She lifted up the document and said, 'Would you like me to translate for you?'

'Please,' I said, my voice no more than a squeak. I felt very anxious, the room tilting, my thoughts swirling.

Marcus reached for my hand and this small movement grounded me and brought me back into the present. I threaded my fingers through his and concentrated on the warmth of his palm. Then I sat still and straight while Ursula adjusted her glasses, cleared her throat, and began to read.

> *My dear Papa,*
>
> *I write to you, knowing you may never receive this letter, but I have little time and must do what I can for my Amadora.*
>
> *Papa, I have committed a grave sin and now, as is fitting, the beloved child born of that sin is to be taken from me. I need you to know that you have a granddaughter before she is gone from me and I am gone from this earth.*
>
> *As I write, I can hear my child's delighted gurgle, that sound from deep in her throat*

that tells me I touch her heart. Soon they will come for her, and I will not see her again. It is the way of this place to take daughters from their mothers and mothers from their daughters.

This is my story too, Papa. I remember the day Mamma led me to the gondola to bring me here all those years ago, and I saw you watching from the campo opposite our palazzo. Why did you never come to see me, Papa? I know that Mamma was busy with Licia and Antonella and had no time for a daughter scarred as I was by birth. But why you, Papa?

As you can see, I have learned to read and write, but even if I have not used these gifts for the glory of God, but have instead brought shame by my actions, I can still use them to write to you.

I beg you to find my Amadora, Papa, and take her to you. When I die, they will ask you to collect my cassa. As is the custom, they will keep what is inside, so this letter will be sewn into the lining in eternal hope.

Sadness envelops me like a pall.

Your daughter,

Prudencia.

I groaned and sat back in my chair. 'Did her father ever see the letter, or the baby?'

'We guess not,' Ursula said. 'As I told you, I found the letter stitched into the lining of her chest, and then she died, and the letter wasn't found for over four hundred years.'

'I'd like to go to San Michele and have a look at the so-called burial place there,' I suddenly said. 'Also, the one in the garden.'

'Yes, I can understand why you would,' Ursula said. 'Come and I'll give you directions to the site on the island. Also, there's a photo taken some forty-odd years ago by another sister who was interested in her fellow nuns. I'll drop it into your room later today. And just let me know when you want to see the grave in the garden. It's in a closed-off area and you'll need the key to the padlock on the gate.'

Then she turned and took my hand in that calm but concerned way peculiar to those at some remove from everyday life. 'For what it's worth, I don't think you should stop at the gravesite, wherever it is. I think there is more to your mother's journal than what I've told you.' She squeezed my hand. 'Venice has taught me there is always a story beneath the story.'

Marcus and I went to San Michele the following day. My head was whirling with thoughts of Eve and Prudencia, trying in vain to pull what I knew into a coherent whole. I wanted to find the gravesite, even though it most probably meant nothing. I concluded that, just as I had come to the Santa Celestina to be in the same space as my mother, I simply wanted to follow Prudencia's story to its end.

Marcus had a headache and spent most of the short trip, chin on hand, gazing out across the lagoon waters. I stared straight ahead, watching the cemetery island creep closer.

The island was nothing like I expected. Only five of us disembarked at San Michele and all funnelled silently along a petunia-lined path that led towards an arcaded building complex. Once there, our three companions, a hunched elderly woman dressed in widow's weeds accompanied by two young children – all laden with flowers – headed purposefully away from the complex, and Marcus and I wandered amongst the bas-reliefs that decorated its outer walls, some with simple Latin inscriptions. One of a later more romantic period showed an angel leading a slight girl upwards from the grave. It was calm and quiet and an enchanting blend of watery sunlight, flowers, and old stone.

'I think I understand now,' Marcus said.

'Yes,' I agreed. 'This place has magic about it. I can see why burial plots are sought after.'

I pulled out Ursula's black and white photo of the 'grave' and held it up for us both to see. It was small and taken from a distance, probably with a box Brownie. It had also faded over time, but despite both these factors, there were clearly no markings on the headstone to identify who lay beneath.

'Ursula said Prudencia's "grave" is on the far side of the island,' Marcus said. 'We just have to find the Orthodox Section and apparently it's not far from there.'

We walked slowly past the multi-level stone memorial towers, their stark surfaces softened by flowers, and then past elaborate graves decorated with the epithets of a lifetime: a pair of ballet slippers beside a photo of a small girl, an open book beside that of a bespectacled man. It was sombre but not depressing, a place for memories rather than death, for soul rather than spirit. We searched for Pound's grave and found it nestled amongst rampant ivy. For a good while we circled around, reading the epitaphs, and exclaiming out loud when one was particularly fanciful or poignant. But Prudencia's 'grave' remained elusive, and we eventually found ourselves back near the building complex. When we'd first arrived, there'd been no one around; now a man was sweeping the walls of the complex with a stiff-bristled broom, its swishing loud on the unyielding concrete. He wore a long, brown habit with a wide cowl neck and a white cincture around his waist. He'd knotted the hem of the gown on one side so he could work unimpeded and underneath his jeans were clearly visible. His hair was long, almost shoulder-length, and was brushed back off his face where it fell in evenly-spaced waves – a far cry from the traditional monastic tonsure. What surprised me most was his age. He must have been no more than thirty, and when he saw us, he waved his broom in greeting before returning to work. I assumed he was a monk, but he might just as easily have been a priest.

'He seems friendly enough,' Marcus said. 'Why don't we ask him where the "grave" might be?'

I looked down at the photograph in my hand. 'If we're ever going to find it, I don't think we've much choice.'

We headed in the sweeper's direction, and when Marcus judged he was within earshot, he called out, '*Mi scusi*. Excuse me.'

The cleric turned and beamed at us. 'Good morning.' He checked his watch. 'I mean, good afternoon.' Then without any prompting from us he added, 'We will speak in English. For me it is the practice.'

I showed him the photograph and asked if he knew the 'grave'. He squinted, put down his broom in order to adjust his glasses, and studied the picture. 'It seems much older than many of these.' I indicated the surrounding graves with a wide sweep of my arm.

'*Si*,' he said as he handed the photo back to me. He bent and picked up his broom, aligned it sideways along the edge of a paving slab, and swept the crevice carefully. Marcus and I exchanged glances and waited while he picked up the few leaves and crumbs of dirt with a long-handled pan and brush. His furrowed brow and the way he sucked on his lower lip suggested he was deep in thought.

'There is a section over there' – 'there' was indicated by an elaborate flourish – 'with the graves with no inscriptions, which are perhaps not the graves.'

He smiled, as if speaking in riddles made everything clear.

'The first real burial here was in 1813,' he said. 'Then the funerals were magnificent events. Triumphal processions to this island across the dark water with funereal gondolas and gondoliers in gilded uniforms, and so many bright flowers.' He was now in full flight. 'Ah, so many flowers.'

We didn't interrupt as it was fascinating, and our cleric was clearly enjoying himself.

'So it was dark and light, you see. Sadness, but also hope. But now the funerals are not so' – he cast about for the right word – 'flamboyant. Death is seen as an end instead of part of a journey.' He shrugged his shoulders. 'It's a sign of the times.'

'This island has great history,' Marcus said respectfully.

'*Si*.' The cleric nodded.

Marcus took the photo from me, held it out again, and said, 'And this "grave"?'

'Ah, si,' he said again. 'Over there.' Then with poetic precision, 'Walk the curving line of the cypresses, turn left at the water's edge, and it is in the middle of the ivy. And may God bless you.' He made the sign of the cross and resumed his sweeping as if we had never arrived.

<h1 style="text-align:center">15</h1>

I found Prudencia's 'grave' by accident, half-hidden by long grass. Someone had buried a large, square slab of grey stone in the earth. At its head two thick, intersecting stone rods formed a Latin cross the same size as the slab, the crossbar secured by a niche hewn into the vertical shaft. There was no other ornamentation, no stone angels or flowers, just some wild geranium that had draped itself sash-like over the cross. There was also no name or date to suggest who lay there. I called to Marcus and drew disapproving stares from two women bent over a nearby tomb. Thankfully, he heard me the first time and hurried over. I triumphantly held up the photograph again. 'I've found it,' I said too loudly.

'Shush.' Marcus put his finger to my lips as he glanced at the women. He moved sideways until he stood directly in front of the cross, and then he crouched down and bit thoughtfully on his thumbnail. 'Ursula's probably right. This is either a very short grave or, as she said, a memorial. If it's the latter, I wonder who erected it. And I wonder why there isn't a name on it?'

I went and stood beside him and pondered what appeared to me to be another ending. I thought about Ursula's twists and turns and noted idly that the length of geranium was thicker at the base of the cross. I followed its trail along the ground with my eye until it changed direction where a brownish object obstructed its path. I looked closer. 'There's something on the ground,' I said. I walked toward it and motioned for Marcus to follow me.

We knelt down, and Marcus touched what turned out to be a fallen piece of timber with his finger. There were frayed lengths of twine hanging from each end. 'It must have been tied to the cross,' he puzzled. 'It must have fallen. I wonder how long it's been there.' He picked it up and scraped away the dirt that coated the surface. 'I can't read it, but it looks as though something's been whittled into the wood.'

Then I felt a punch to my chest that I thought might stop my heart. I stood up and stepped backwards, stumbled on a rock, and flailed about for support. There was none. Marcus leaped forward and grabbed my arm. 'What's the matter?' he cried. 'You're as white as a sheet.'

'It's the sign,' I gasped. I knew I made no sense, but my thoughts had scattered and with them any chance of speaking clearly. I leaned heavily on Marcus's arm. I was standing in the eye of a storm and with mocking clarity could see the truth swirling about me but refusing to take coherent shape. My stomach churned and I pressed my hands to either side of my neck in an effort to breathe normally.

'Iris! What is it?' Marcus insisted.

'The sign,' I said. I sat on the damp grass and picked up the fallen piece of timber.

Marcus sat beside me and cupped my face in his palms. 'Talk to me,' he said.

'It can't be ... It's ... It's all been a lie. Don't you see?' I cried. 'My mother didn't die. It's not her grave. It's ...'. My voice broke. I was shaking and tears ran down my cheeks.

I rubbed at them impatiently. I must have looked like some wild creature.

'I don't understand,' Marcus said. He held my gaze and continued, 'Iris, it's okay. Calm down. This memorial has nothing to do with your mother. It's a memorial for Prudencia. It's good that we've found it.'

I shook my head in frustration and tried to stand, but stabs of fear made me double over and clasp my knees for support. I breathed in and out until it felt safe to stand upright. Finally, I managed to say, 'Look, I'll show you.' I reached up, tugged the geranium from the cross, and pointed to some straggly bits of twine wound around the crossbar. The greenery had hidden them. 'When I was a child, my father took me to visit my mother's grave in Curdies River Cemetery.' I held the wood against the cross. 'Her grave was marble. There was a wooden sign bolted to it with my mother's name.' I stopped, my next words like boulders in my throat. I gulped and said in a low voice, 'I was too young to realise that it wasn't a grave.'

Marcus still looked puzzled.

'Don't you see?' My voice rose hysterically. 'It was a memorial to my mother. Just like this so-called grave is a memorial to Prudencia. Both have wooden plaques. And if my mother's grave is a memorial, maybe she isn't even dead. Maybe everyone's lied to me.' I frowned, dug my heels into the grass, and threw the piece of timber hard at the stone cross. It had softened with age and fragmented rather than splintered, falling without a sound onto the ground below. 'I remember it was a long drive,' I whispered. 'But I never wondered why my mother's grave was so far from home.'

Marcus said nothing. I could see him piecing together my fragmented sentences. 'You can't be sure,' he finally said. 'I mean the situations are similar, but there's no proof.' He meant to console me, but there was enough doubt in his voice to fuel my mounting despair.

The two women who were exploring the area near us had moved hurriedly away at my first outcry and now stood at a distance, watching. Then they put their heads down and moved off in the direction of a small chapel. The tombs around me lurched menacingly and I reached for Marcus's arm for support. He put his hand on mine and pressed on it. My initial shock dulled, leaving me woozy and off-balance. Heaviness blanketed me. I thought of my father and the long silences that had shaped my childhood and made me search so hard for certainty now made sense. I recalled our trips to the cemetery and how Lawrence had stood without a word watching the grave, while I flung out prayers in its direction and then plucked out the weeds from its base. There had been no sharing of grief followed by the comfort of memories. There had been only a small girl, who knew nothing of grief's protocol and had received no guidance, trying as hard as she could to make contact with a mother who was not there. My shivering escalated, and Marcus shifted his arm to my shoulders and held me tightly. Then, without a word, he steered me away from Prudencia's memorial towards the vaporetti pontoon on the other side of the island.

I have vivid but discrete memories of the trip back to Santa Celestina: the choppy waters of the lagoon, the sour taste of seasickness for the first time in my life. There was the blur of faces: laughing tourists flourishing their cache of Murano glassware, Venetian businessmen stiff-backed behind their newspapers, school children in noisy clusters. But time had warped and the journey itself could have been three minutes or three hours.

That night Marcus stayed in my room, and I slept in his arms. In the dark hours of the night, I dreamed of my mother's grave, as I'd not done since childhood. This time I was tugging at her marble slab while goblin-like figures cavorted around it, demonic creatures with twisted faces. They wanted to return to their world beyond the slab and when they couldn't find an entry point, they grew angry, plucked out small clumps of violets, threw them onto the slab, and then crushed them underfoot.

I woke with a start and sat up in bed. Marcus's hand slipped from my belly onto the sheet between us. He stirred and then settled back to sleep. It was cold, so I pulled the doona up under my chin and hugged it close to my chest. Marcus was lying on his side with his other hand tucked under his cheek. I touched his face but when he didn't stir, I wound my arm around and under his neck and lay my head on his chest. I didn't want to be awake alone. His body was warm. I spread my fingers across his chest and lay very still, listening to his heartbeat in the same way as a child might look for comfort. After a while his fingers moved gently over my face and then circled my breasts and pushed against my belly button.

'Are you okay?' he said.

'I could smell violets,' I whispered.

'Violets?'

'Yes. They've always been there. From the first day Lawrence took me to my mother's' – I corrected myself – 'from the first day Lawrence took me to the cemetery.'

'Why violets?'

'Lawrence told me it was Allegra's favourite scent. I don't remember much about her, only long blond hair and violet perfume.' I thought for a moment. 'I remember her laugh and the way she used to swing me around in circles.'

As I reached back, the paucity of these few memories washed over me. It was no wonder the journal had retained its drawing power. No wonder that for so long it had glowed like hot coals. It was all I had and I'd stoked its fires with my own need. 'Why did he do this,' I said.

'You mean your father?'

'Yes, why did Lawrence do this to me?'

'You can't be absolutely sure, you know,' Marcus again said gently. 'Did your father ever explain to you how your mother died?'

'When I was very young, he told me she had a stroke. He said it was rare and quick. Then he shut down and there was really nothing for me to say. I was only a child.'

'And therefore meant only to receive knowledge, not question it,' Marcus said.

'I suppose so.'

'What about Monica? And, for that matter, the rest of your family?'

'Monica,' I repeated. I shook my head in disbelief. In the face of all that had happened, I had forgotten about Monica. 'She told me my mother had gone away. I don't remember her ever using the word "die". She must have known everything all along yet said nothing. I trusted her and she lied to me.'

'There's a difference between lying and not telling the truth,' Marcus said.

'What do you mean?'

'If your father chose to tell you one thing, she might have felt it wasn't her place to tell you any different.'

'So she just chose words that were suitably ambiguous.' It seemed unfair of Marcus to find excuses for Monica's behaviour. I recalled her annoyance at Lawrence taking me to my mother's grave. I'd been too young to pick up on the nuances of their conversation. Nor had I questioned its contents. I had simply accepted what I heard at face value.

'What about the rest of your family?' Marcus repeated.

I shrugged and said, 'Dead. Or so far removed they may as well have been.'

Marcus rolled onto his back and sighed. 'This is incredible. But, Iris, remember this epiphany of yours on San Michele is still just a hunch. I think the only way you can find out anything is to ask Monica what really happened to your mother.'

I sat up and turned my head to look at Marcus. A few seconds passed before I said miserably, 'If my mother wasn't dead, then where was she? Actually, if my mother isn't dead, then where is she?'

The next morning, we explained to Clementina that we would be away overnight and reserved our rooms in Santa Celestina until we got back. We took the train to Mestre and hired a car to drive to Montespertoli. I was glad of the long trip and didn't offer to help Marcus with the directions. I settled back in my seat and thought about what I had learned. My mother wanted me to find her journal. She left me fragments – four postcards, a few pieces of script – for me to pick my way through. Odd stones and pebbles more likely to trip me up than set me on my way, but I knew now that I had followed them because they were a mother's map for her daughter.

After this my reasoning faltered. There was simply no way to accommodate my revelation on San Michele. Like an earthquake it had fractured my world from the bottom up and cracked it wide open. Until then I had been following the trail toward Allegra. Now I knew she had never even been there.

We arrived in Montespertoli in the early afternoon, and I expected to have to wait until Monica returned from the university late in the day, but from the ridge road above her house, I saw a figure moving against the stone walls.

By the time we drove down the long driveway, she had gone inside. I knocked and listened to the click of footsteps on the tiled floor grow louder as she neared the door. Monica peered through the side window and when she saw who it was, she hastily pulled back the bolt, threw open the door, and reached out to hug and kiss me. But I drew back, my body rigid with anger. She dropped her hands, and a shadow crossed her face. It was fleeting, but I saw it nonetheless. A sliver of doubt and guilt, brief as a bird's wing against a blue sky and, yes, the cold snap of fear that took the light from her eyes and turned them slate grey. I steadied myself by spreading my feet apart and pushing both hands deep into my pockets. I leaned forward. 'Why did you let me believe that my mother died?'

Monica closed her eyes. She stood quite still, and I watched the blood drain from her face, drawn by those icy ghosts she had warned me against on the first day Marcus and I visited her.

I leaned forward and gripped her arm. She flinched. 'Why Monica? Why?' I tried to keep my voice calm and drew breath down into my feet in an effort to stay anchored, but the house wall beside me wavered and my body jerked involuntarily, as if that puppeteer was again pulling strings attached to the top of my head. Neither of us spoke. We just stood there, in the face of something we hadn't yet named but knew might blow our world apart when we did.

'I think we should go and sit down.' Marcus touched both of us at the same time and the spell broke. In silence, we walked down the passage to the kitchen.

'How did you know?' Monica said. She made no attempt to refute what I had claimed.

'Because of Prudencia.'

'Prudencia?'

'Do you remember telling me that my mother kept a journal? Just before you left for Italy.'

'Yes,' she said. 'But what's this got to do with anything? And who's Prudencia?'

I shook my head impatiently. 'On the visit before that last one, I heard you and Lawrence arguing.' Monica looked up, surprised by my recollection. 'After you left, I saw my father throw something into the bin late that night. I pulled it out. It was the journal.'

'So you already had it?' she said. She drew a deep breath, breathed out slowly, and then her body sagged forward. 'I wondered what had happened to it.'

'Yes, but it made little sense. There were just postcards and bits of writing. But then there was Prudencia, you see' – I stopped, unable to put into few words the trail that had led me to this point – 'and I found out through her.'

Not surprisingly, Monica looked puzzled and then Marcus told her about Prudencia. She listened without speaking, her head in her hands. Occasionally, she raked her fingers through her hair and then bit hard on her knuckles. The faint worry lines between her brows were white like scars, her forehead was creased. When he finished, she looked up. I noticed with surprise that some of the light was back in her eyes.

'When you were born, Allegra said she wanted you to have her journal. We were talking one morning about all sorts of things. We were – are – twins. We shared a lot.' Monica looked at me as she spoke, but her gaze was focussed elsewhere. 'She said mothers and daughters were destined to misunderstand each other. She laughed and said that perhaps a journal would help you understand her. When she went away, I waited until you were eleven before I asked Lawrence if he was going to give it to you. He got so angry. I can still hear him.' Her voice cracked. 'I want her to believe her mother's dead, he said, why on earth would I give her something like that.'

'What did my mother do?' I was confused. Monica's last words did not gel with the image I had of my father. I could not associate Lawrence with anger. It was too forceful, too external. My father was an artist and drew from the soul. I believed, perhaps childishly, perhaps from some deep-set need, that he told the story of his grief in the slope of a bird's wing or his longing in a sculpture's sensual curves. Such beauty could not be born of an emotion as base as anger.

'Before I tell you, there are things you need to know.' Monica paused. She got up from her chair and walked slowly to the other side of the room where she leaned against the wall, facing us. There was something reverent in that slow walk. A thick strand of dark hair had fallen from the jewelled clasp at the nape of her neck, and she twirled it distractedly with her finger. Neither Marcus nor I spoke. The space separating us from Monica was holy ground and I had the feeling that the wrong words might frighten away its spirits. Marcus must have sensed this, too. Because he clutched my hand and pulled it slightly, warning me to be silent. 'Allegra was my other half. I shared her soul,' Monica finally said. 'Remember when you were little and I told you how she met Lawrence and fell in love.'

'That was the day you told me my mother was a dreamer, and that this was dangerous.'

'Did I?' Monica looked surprised.

'Well, I'm not sure of your exact words. But from then on, I associated dreamers with dying. I became' – I looked sideways at Marcus – 'a very literal sort of girl. It seemed safer.'

'I guess Lawrence didn't tell you much about Allegra.'

I grimaced and shrugged my shoulders.

'When they met, Allegra was not yet twenty. To her life was love and romance, poetry and music.' Monica smiled.

'She fell pregnant with you quickly and sailed through the pregnancy. She held crystals over her belly to guess the sex and made Lawrence paint a garden on your bedroom wall. It was beautiful.'

'Just like *Primavera*,' I said.

Monica made no sign that she had heard me.

'But when you were born, something happened to her. She spent a great deal of time walking on the beach. She lost weight. Oh, so much weight that I thought she might disappear. Then one day' – Monica swallowed hard and tears pooled in her eyes – 'she vanished. It was as simple and complicated as that. Lawrence was out of his mind. The police were called, and they traced her to the airport. There was conjecture that she had flown to Italy, because our parents came from here.'

'And then,' Marcus said.

'There were missing person searches, but nothing came of them. After a time, your grandparents returned to their village near Florence, perhaps in some vain hope that she would surface. And Lawrence cocooned you in Peterborough. He held on to you so tightly. Perhaps he thought you might disappear as well. I fought like crazy to keep on seeing you.'

'You mean they never found her?' I said, incredulously.

There was a pause, slight, like the beat between breaths. But it was enough. I banged my fist on the table. 'You know what happened, don't you? You knew all the time and you didn't tell us.'

'No, not all the time.' Monica walked quickly back to the table and reached across for my hand, but I closed my fist.

I stood up, knocking over my chair as I backed away. Its cast-iron frame resounded as it hit the tiles. I wanted to flee but instead I laid my head in Marcus's arms and sobbed.

There was a long silence. An unexpected strip of yellow sunlight cut across the terracotta tiles and lit up the edge of the table. At the same time, a bird struck a pane of glass in the kitchen and beat its wings frantically. We started and turned to see what was happening. The bird fell to the ground and for a few seconds lay stunned. Then its wings twitched and it flew away.

'I didn't know what had happened to Allegra until I returned to Italy,' Monica said flatly. 'How could I tell you? I knew what Lawrence had done. But I received a letter from her not long after I finished my thesis. Allegra said she had discussed it with a nun on one of her visits to Santa Celestina. She said she was pleased I'd done what I needed to do.' She stopped and tilted her head to one side, on her face a look midway between regret and sadness. 'As girls we were always there for each other's triumphs and disasters. She knew what my study meant to me. Old habits, I guess, die hard. But there was no address on the letter.'

'Perhaps she was the woman Ursula said came from Vicenza to see the chest,' Marcus said.

For me there was no longer any doubt. I was tired and my anger had dulled to bewilderment. 'But why did she leave?' I said. I shook my head from side to side as if this might clear away the confusion and again said, 'Why did she leave?'

Monica walked over and rested her hand on my shoulder. Her grip was surprisingly light, as tenuous, I thought irritably, as the saints and sinners who peopled her life. I reached up, lifted her hand away, and held it between my fingers. I saw her swallow, and then she broke away and paced to the window again and turned toward me.

'Allegra was alive,' she said. There was defiance in her voice. 'She was too alive to be kept in such a small space.'

In a flash it came back to me. The filigreed silver frame surrounding my mother and father. Allegra's half-smile, half-pout, eyes that stared out and not down holding, as fragile and delicately tapestried as butterfly wings, dreams dreamed but not lived.

'Yes, but why did she leave,' I insisted.

Monica didn't answer. She turned to look out the window, her outline gilded by the afternoon sun. My thoughts slipped sideways and for a second she was Saint Ursula in that moment of apotheosis, caught in the enchantment of some other world, the golden light protecting her from we mere mortals.

'And you call my mother a dreamer,' I said scornfully.

She turned back and for several minutes we faced each other across the room. I wanted her to say something – anything – but the silence only grew until no words would have been large enough to breach its chasm. I drew a deep breath into the pit of my stomach and held it for a moment before letting it out. Then I turned to Marcus and said, 'I want to go, now.'

Monica moved towards me, but I put out a hand to block her and she backed away. I held her gaze for as long as it took to pick up my bag and reach for Marcus's hand before heading to the doorway. Once there, I looked back

– perhaps in some vain hope that all this hadn't happened and she would be smiling and holding out her arms to me – but Monica had again turned to face the window.

We returned to Venice that same night, driving through sluicing rain in the empty hours after midnight. Around us the traffic sped on unperturbed, and the trucks thundered past in the far lane splashing arcs of water coloured red and yellow by street lighting. We slept for a short time in the parking area of the car rental firm in Mestre and woke surrounded by the lagoon's low mist.

The first worker arrived just after eight o'clock and we handed over the car before hailing a taxi to take us to the station, where we caught the train into Venice proper.

Clementina was on duty when we arrived at Santa Celestina. I must have looked wretched because I saw first surprise and then concern disturb her usually impassive features. She pulled a towel from a cupboard behind her and draped it around my damp shoulders. Then she phoned the kitchen and ordered English tea to be sent to my room – all without a word passing between us. She gave Marcus the keys to both our rooms before finally placing her hand on my shoulder and saying, 'Would you like to see Ursula?' Initially, I was surprised at the question, but Clementina must have seen what had passed between the three of us in recent days and rightly guessed Ursula's knowledge of whatever had brought me to this state. I nodded and she picked up the phone. I heard the beginnings of their brief exchange before Marcus guided me out the door and into the corridor.

To my surprise, in the brief space between our leaving the Dottoressa's office and arriving at my room, someone had turned down the bed coverings as if it were night instead of bright daylight. I kicked off my shoes, laid flat on the bed, and stared at the ceiling. I didn't cry. Instead, large tears dripped from my eyes as if some inner mechanism sensed the need for release even before I summoned up the energy to cry for myself. Marcus curled sideways on the bed beside me, his right arm awkwardly cradling the top of my head. Ten minutes or so passed before there was a knock at the door.

'It must be Ursula,' Marcus said before he called out, 'Come in.'

I heard something – a tea tray – clatter on the floor outside. Then the door opened and there was a brief pause before Ursula appeared, during which time she must have bent to pick up the tray. She nudged the door shut with her elbow, placed the tray on the table beside the bed, and pulled up a chair. She poured tea and handed it to us. I took the cup automatically, registering the sweet biscotti on the saucer.

While we drank, Marcus told Ursula of my revelation on San Michele and our subsequent trip to Montespertoli. She didn't move during the whole of the telling but sat, head down and brow furrowed, as if to fully absorb what was being said. When he finished, she lifted her head, looked at me, and said softly, 'Stories within stories.' From anyone else this might have sounded clichéd, but from her it felt real.

'We always believed – knew really – that the grave on San Michele was a memorial,' she mused. 'But there is no absolute proof one way or the other.' She looked distressed, as if she wanted the grave to belong to a real person, so that my revelation would never have taken place.

'It doesn't matter which is real and which is not,' I said. 'Prudencia has led me to the truth, you see,' I continued. 'Marcus didn't fully explain the impact of the plaque to you. It was' – I searched for an appropriate hyperbole – 'cataclysmic. I think someone of romantic disposition – some tourist perhaps who had heard of Prudencia's story – must have gone so far as to carve her name in wood and fasten it to the cross with twine. We know the plaque isn't old because, of course, the timber would have perished.'

Marcus turned from me to Ursula and enunciated his next words in a sing-song staccato for emphasis. 'We know that Prudencia's child went to Vicenza, with the anchoress. Yes?'

Ursula nodded and said, 'There's a family in the city which links itself to Prudencia. It's commonplace in Italy to ally yourself with people from the past – famous or infamous. The family has a workshop where they decorate miniature chests for discerning collectors, and they also make a living from tourists.'

'Okay,' Marcus said. 'Perhaps Allegra went to Vicenza for sentimental reasons – to follow in Prudencia's footsteps.' He turned back to me. 'Monica did say your mother was a dreamer. We also know that she was the woman who visited this convent.'

'Another yes.' Ursula pursed her lips. 'I'm not sure where you're going with this, but I remember speaking to

Iris's mother about Monica's thesis quite clearly. She told me that she came from a great distance but didn't go on to explain. I've always enjoyed talking to people who come to the museum. There are not many opportunities in my line of work.'

'Can you remember anything else she said?'

Ursula hesitated. 'The memory of her is clear because of her frequent visits. I do remember her saying that she had previously visited with her husband but had come back alone to find out more about Prudencia. She told me she was going to San Michele to visit the "grave".'

'Just as I thought,' Marcus said triumphantly. 'The plaque, you see.' He raised his arms, palms upturned as if they held the truth. There was no need for him to say more, as the knowledge dawned on the three of us at the same time.

I gasped. 'Allegra must have ...'

'Yes,' said Ursula. 'Perhaps she did ...'

At that moment each of us saw Allegra tying timber to a stone cross in a remote part of San Michele in Isola.

There was nothing more to be said. I'd begun to cry softly, tears dripping down my cheeks onto the pillow. Ursula rose from her seat and began to stack the cups onto the tray. When she'd finished, she came close to me and took my hand. 'I'll go now,' she said. 'You look exhausted. You need rest.' Uncharacteristically for a nun, she bent over me, and I felt her lips brush my forehead. 'If there's anything I can do, if you'd like to talk more, I'll be in the museum most of tomorrow. If not, Clementina will know where I am. Sleep well, Iris. And may God bless your dreams. I'm so sorry this has happened.' Fatigue such as I'd never experienced flooded through me, and I barely heard her quiet exit from the room.

Marcus pulled the quilt over us and edged closer. I could feel his body cupped around my own and the slow, steady beat of his heart against my back. God, I thought, as I drifted into sleep. Why would any god play such a trick?

We slept until the convent's midday bell, sonorous but musical, chimed close by and pulled us slowly awake.

16

Four days passed before I had the strength to face Ursula again. During that time Marcus and I walked the labyrinthine *calli* of Venice, while the deep bruise caused by my father and Monica's betrayal bloomed inside me. When we met Ursula on our way to and from the convent, she greeted us in her usual friendly manner and then commented on the weather or suggested a painting or a site we might like to visit. She gave no sign that she was perplexed or hurt by my silence.

Marcus didn't bring up the subject of my discovery himself but instead responded to each of my outbursts – which were frequent and vehement – with gentle empathy and another long walk to a tourist site. It was only much later that I realised he had chosen our various routes and paid for our entry tickets. He must have understood that I lacked the energy for making decisions and simply let me mourn for what I had lost, which for me seemed harsher than when I first learned as a child of my mother's death. Death, at least, scythed cleanly. Of course, there was my childish anger at being deserted by the dead. After all, what were those left to do with only the trickery of memory or piecemeal collections of bits and bobs for comfort? Oh, yes, at an early age the journal had taught me all about anger. But with death, at least the cause of it was writ in a reality as hard as stone. It was free of subterfuge and lies. I could cope – barely – with a dead mother, even one who left her daughter nothing more than a set of cryptic clues. But what was I to do with one who had walked coolly out of my life? And whose actions had been kept from me by those who professed to love me the most? There were a few moments during those days when I allowed myself a glimpse into the sham that I now felt underpinned all I had known, but I pulled myself back quickly because all I could see was a past as empty as those two graves in windswept Curdies River and silent San Michele.

It was the beauty of Venice that saved me in the end. Not because it distracted or uplifted me but because it lured me deep into myself and let me cry. It let me see through to something beyond the emptiness, something bigger than my disillusion, something mired deep in a vast space that I could only glimpse. It was only by entering into that place that I would begin to understand my mother. It was Venice who completed what Marcus had begun on the day he took me to Carmignano.

It was late afternoon of the fourth day when we reached the church of San Zaccaria, which stood in a stark piazza just off the main trail of restaurants and shops that stretched between Saint Mark's Square and the *sestiere* of Castello. As usual we stood in the centre of the piazza in order to take in the facade. Blinded by the promises of richness inside, visitors often forgot that the outside of Venetian buildings held treasures of their own.

'It's a bit of a mixture, isn't it?' Marcus said. 'Impressive enough but, if you look closely, a real hotchpotch of styles. See' – he pointed towards the first course – 'those low buttress-piers are nothing like the curved piers above them. But when Codussi took over the construction, he somehow managed to pull it all together. Clever really.'

I listened closely, following where Marcus indicated. His practical comments soothed me, and while I searched for a light source or identified a style of architecture, I was able to pretend that the world was still spinning on the same axis as two months ago. When we finally went inside San Zaccaria, I was disappointed. I don't know what I'd expected, but it wasn't the grey Gothic expanse that stretched from nave to altar. Despite the church being open in design, the busy biblical and historical paintings on the side walls cluttered the interior but, I suppose, this only served to highlight the studied gravity of the third postcard in my mother's journal – Bellini's *Madonna and Child with Saints* – on the left wall. Of course, I knew of Bellini's painting; I had come across it during my studies. I was aware of the figures' deep concentration; the way they appeared to take no notice of each other yet somehow form a connected whole. But seeing it in person was an unexpected shock.

'It's beautiful,' I whispered. 'But I don't fully understand why.'

'What do you mean?' Marcus said.

'Well' – I hesitated – 'the figures appear to be unaware of each other, but we don't feel as though they are in any way distant from each other. It's peculiar really. I mean, if emotion is the driving force behind art, why do we feel their connection to each other so strongly when they are actually ignoring each other.'

I walked forward and peered up at the painting. On my left, a reflective, if grim, Saint Peter faced the viewer but gazed down towards his clenched fist. Next to him, Saint Catherine stared at the tip of her palm branch from under lowered lids. On the other side an upright Saint Lucy, in a blue-gold brocade dress that echoed her red-gold hair, gazed into the bowl that was said to hold her eyes. A stolid Saint Jerome in Cardinal red was focussed on his book. Even the Virgin and Child between Catherine and Lucy stared downward. But to me the naked little child looked knowing, this perhaps exacerbated by his broad forehead and the placement of limbs with their ripples of flesh that implied movement. The only figure facing outward was the angel playing the viol, although even she was clearly engrossed in the heavenly music she was making.

Except for Marcus and me, the church was empty. It was very still. There was a faint smell of incense left over from an earlier Mass. A stand of votive candles flickered nearby. I noticed that they were not the usual fat, little round candles that slotted neatly into multi-clawed brass fixtures. These candles were tall and thin and were stuck haphazardly into a bowl of sand. A few had fallen sideways, and I wondered if this meant the fervent petitions that had put them there in the first place were doomed to failure. We had been in the church for some time, and the cold was pressing. I rubbed my hands together and shuffled my feet to try and warm them. I looked back at the painting and straight into the eyes of the little angel who seemed to stare at and through me. On impulse, I turned around, but there was nothing there. Then I ranged from figure to figure. It struck me that while the other figures remained transfixed, my angel was actively drawing her bow across the strings of her viol.

'They look blissful,' I said, pointing to the angel. 'Perhaps it's because of her. Perhaps they're all listening to the invisible strains of her music.'

'Maybe "blissful" is the right word,' Marcus mused. He moved a step closer to the painting and said, 'Bellini's concern is not with human conversation but with a greater sacred conversation. Maybe he wanted to see past our petty little human stories and glimpse into a beyond where we understand each other via the music of the soul, instead of the jangle of psychology.'

'Go on,' I said, intrigued.

Marcus frowned and turned to me with a worried look. 'Psychology is great. I mean, we all know that. I don't want you to think I'm suggesting anything else.' His voice trailed away, and he was again lost to the painting for a short time. I didn't interrupt. Finally, he said, 'But sometimes I think it's best to let things be what they are without straining too much to work out why, or change someone, or even change ourselves. Sometimes there just isn't anything else to do. I mean, look at the saints. Their destinies were bizarre, so we have to try and see beyond them to understand anything at all about what motivated them. For someone who doesn't believe in God, their lives must seem incomprehensible.' He paused. 'Perhaps if we are wise, we stop trying to work out why and just accept life's silent music – like the saints.'

I peered again at the little musical angel in the centre of the painting and smiled. She looked, I thought with surprise, quite wise and also a bit world-weary. 'Perhaps she wishes she could turn up the volume so we could all hear her music but knows she's destined to play to mostly deaf ears for all eternity,' I said.

Suddenly I felt as if I was reading the painting by lightning flashes. 'It's all about stories, isn't?' I exclaimed. 'Everyone in this painting had a tragedy in waiting.' There was a faint thrill of discovery as I ticked off each tragedy on my fingers. 'The woman would lose her son. The son would be crucified. Peter would also be crucified, but upside down. Catherine would be tied to a wheel and martyred. Lucy would pluck out her own beautiful eyes to evade her suitor. And Jerome would be persecuted to the point of martyrdom for his ascetic stance. Everyone had a journey to take. But the journey wasn't meant to destroy them.' I stopped, frustrated by my inability to express what I had discovered, and sat down in a nearby pew. A few minutes passed. Neither of us moved. The sun broke from behind the clouds and turned the grey interior silver. I started, caught off-guard by jewel-like flashes as sunlight refracted off the marble balustrade around the altar. I felt weightless and flooded with light. 'The journey would help them to see beyond themselves,' I finally said. 'It would help them hear the music.' I shivered.

'Ah!' Marcus said.

I thought of my mother. I saw her blond hair; smelled her violet scent, incongruous in the salty Peterborough air; and felt her hands cool against my own as she swirled me around. We were together for only a short time and could not have known where our stories would lead us. In that moment, I realised with a start that nothing could dissolve what we had once been. My mother's story had taken her from me, but she was still my mother. It was blindingly simple. All I had to do was see beyond our stories to the music we shared. The first word that came to my mind was forgiveness – I would forgive Allegra – but this word was too biblical, no doubt drawn from me by my surroundings, all of which pleaded its assurance. But the feeling I had ran deeper and felt better than the notion of forgiveness, with its uneasy righteous shadow. The feeling I had was more akin to acceptance. It was as if I had let out a great sigh, on its breath the weight of all I'd been carrying.

We sat with Bellini's painting for a long time. Occasionally the entry doors to the church creaked open, followed by the hollow slap of footsteps on the stone floor and then, once again, the creak of the doors. During that time the painting imprinted itself on my mind and with its image the realisation that Bellini had not just painted a commission for San Zaccaria but had done so with the full fervour of spiritual conviction. Artist and painting were one and the same and in that, perhaps, lay its power.

Finally, I turned to Marcus. 'I've heard it said that art can heal but only ever paid the notion lip-service. You told me Pontormo's *Visitation* changed your life. Perhaps it was more than that. Perhaps it healed your life?'

We both looked back at the Bellini with its meditative figures framed by richly ornamented columns, over their heads the intricate tesserae of a painted Byzantine dome and around them, if one listened hard enough, the strains of their silent music.

17

That night my sleep was dreamless. I woke once in the early hours of the morning and heard the engine of a motorboat fade off into the distance until all was once again quiet, and I drifted back to sleep.

When Marcus knocked on my door, I was sitting in the wicker chair next to my bed, drinking tea. Each morning since my return from Montespertoli, there'd been a rap on the door about eight o'clock, after which I'd find a tray with a pot of tea, milk, and two pastries on the floor outside my room.

Marcus waited for my response before coming in. He perched on the side of the bed and we looked at each other. 'I have no idea how you must feel,' he said. 'But to me, sitting here now, it's as if we're two survivors after a shipwreck.'

I smiled, wrapped a serviette around my night water glass, filled it with tea, and handed it to him. He sipped at it.

'You're right,' I said ruefully. 'It's like the silence after the apocalypse, that brief moment when the world has been blasted and all you can hear is your own breath' – I paused and then added poignantly – 'and there is nowhere to go until some green shoots sprout and you can follow them into the light.'

Marcus instantly picked up on my poetic imagery and said, 'Was Bellini the first of those green shoots?'

I held my cup to my mouth and brushed its hard surface against my lips. Finally, I rested my chin on its rim and said, 'You know, it might very well have been.'

Marcus rang Clementina after breakfast and arranged for Ursula to meet us in the breakfast room before she began her daily duties in the museum. There was one more thing to do in order to complete my journey: I needed to see Prudencia's grave. I might not know what happened to my mother, but the young nun's grave was clearly signposted, or as near as one could be after four centuries. I could stand there and know that the person lying in it was the girl who had led me to Allegra's story. I could thank her and, maybe then, begin the long task of rebuilding my life with new, reliable foundations.

As we sat in the breakfast room drinking strong coffee and nibbling toast and jam, Ursula walked towards us, concern evident on her face. 'Something's happened?' she asked.

'Yes, it has. But it's all right,' I said. 'We were wondering ...Would you mind taking us to see Prudencia's grave?'

'Of course,' she said. 'I'd be delighted.'

I paused and then glanced around the room. I felt I owed Ursula an explanation for this sudden summons. But the number of visitors to Santa Celestina had increased steadily over the past two weeks, and the small room now buzzed with conversation and rustling tourist maps. It wasn't the place for intimate exchanges. Ursula read my hesitation and said, 'We can talk later in the convent garden if you like? How about we meet in the cloister after lunch?'

'That's a good idea,' I said. 'I'll tell you all then.'

At one o'clock Marcus and I sat on a low wall in the sunlit cloister and waited for Ursula. She came through the door behind us, and before we saw her, we heard her exclaim, 'What a beautiful day!'

We both spun around. She stood in the sun, her arms spread wide, and said, 'The shift from spring to summer in Venice is not clear cut. As you've experienced, the weather can be ice cold and the wind bitter, but around now the sun begins to appear more often and lasts longer. Such a relief!' She smiled and looked up to heaven. 'Come with me and I'll take you to Prudencia.' Without waiting, she led the way across the cloister courtyard to a small wooden door in the far corner, which opened into an arcaded colonnade. This walkway took several sharp turns before reaching what appeared from a distance to be a dead end but was actually a plain door set into a wall. Ursula reached into her pocket and drew out a bundle of brass keys on an oversized key ring. She tried a few before finding the right one and led us through and into the convent garden.

The garden was about the same size as the cloister and consisted of beds of various sizes edged with diagonally set bricks. Most of the beds were empty, but there was a compost bin in the centre of one, and another bed was newly planted out with what looked from a distance to be vegetable seedlings. In the far corner there was a small area fenced off with iron railings.

'The archives tell us our Prudencia grew the convent's herbs,' Ursula said. 'She was supposedly knowledgeable with regards to their healing powers and before her fall from grace often went out to wealthy families to supply remedies.' She gestured around the surrounding area. 'This was all planted out in past times, but now there is only our summer supply of salad vegetables, and these are looked after by old Giovanni.'

She led us towards the fenced area, opened its ornate, rusty gate, and we walked into a small graveyard.

I counted eight graves set in rows of four, with a wide enough space between the rows to allow for walking. Each grave was no more than a plain slab with an initial carved into the top centre and the date of death directly underneath. Carved rays – like the rays of the sun – spread out from either side of each initial.

It was a quiet but peaceful place. Maybe it was the stone convent walls nearby or the fact that believers had walked these gardens armed as much with prayers as with garden tools, but it was also intimate, the cut between the living and the dead not quite so deep. I thought back to my mother's grave under its vast sky and my stumbling attempts to pray and saw my furtive glances at Lawrence for reassurance that didn't come.

I reached into my bag, gently pulled out a small bunch of cultivated violets, and placed them under the 'P' on the grave second in from the top right. Neither Ursula nor Marcus spoke, and I straightened and said, 'I wonder about Prudence.' I corrected myself. 'The virtue, not the girl. If you'd asked me a couple of months ago if Prudencia behaved prudently, I'd have said no. But now I'm not so sure.'

'How so?' Marcus said.

Ursula had picked up a thin twig and was clearing small clumps of moss from the grooves radiating from the initial 'P'. 'I think I know what Iris means,' she said.

I walked over to the stone wall at the rear of the little cemetery and leaned against it. The stones were warm. 'Well, when I first met you, Ursula, you translated the Latin words above the *cassa* for me,' I said. 'And then Marcus did a little performance in the Accademia to explain his version of Prudence. Both of them involved looking behind, looking forward, and looking around, while looking at yourself. At first it appears that Prudencia was not prudent. She should have stayed in the convent and avoided all the drama.'

Marcus thought for a moment. 'What, are you saying she acted prudently?'

'I'm saying' – I stumbled for the right words – 'I'm just saying it's debatable.' I paused. 'This is hard to put into words but, to me, a prudent decision is made carefully and doesn't favour one thing or person over another. Often that decision means a thing or person is cast aside and perhaps even hurt. Often the choice – the answer – puts the seeker squarely between the devil and the deep blue sea. Perhaps what is good for someone doesn't seem so to others. I mean, we only see through our own narrow window, don't we?' I raised my hands palms upwards in a gesture of helplessness so as to emphasise the complexity of my argument. Then the nub of it all came quickly and I added, 'Hard deeds are carried out in the interests of a good end result.'

'What I think Iris is saying,' Ursula said, 'is that Prudencia was true to herself, and that her decisions were prudent for her, despite everything she went through.' She looked at me for approval and I nodded. She continued, 'What you're saying is that she lived her own story.'

'Yes,' I said. 'It was the Bellini painting in San Zaccaria that did it. It made me realise that our stories are our own. Even though we live with loved ones and share a greater, common humanity, we still have to live true to ourselves within all that.'

'What about your mother?' Marcus said. Even though I was expecting the conversation to move onto Allegra, I suddenly felt weak at the knees and my mouth dried. I licked my lips 'It's all about Eve, again, isn't it,' he murmured, more to himself than to either of us.

'Eve?' Ursula said.

'Iris, tell Ursula your thoughts about Eve.'

'Remember the four postcards in the journal?' I said.

'Yes.' Ursula looked intrigued. 'You told me that Giovanni Bellini's *Allegory of Prudence* was one, and the last few days have highlighted his *Madonna and Child* as another.'

'Well,' I said. 'The other two were Botticelli's *Primavera* and Masaccio's Adam and Eve. I've always known that there was a reason my mother chose these pictures. I've thought and thought' – I hesitated, painfully aware of the shortcomings of my carefully thought-out hypothesis about Eve and my mother – 'and wonder if my mother felt like Eve. A woman driven from paradise. That something bad had happened to her.'

'Ah!' Ursula said gently. 'I think you've come to the conclusion that your mother made a decision. But this doesn't mean she made her decision easily.'

'I know,' I said. 'But it's hard to believe my mother wanted – needed – to leave me and Lawrence.'

'Iris, I know this is hard, but I think you're right. Perhaps your mother saw the naked truth and had to leave.' She stopped, cleared her throat, and continued, 'Anyway, despite all our talk about the virtue of Prudence, I think the simple words in Prudencia's diary spoke to your mother, and I think they tell us a great deal. You ask why your mother left? I think she left because she loved you so much. And her link to Prudencia? Well, I don't think it was overly complicated. I think she felt for a woman who had lost her child.'

I stood away from the wall and was conscious of cool air filling the space between the wall's warmth and my back. I walked over to Prudencia's grave and thought about the young nun whose story had taken her beyond the safety of her convent walls. Then I recalled the childhood photograph of my parents and realised that the observation I'd made when eleven years old was right. Allegra – like Prudencia – had been too alive to stay within her frame, be it silver or the small coastal town of Peterborough. As much as she loved him, Lawrence was too self-contained to hold her. My mother – Allegra – needed a larger embrace. It was no one's fault.

In my mind's eye I saw the angel in Bellini's painting. She was staring straight at me and daring me to look away. For a second I resisted and went to turn aside, but then I heard a sweet sound as clear and pure as a fingernail on glass, and I shook my head. But the music – yes, I believe it was music – only intensified, and what was left of my sadness dissolved in its fierce pale light.

18

Two days after our conversation with Ursula, Marcus and I walked as far as we could along the Fondamente Nuove and stopped to rest on a bridge near the turn off to the church of the Gesuiti. Marcus wanted me to see its green and white walls with their tiny pseudo-opera boxes, over which he promised the marble was sculpted to hang like drapes, but I stalled on the bridge, pierced by the lagoon's serene beauty. He stood close to me, his hands deep in his coat pockets.

I leaned over the side of the balustrade and peered down at the gently lapping waters. There was no sun, only streaks of white cloud that lay in thin parallel lines across a grey sky. The brightness of recent days had vanished. A few small boats scudded over the waters, dipping obediently around the marker buoys. A vaporetto loaded with tourists lumbered past. I watched people spill out and through the pontoon; the well-dressed Venetians clearly discernible from the sneaker-clad visitors.

'You know, I don't feel like the same person,' I said. 'It's as if I've been spun around and now see life – see everything, really – quite differently. But what I've discovered still feels raw, as if it might fragment and disappear if I blink too hard.'

'Green shoots,' Marcus reminded me, 'are tender.'

He was right. My very nerve endings felt tentative, as if they had no outer coating for protection. I sighed.

Marcus leaned back against the bridge, and I felt his gaze on me as he said, 'Time does make a difference but, Iris, your story's been a long time in the making, and my mother always said that emotions are like seesaws. The journey back up can take as much time as the journey downwards.'

'I don't think I can wait until I'm nearly fifty to feel better,' I said.

He laughed. 'It won't take that long.'

Our musings were interrupted when two Japanese couples joined us on the bridge and looked at us hesitantly. The taller of the men brandished a camera at Marcus and asked in halting English if he'd photograph them. They were polite and grateful, and after a brief exchange about Venice's attractions, they bowed and moved on.

Marcus resumed his place beside me and suddenly said, 'What happened to Lorenzo Monaco?'

'What do you mean?' Then the truth of his words dawned and I smiled. 'Oh! I'll always love the art of that period. I love its certainties, its proud and easy confidence. That'll never change. But' – I measured my words carefully – 'I didn't realise that I liked it because it allowed me to feel safe. While I interpreted the signs and symbols, I could avoid anything that took me outside my comfort zone.' I looked up at him thoughtfully. He was now staring straight ahead over the lagoon. 'Do you remember when you told me about Pontormo's impact on your life and how you suddenly saw past all your obligations to your own story?'

'Yes ...' He sounded cautious, as if he was wary of what I would say next.

'Well, I think I've gone one step further. I've stepped from behind my walls and seen that other people's stories

– even parents' – actually exist, and that their stories, their lives, have as much validity as my own.' I stopped, unable for a moment to capture in words the discovery that had lightened my life. On impulse I reached up and touched his face with the palm of my hand. He bent to kiss me, but just before his lips touched mine, what I needed to say came to me and I whispered, 'It's just so ridiculously simple. There really is a truth for each of us.'

He brushed his lips against my cheek and said, 'Yes, I think there is.'

We stood apart and rested our hands on the balustrade of the bridge.

'Perhaps this is what being human is all about?' I reflected.

'How do I know?' Marcus rolled his eyes and drummed his fingers thoughtfully. 'But, yes, perhaps it is, with a bit of empathy, a love of beauty, and an appreciation of the moment thrown in for good measure.'

'Perhaps it's also forgiveness,' I added.

Marcus looked rueful and said, 'All things so easy to speak of but so very, very difficult to practice.'

'When we first met you told me that, to you, women in art embody what can't be touched,' I said. 'I think you said they speak to the longing in us. You know, I might very well have proved your theory.'

Marcus whistled softly under his breath and said, 'Your mother left you a journal. You followed its trail and read her story between its lines' – he smiled – 'actually, between its brushstrokes. Yes, I suppose you could say you've lived out my theory.'

I looked out at the choppy, blue-green water and said slowly, 'You know, maybe I'm more like her than I think.

After all, I deciphered the journal.' Then I reached into my jacket pocket, pulled out my city map, scrutinised it, and said, 'What say we head for the Gesuiti?'

Marcus reached for my hand. 'The Gesuiti it is.'

When we returned to Santa Celestina late that afternoon, I was not surprised to learn that Monica was waiting for us. It had only been a matter of time.

Clementina told us she'd arrived around lunchtime and been shown through to the communal lounge room where she'd stayed ever since. When we entered, Monica was sitting in a deep leather chair, her head thrown back in order to study the decorations on the cornice high above.

'Monica,' I said.

She started and stood up. There was an awkward silence before she said, 'Iris ...' Her voice held an undercurrent of fear. Perhaps she thought I might simply tell her to go away, but I wasn't going to make it that easy. So I said nothing and just stared at her. She blinked and bit her bottom lip. 'I don't expect you to forgive me. But I've thought of nothing else since you left – and there is more I need to tell you.' She sighed as if for all this time she had been carrying a great weight and was now about to lay it down. 'I want you to have this.'

She reached into her bag, pulled out a tissue-wrapped parcel, and handed it to me. I unfolded the creased layers of paper and exposed a small ornamental box. 'It's a *cassa!* A miniature marriage chest,' I marvelled.

'It's beautifully made,' Marcus said. 'Look at those tiny panels! And that detailed brushwork.'

'Yes,' Monica said. 'Allegra was an artist in her own right.'

'You mean my mother painted this?' I reached over and took the box. It fitted neatly into the palm of my hand. It had two panels on the sides and one at each end, which were painted with individual geometric designs in shades of green that ranged from light apple to the deepest jade. Each panel was bordered by inlaid mother-of-pearl. Gold-leaf decoration defined the box itself. I lifted the lid. The box was lined with stiff, gold satin. It had been carefully cut and fitted, the seams aligning with the sides and base. A single piece of fabric lined the lid. I ran my hand over each surface. They were tight and flat. There could be no letter hiding behind this lining. In the bottom right corner, however, I saw some embroidery. I bent over to take a closer look and in gold thread slightly brighter than the satin fabric were the initials 'A.M.', followed by what looked like a symbol or trademark.

'Allegra Maddison?' I gasped and looked up at Monica.

'Yes,' she said.

'What's beside the initials?' I angled the box towards the window. The shape of the mark beside the initials was hard to determine. The edges were feathered and the script inside the mark was embroidered in a minuscule, ornate cursive script. I looked up as a weak sun broke through the clouds and brightened the room. Then I turned back to the box. In the clearer light the shape of the mark was suddenly plain to see. It was a feathered heart with the single word 'Iris' embroidered inside. Until then I had held myself together, propped up by anger, but the tenderness of this small heart shattered my resolve. My legs suddenly felt weak, and I sat down on a nearby chair and whispered, 'My mother didn't forget me.'

Monica came and stood beside me and said, 'Allegra embroidered the heart with your name inside every *cassa* she made. She loved you, Iris.'

I looked up. 'Where is she? Where's my mother?'

Monica again reached into her bag but this time took out an envelope. She slid out a photograph, laid it right side up on the palm of her hand, and held it towards me. It was a tombstone, just a slab of marble with a headstone surmounted by a simple cross. But clearly visible were the engraved words 'Allegra Maddison'.

I felt dizzy and leaned forward, my elbows on my knees, my head resting in my hands. 'It's another grave,' I said. At first my voice was muffled but then I laughed, a high-pitched hysterical laugh. Weren't tragedy and comedy supposed to be linked? At opposite ends of the line but if you pull it into a circle they merge and become indistinguishable. The situation was incredulous. I swallowed hard and said, 'Just how many graves can one person have?'

'Iris!' Marcus reached out, but I pushed his hand away.

'When did she die this time?' I said.

'1985,' Monica said flatly.

Something – a note of resignation, the weight of what Monica had carried for so long – stopped me before I went too far and I said, 'What happened?'

'A blood clot. It was ridiculous. She went into hospital with a severe headache and didn't come out. I received a phone call late one night. She'd left instructions that I was to be contacted if anything happened to her. She wanted to be buried where she had lived – in Vicenza. I made sure this happened.'

'And this *cassa*?' I said.

'An obsession. A homage to Prudencia. I don't know, really,' Monica said. 'But Allegra had a senior position in a thriving business supplying these boxes to up-market tourist outlets. They were sorry to lose her.'

The room swayed and I shook my head, but it didn't right itself, and I reached toward Marcus who steadied me by holding me close. I leaned my forehead against him and cried.

We talked long into the afternoon, trying to give shape to my mother's ghost. At one point I thought I saw Ursula walk along the corridor. Not long after, Clementina silently brought scalding coffee and tough little almond biscuits.

Monica had arranged to fly back to Florence that evening and when it was time for her to leave, she reached out to hug me. As she pressed me close, I noticed that she was thinner than I remembered, and when she stroked my face, I put my hand over hers and was surprised by the soft protruding veins and fine wrist. Small lines fanned out from her eyes and there were traces of other lines stretched across her cheekbones. She stepped away, left the back of a cool hand against my cheek, and looked into my eyes. 'What will you do about Lawrence?'

'What will I do about Lawrence?' I repeated. 'I don't know, really.' Until now I had drawn a line between what I had discovered and what I would now do.

'Go and see him, Iris.'

'I suppose' – I looked from Monica to Marcus but neither spoke – 'I suppose I have to.'

'I've rung him,' Monica said. 'He knows.'

I laughed before tiredly adding, 'Why aren't I surprised. Of course you have. It didn't occur to you to talk to me first? To actually include me.' Secretly, however, I was relieved Monica had spoken to Lawrence. It was one less explanation for me to make.

'I only spoke to him yesterday,' Monica said. 'Just before I came here. I knew what I had to tell you was life changing. I needed him to be aware.'

'I'll go and see him,' I said. 'But I need time before I do. I want to stay here and let this settle.' I was suddenly bone weary. My father had underpinned my life with a lie, and I needed time to shore up my foundations. I instinctively knew that to see him, at this point, had the power to undermine me. I looked at Marcus. 'I need my walls,' I said. 'Just for a little while.'

A week after Monica's visit, Marcus and I moved into a small apartment in Castello. There was a combined bedroom and sitting room and an apology for a kitchen, and each morning when I opened the shutters I looked straight into the opposite window. As the changeable spring weather gave way to summer heat, the cyclamens on the sill wilted and were replaced by a gaudy plastic arrangement, which was vigorously dusted every few days by my house-proud neighbour. After I made tea for Marcus and coffee for myself, I returned to the bedroom and found Marcus propped up in bed with a book on art or history, and we discussed or argued. We made lists of things to do but were invariably sidetracked. Despite the ravages of time, Venice was a world unto herself and she seduced us. This tiny waterborne stone city scorned the outside world, but there was no sense of confinement because instead of reaching out, she traversed back through centuries and high into the cosmos.

We avoided the crowded tourist areas and spent much of our time among the lagoon islands. We sat in deserted vaporetti pontoons and looked out over the grey waters at tilting belltowers or clusters of stone buildings. We searched out old paintings in damp, unrestored churches and felt often as if time had stopped.

We stayed in Venice for six months, and during this time I did not contact my father. I knew I would eventually come to a decision as to what to do, but I needed this time to let the events of the past reassemble into a shape I could recognise before confronting the problem of Lawrence.

Two weeks before I was due to fly back to Australia, Marcus and I took the train to Vicenza to visit Allegra's grave. In the early days after discovering the truth, I had decided I didn't need another grave in my life. The photograph would suffice. After all, the trajectory of events veered toward the farcical and to visit another grave bore elements of the surreal. But then I was still in shock, and my decisions were skewed by the need to protect myself. As time wore on and the reality of my mother's real death took hold, I made the difficult decision to go.

We found Allegra's grave in a small cemetery tucked behind the ruins of an old church. It was one of a line of graves that ran parallel with the length of the cemetery's back stone wall. It was surprisingly well kept. Monica had said that my mother was highly regarded, and it appeared that even after all these years someone was tending her grave. There were no weeds around the slab and the headstone looked as if it had been recently cleaned, and there was a glass vase in the centre filled with fresh white lilies. I reached over and ran a finger along my mother's name. The engraving was free of dust or dirt. As I looked at it, I felt a door shut, softly, with no pique or anger. I stepped away and reached for Marcus's hand. 'There's nothing left for me to do,' I said. 'This part of my story is over. It's time for me – for us – to go.'

It was during this time in Venice that I, to put it simply, learned to trust and to love again. Marcus stayed by my side, but this time he gave me what I needed, not what he felt was good for me.

It was also during this time that my child was conceived, just as I had been, between a walk and a dream, but this time in a city that floated on water.

Peterborough

Australia

1991

19

I returned to Australia late on a Thursday night at the beginning of December. I'd been away just over nine months, but in the light of all that had happened it might as well have been nine years. I'd organised a four-day stopover in Singapore, as I didn't want to arrive home carrying the full impact of a long-haul flight.

Singapore had been hot and humid and, apart from a few forays to nearby shops, I'd eschewed tourist sites in favour of the hotel pool. I phoned Louise on a whim a few hours before I flew out, and she insisted on meeting me at the airport and taking me to her new apartment for another short break before I returned to Peterborough. I didn't argue, as the time with her would allow me to adjust to the change of skies before I confronted my father.

Louise had moved from the shared house to a small apartment in the upper story of a renovated terrace house in North Fitzroy. She led me to her spare room, dumped my luggage beside the bed, and left me to sleep off the residual effects of my week's travelling. By the time I woke the next day, she'd gone to work, and by the time she came home, I'd gone back to bed. I reflected that in our university days, we would have stayed up half the night having long conversations. Now, it was the weekend before we caught up properly.

I surfaced late on the Saturday morning and wandered through Louise's apartment. The fog in my head had cleared and I noted idly that it had none of the shared house's ethnic eccentricity. On one side of a long hallway, a narrow lounge room ran the length of the building. Half-drawn blinds filtered the light. There were two low cream couches, which intersected at one corner, each with a symmetrical arrangement of ruby-coloured cushions. Propped up on the centre coffee table was a note, which read:

> *Work called. Can you believe it on a Saturday! Be back just after lunch. Looking forward to hearing all about it.*

At the rear of the room, there were French doors that opened onto a small, covered balcony, onto which Louise had squeezed two low-slung striped canvas chairs. It was a cool but sunny early summer day, so I made myself a drink, sat out on the balcony, and pondered the tiny parterre garden below. Half an hour later, I heard a door slam and then quick footsteps on the wooden floor.

'I'm out here,' I called.

The footsteps grew closer, and I looked up and saw Louise at the French doors. She stood for a few moments, her smile widening into a grin. Then she covered the space between us in two steps and threw her arms around me. 'It's good to see you up and around at last.' Then she drew back and held me at arm's length with her hands on my shoulders and cocked her head to one side. 'You've lost weight. Your face is thinner' – her voice softened – 'you poor thing. It must have been quite a time.'

I blinked away tears and nodded. I'd looked in the mirror that morning and seen the fine lines at the corners of my eyes and felt my skin, like parchment after the long time in the dry air of the plane's cabin.

'Don't move,' she said. 'I'll make us coffee, and we can sit here and talk.'

She returned ten minutes later, placed a tray on the table between us, and sat opposite me. 'So, all this happened because of your Aunt Monica's Saint Ursula,' she said.

'I suppose so.' I'd almost forgotten about the exhibition. It seemed light years ago. But Louise was right. Finding the marriage chest had propelled me to Italy and led me straight to Prudencia and finally to the truth about my mother. 'It makes you think, doesn't it?' I said.

'Tell me,' Louise demanded.

I talked until shadows crept over the garden below. Louise interrupted only if something I said was unclear.

'So, you see,' I finally said, 'I can't say that I understand why my mother did what she did, but now I can accept it. I can forgive her and begin to think about the future without Allegra's journal at the centre of it.'

'I don't get it,' Louise said. 'How can you forgive someone who's dead? You can't see their face. You can't meet their eyes. Nothing can pass between you.'

'It's hard to explain,' I said. 'It's not really something that had to go on between my mother and me. I had to arrive at a point' – I groped for the right words – 'where I could see my mother's story as exactly that – her story – separate from mine and not meant to hurt or destroy anyone. Just meant to be lived.'

'But she left you?'

'Yes, and, as I said, I'll never fully understand why. But, you see, the point is I don't need to understand any more. I've been lucky. My mother left me her journal and, if you like, her story in postcards. She also left me Prudencia, who told me that some places and circumstances separate us from the ones we love. Some people have to forgive without anything to help them. From what I can make of the letter Prudencia wrote to her father, he was watching from a distance when her mother took her to Santa Celestina. She didn't hold a grudge against him for not saving her from a life of confinement. Instead, when she had her own child all those years later, she wanted him to know about his granddaughter. So she wrote the letter he never received. We can only hope that her father met his granddaughter.' I shrugged my shoulders. 'I really believe that my mother felt the price of separation. What drove her to it must have been monumental.'

Louise looked bemused. 'But still ...'

I shook my head. 'No buts. I feel freer and lighter. The knot in my stomach has gone. I don't think I can explain it any better.'

'And you've fallen in love,' Louise said.

'That, too.' I smiled and drummed my fingertips lightly against my belly. What I had suspected in Venice had become reality. I was to have a child. The fact that Marcus and I had known each other for only eight months didn't concern me. He had walked with me while my world collapsed and stayed with me while I drew it back together. I felt no doubts about us, just the hard-won confidence that comes when you learn to trust your intuition. And to those who say it is impossible to love in so short a time? Love isn't measured by the time you spend with a person. Love arrives full-blown when you understand a person's story. It weaves together all parts – the beautiful, the unlovable, the poignant, the bizarre – and holds them together ever so gently. Love doesn't waste time searching for perfection.

'And when do I meet this Marcus?'

'Marcus is coming to Australia after I've spoken to Lawrence. I need to be alone with my father for a while.'

'I'll look forward to it,' Louise said. 'But you won't stay in Australia, will you?'

I thought for a moment. Marcus and I had discussed the possibility of completing his research together in Italy. This was still possible but the child, I felt, must be born in Australia. For a minute I was tempted to tell Louise I was pregnant, but I held back.

'Perhaps not in the short term. But I'll return and, after that, who knows?'

Louise offered to drive me to Peterborough, but I wanted to travel home by bus as I had always done when I'd returned from university. I wanted to glimpse that first expanse of sea as we neared Geelong and follow it along the winding roads that hugged the coast. The sea had always brought sensations of freedom and clarity, and I suppose I wanted these now. But I was not the same girl, and instead of being comforted, I felt exposed. Similarly, the paddocks and sloping dunes that had once also offered solace now merged into an endless horizon. There were no boundaries. Nothing was certain and I didn't feel safe. Amidst the stones of Venice – with Marcus at my side – I had reached a form of equilibrium. Here the churning ocean was relentless and the open countryside daunting, and I felt vulnerable.

In Venice my father had been far away. It had taken many months for me to be able to think about him rationally. When I did it was painful and often I would push the thoughts away and look for distraction, but now I had no choice but to face him.

As the distance between the Ocean Road towns grew, so too did the familiar tracts of stunted, ghostly-green cushion bush and spiky daisy bush, kept low by the winds that blew in from the sea. I felt shaky and wryly reflected that I was just like the vegetation, buffeted by something over which I had no control. By the time I reached Peterborough, comforting thoughts of Marcus and our child had been replaced by my father's anguished face. There was no avoiding the past; it lay behind me like a shadow.

When the bus arrived in Peterborough, I stepped out and stood by the side of the road. It was preternaturally quiet, the only sounds the familiar rush of waves and the squawking of hovering seagulls. I felt as if I'd travelled a million miles through time and space only to return to where it had all begun.

I took a deep breath and walked unsteadily up the hill to our house. It looked deserted and the large expanse of grass that swept down to the verge was uncut. I climbed the few steps onto the front veranda. There was a patina of dust over the outdoor furniture. I ran my finger over my father's prized mosaic tabletop and stared at the shiny slick. Then I fumbled in my bag for my key, long since relegated to the bottom of a zippered side pocket, and let myself inside.

My footsteps were hollow on the wooden boards, and I walked slowly and almost on tiptoes to lessen the noise. When I reached the far end of the corridor, I could just make out the rhythmic swoosh of sandpaper. A radio – tuned slightly off frequency – crackled in the background. I smiled, despite myself. I had never understood why Lawrence bothered with the radio. When he worked he was deaf to the world. I opened the door to the studio. At first my father didn't notice me, but when he circled to consider his sculpture from behind, he saw me. He raised one arm but seemed not to know what to do with it and quickly dropped it to his side. He was pale and looked unkempt, his clothes crushed and his face unshaven. I felt as if I was facing a stranger and when I said, 'Dad', I was startled by the sound of my own voice, and my heart began to pound. 'Dad?' I said again. 'Why?'

'Why?' he echoed. He looked perplexed, like a child who has been caught out doing something wrong. He sat on a nearby bench, rested his elbows on his knees, and let his hands dangle between his legs. I could tell by the shape of his jaw that his teeth were clenched, and he absently flicked his thumbs against his middle fingers, but he still didn't speak.

'Dad?' I repeated, but this time with an undercurrent of urgency. I understood that over the years, Lawrence must have convinced himself – with any number of reasons – that the motivations behind his actions had been right and that these reasons would have bound him ever more tightly as time passed. My request for one single reason would force him to loosen the tangle, unravel it, and find what lay beneath. I instinctively knew that this was dangerous and my love for him – that compassion felt when a loved one is in pain – stayed any frustration or anger I might have shown. I walked over and sat down beside him. 'Lawrence? Why?'

He began to talk slowly, drawing up words as if from the bottom of a well. 'I loved your mother.'

I waited. He sighed and his shoulders sagged. He concentrated fiercely on his hands, the thumbs and middle fingers now tapping each other noiselessly. A shock of hair fell over his face and he brushed it back with the flat of his hand. 'But she left.' His three blunt words exploded with the force of a bomb. 'One day I went to Warrnambool for supplies – oil paint, I think it was – and when I returned, she had gone.'

'Did she leave you a message or a note?' I was incredulous. 'And where was I?'

'I'd taken you with me to give her a break. You were only two years old and as busy as a bee. And, no, there wasn't a note. I thought at first she'd gone to visit someone or maybe to the beach.'

'There must have been some reason for her to go,' I said. Impatience replaced caution and I pushed harder. I could feel frustration building. I'd mulled over so many possibilities for mother's departure. Suddenly, my repressed anger broke through and my voice rose. 'No one does something like that without a reason. Can't you see how difficult this is for me to understand. Not knowing what happened. Living with the belief my mother was dead and then discovering she was alive.'

Lawrence reached out and ran his hand over the smooth surface of his sculpture. I noticed that it was a woman. I had never seen him sculpt a person before. The woman was kneeling back on her haunches, her hands pressed neatly between her knees. Her back was straight and her head erect, her gaze on the middle distance. She was thin, fragile even, her shoulder blades piercing her flesh like budding wings.

'But I always believed she died,' I said petulantly. 'When people asked me about my mother, I told them she was dead. No one said any different. Surely, someone noticed.'

'Why should they have?' Lawrence said. 'We'd only lived here for a short time. Not long enough to be well known. For all anyone knew, Allegra' – he stopped and I realised I had never heard him mention her name before – 'was never meant to live here permanently. The townsfolk saw us as a hippie couple with a baby. If the woman disappeared, so what? There was nothing unusual in that.'

'And the Curdies River Cemetery?'

'It's far enough away. I knew there was an unmarked grave.'

'But to go to all the trouble of making a plaque and securing it to the grave? I mean, surely, someone ...' My voice trailed away. After a short silence, I returned to the question that haunted me. 'But why, Dad? Why?'

'I wish I knew the reason,' Lawrence said. 'It would have been easier.' I watched his finger trace over the face of the sculpture, and then he looked up at me and on his face was anguish such as I'd never seen before. 'It's bad enough to have someone leave you,' he said. 'But for them to leave for what appears to be no reason is unbearable.'

'Did she love me?' My voice was small and far away.

'Oh, yes,' Lawrence said. 'She loved you, all right.'

After these last words there seemed nothing else for us to say. My father wearily put down his sandpaper and walked towards the door, leaving me to follow along behind. In the kitchen he made tea – all without further conversation – and placed a mug in front of me. We sat opposite each other at the kitchen table, the weight of all that had happened piled high between us.

20

For the two weeks in between my return to Peterborough and Marcus's arrival in Australia, my father and I circled each other in the house in which I'd grown up. I didn't expect things to be easy. How could they be? But I was not prepared for the emotional impact of our estrangement. It was as if a giant hand had destroyed our shared web of feeling, much as we carelessly brush away a spider's intricate weaving without a second thought. I cooked our meals, laid the table, and even washed our clothes but hardly spoke except for when necessary. We had one long conversation about the future of the shop. Lawrence had only opened four days a week while I'd been gone. Annette willingly covered Thursday to Saturday, and my father now did Sundays. There was no reason, he said, why this shouldn't continue. Other than this, Lawrence spent much of his time walking for long hours or simply sat in his wing chair listening to music. He didn't once return to his studio, which disturbed me because it was so uncharacteristic but left me feeling vindicated, as if he deserved this as a punishment for what he'd done.

I didn't tell my father about Marcus's impending arrival until the end of the first week. Both of us had plummeted to that empty place where long-held beliefs lie ruined like giant buildings from a past age fallen to wreckage. In my mind's eye I saw the palazzos of Venice sinking into the lagoon, waiting for a benefactor to shore them up before they completely disappeared. And I wondered who, if anyone, would be our benefactor? And how we would summon the energy to rebuild?

We were sitting in the living room after dinner on the Friday of that week watching the news. I waited until the end of the weather report, drew a deep breath, and summoned up my courage, at the same time wondering why I felt the need to do so after all that had happened.

'Marcus is arriving next Thursday,' I said. 'I'll go to Melbourne on Wednesday, stay the night with Louise, pick him up at the airport on Thursday, and be back here by nightfall.'

Lawrence nodded absently. He looked bewildered – punch-drunk – reeling from too many bouts in the ring.

'Do you mind if he stays with us?' I said.

My father shrugged and with a resigned grimace said, 'As you please.'

There was no mention of sleeping arrangements, and it didn't seem necessary to raise the matter. If Lawrence wondered how our lives together would proceed, or even if I would stay in Peterborough, he didn't ask.

I saw Marcus before he saw me, and the relief I felt surprised me. A shiver, a combination of nerves and excitement, ran through me and I shook myself. I'd thought I loved him, but in this moment a hazy belief became solid reality. I watched as he walked through the international arrival exit doors, stood to one side, put down his cabin bag, and dragged his palms tiredly across his cheekbones. He had the bewildered look of the jet-lagged traveller. His collar was half tucked into his shirt, and his hair was flattened and uncombed. I almost caught his eye, but he suddenly bent forward, picked up the bag, and joined the stream of passengers walking alongside the metal barricades into the terminal proper. I hurried after him and halfway along reached out and grabbed his arm. He turned and, despite the barricade and the crowd, dropped his bag and put his arms awkwardly around me. My mind leapt back to our early meetings when I'd waited eagerly for the feel of his wool coat, as if it were a talisman portending good things to come. This time he wore a long-sleeved checked shirt, folded back a few times at the cuffs, and I could sense the outline of his body – his ribs – through its fine cotton.

'Your father's expecting me, I hope,' Marcus said. By this time, we were walking across the road to the car park, and I could see him growing visibly more tired as bright sunlight hit him.

'I think he's taken it on board,' I said. 'But he's absent. He's there in body but not in spirit. And he's not sculpting, which is unheard of for him.'

'The fact that you've found out the truth must have hit him hard.' He yawned and said, 'If I lived here and had to go through that length of time in a plane every time I travelled abroad, I'd never go anywhere.'

Marcus slept nearly the entire way to Peterborough, seeing nothing of the rugged Ocean Road coastline, only Melbourne's disjointed western suburbs before he closed his eyes and his breathing deepened. So be it, I thought, the beauty of my Peterborough will only come as more of a surprise.

Lawrence must have heard the car because he was waiting outside the house when we arrived. In the few seconds between first sighting my father and pulling the car up in our driveway, a wave of panic sharpened all around me; feelings, landscape and people heightened and intensified so as to be almost surreal. I gulped and sweat broke out on my upper body, but I kept driving, the physical business of driving the car a saving grace, otherwise it is quite possible I would have turned and run.

Marcus ran his hand through his hair and made a vain attempt to straighten his clothes, and then we arrived and the pantomime of greetings unfolded in slow motion until suddenly we were on the other side of these anticipated introductions, and all around me resumed normal shape.

The conversation on that first evening was surprisingly easy. After dinner we went to the living room where my father sat in his usual chair. I took the one near the window and Marcus the chair in between us. I saw his glance linger briefly on the print of *Primavera* on the wall above the mantelpiece. The television droned in the background, a long nature documentary on animal migration patterns providing both a source of and a respite from sustained conversation.

I watched my father closely, but he didn't show any signs of resentment towards Marcus and was not defensive in either his manner or his replies. Instead, he asked him about his work, and they discussed shared areas of interest. I even sensed a slight lift in Lawrence's demeanour and wondered if perhaps he was glad to have been found out. Marcus, as well, was courteous and carefully avoided contentious topics. No mention was made of what had occurred, which I'd expected would be the case, but I couldn't shake the feeling that I was participating in a bizarre comedy of manners, where darker truths lurk like pond life beneath the current of civilised conversation. I also felt slightly annoyed. The child in me wanted a scene and craved the physical rush of adrenalin afforded by a confrontation and, to my shame, I had to subdue the desire to see my father cowering further under the weight of our combined righteousness.

At half past nine Marcus stood up. He still looked tired and was now pale, and his bleary eyes clearly showed that he was disoriented.

'I'm afraid the last few days have caught up with me. But' – he looked at my father – 'I'm so glad to be here.'

Lawrence rose and put one hand on his shoulder and shook Marcus's hand with the other. 'It's good to finally meet you. Europe to Peterborough is no mean feat.'

There was an instant during which neither man moved, and I observed through stalled time my father and my lover. Lawrence was now in his late forties, still handsome in the endearing way of an ageing hippie. Marcus sat squarely between my father's age and my own, old enough to have experienced life and know how to behave in difficult circumstances but young enough to still carry optimism. His presence was loosening the knot binding my father and me, giving us space to step back and breathe again, and in that to begin to see the possibilities of rebuilding. I also realised with a shock that it was quite possible that Lawrence was relieved that our intense relationship was now diluted by the presence of another.

The following day, I took Marcus along the poplar walk and then made him climb with me to the crannies. The sea was calm, pale blue with small waves rolling soundlessly into the sand of the half-moon bay below us. I pointed out the visible segments of The Twelve Apostles, and then we sat where Monica and I had sat all those years ago when I first pestered her about my mother.

We walked down the main street, past Mr Calder's shop – which had long since closed – and then across the highway and up the stony hill that overlooked our house. At that height, there was a slight breeze, but it was warm enough to sit contemplating the view in front of us. The layout of our oddball house was more obvious from this vantage point on the hill, and I began to point out the provenance of its various rooms to Marcus. There was a sudden movement in the still scene in front of us and I stopped talking and exclaimed, 'Lawrence!' My father's outline was clearly visible to me as he walked across the windows of his studio from one side of the room to the other.

'Where?' Marcus looked puzzled and peered in the direction from which we'd walked. 'I can't see him.'

'Look! He's in his studio. My father's begun to work again.'

Lawrence settled on what I guessed was his stool in front of the sculpture of the woman.

'Are you pleased?' Marcus's unexpected question broke into my reverie, and I looked at him through narrowed eyes and said, 'What do you mean?'

'I mean, are you glad he's sculpting again?'

I thought for a moment. 'Yes,' I said. 'Yes, I am.'

We both turned and watched Lawrence. His movements were as familiar to me as my own: the lift of the arm with the chisel poised mid-air, its measured descent on to the sculpture. It took little imagination for me to see his concentrated frown and the strained muscles in his forearms. Perhaps for all the years he'd hidden the truth from me, he'd also hidden part of himself and now, by sculpting this woman, he'd be set free.

Suddenly my thoughts returned to my mother's journal. 'It's incredible, really,' I said. 'If I hadn't seen my father throw the journal into the bin in that fit of pique … If I hadn't got out of bed and collected it from the bin … If I hadn't allowed Louise to push me off to Italy … So many ifs …'

'You'd never have met me,' Marcus quipped.

'No, seriously, if I hadn't met you, I'd never have discovered the truth.'

'That's not true,' he said. 'Prudencia was always your secret, and you followed her trail yourself.'

'I guess so,' I said slowly. 'Adam and Eve started it all.' I dug him in the ribs. 'And that odd man who began talking to a perfect stranger about Eve's wail.'

'And Prudencia held your mother's story,' Marcus continued.

'And the Bellini in San Zaccaria brought me to where I am now.'

'Yes, I suppose you could say that the Bellini freed you from the need to know,' Marcus said. 'You could even say that knowledge was your forbidden fruit – like Eve's was the apple in the Garden of Eden.'

I sat up and hugged my knees. There was a small patch of yellow spring daisies beside me, and I picked one absently and began to pluck its petals one by one. 'I suppose answers are always seductive.' I looked down. All that was left in my hand was the daisy's black centre, bristling with stamens. 'It's living without them that is the true art, and when you learn to live without them, the answers often come unbidden.'

We sat for a while longer and then Marcus rose to his feet. It was late afternoon, and I knew he wanted to check that all was in order for our return to Italy. He dropped a kiss on my head and headed off down the hill. I watched him pick his way down the stony hillside and stop briefly before crossing the road. He sprinted the short distance to the house and then disappeared from view.

I turned my attention back to the ocean, unfailing in its grand beauty, but knew that soon it would be time for me, too, to return to the house. It was time to talk to Lawrence about the future, rather than the past. It was time to tell him of his coming grandchild and the fact that we were to return to Italy in a month so Marcus could continue researching his documentary on women in Renaissance art. It was ironic that my circumstances had brought us together and then given him the raw material for his work.

It was also time to tell my father that Marcus and I would be back in the early autumn, so that our daughter could be born near the Peterborough ocean.

Acknowledgements

There are many people involved in a book's journey from idea to paper. So to all those friends through to professionals who influenced and helped bring *The Angel's Song* to life, I am deeply grateful. A special thank you must go to Coven Press whose expertise, diligence, and attention to detail made my self-publishing venture a dream run. Special thanks also go to my writing group. It is a privilege to share stories with like-minded people. Everyone needs a tribe! Thank you also to Alice Barker for her excellent editing advice early in this project. And to Francesca Urbini for her assistance with the Italian language. A special mention must go to the British art historian Andrew Graham-Dixon whose sensitive and thoughtful approach to art has inspired me over three decades. Lastly, love to my husband, Ken, and our canine companion, Ivy. The writing journey is labyrinthine and their patience is much appreciated.

Biography

Karen Sparnon works as a freelance writer, editor, and teacher. Her first novel – *Madonna of the Eucalypts* – was published by Text Publishing in 2006 and in 2007 won the Victorian Premier's Literary Award for writing about Italians in Australia. *Madonna of the Eucalypts* was sold overseas and translated. She has recently completed *The Angel's Song* and is currently working on her third manuscript.

Karen has written for major newspapers and magazines and been shortlisted and longlisted for writing awards, most recently the Affirm Press Mentorship Award. Karen lives with her husband, Ken, and canine companion, Ivy, in the Victorian Central Highlands, surrounded by its lush gardens and historic architecture.

Credits

Editing
Proofread by Anna Bilbrough of Coven Press

Design
Cover by Elizabeth McCracken of Coven Press

Cover Elements
San Zaccaria Altarpiece by Giovanni Bellini
Sandy Cove, Peterborough from Karen Sparnon
Other elements from Adobe Stock

Interior
Typeset by Alana Lambert of Coven Press
Format proofing by Elizabeth McCracken of Coven Press
Sorts Mill Goudy/11pt/16pt spacing